PAtly

The Lights of Sheridan Square

Hope you enjoy, t

Bob Ford

Copyright © 2012 by Bob Ford

ISBN 10: 1468015958
SBN-13: 978-1468015959

Published by Deerfield Park, 200 East 69th Street, Suite 7J
New York, NY 10021

Correspondence should be addressed to the author:

Bob Ford
bobfordnyc@gmail.com

Deerfield Park Books.

BOB
FORD

The Lights
of
Sheridan Square

A NOVEL

Deerfield Park Books
New York, NY

Author Contact
bobfordnyc@gmail.com

CONTENTS

To
Bonnie, of course
and to the memory of
Will Holton
No better man.
No better friend.
And to his wife, Mary.

PROLOGUE

It was not like Jay Carraway to strike up idle conversations with people he did not know. The young man seated next to him in first class had said little during the flight, focused as he was on the contents of his briefcase. Only as the 747 began its descent into San Francisco, did the young man decide he wanted to talk. He began by letting out a long, frustrating sigh and then said, "Don't you wish sometimes that you could be clairvoyant?" The question seemed to have been launched like a weather balloon, hovering - suspended - in mid-air waiting for the man next to him to address it.

"On occasion, it would be helpful," Jay replied absently.

"Have you ever thought about how a major event - a death, a marriage, a divorce, losing a job, an illness, any of those things, can completely change the course of your life?"

"Yes," he answered, "but then we expect our lives to change in those situations." For moment Jay said nothing and then added, "What most of us *never* expect, never even consider, is how the most trivial, everyday occurrence can, given the right circumstances, turn your life a full one-hundred and eighty degrees."

"I'm not sure I understand what you mean."

"Think about how many inconsequential events occur in your life every day. Minor things that go virtually unnoticed. Yet, what we seldom think about is that any one incident might set in motion changes that could affect your whole life: A chance encounter with a pretty girl. An airplane not taken. A delay in a schedule. A sudden rainstorm and no umbrella. A phone call from an old friend. An invitation you decide to accept at the last minute - the list is endless. It's only after the fact, sometimes long after, that we realize how some seemingly incidental event, one over which we had no control has had consequential results."

"I hadn't thought about it, but I guess you're right," he said. Then pointing toward the picture Jay was holding in his hand he said, "I don't mean to pry, but who is that? She looks familiar."

"No one you'd know. It's an old photograph. I shot it a long time ago." Jay had taken the eight-by-ten black and white photograph out of his briefcase some time ago intending but a momentary glance. But in looking at the picture he had allowed himself to be transported back in time where, like someone gathering picnic items blown asunder by the wind, he had begun to collect memories that had been scattered by time and distance.

"Looks like she might have been an actress."

"She wanted to be, but it never happened for her," he said glancing up at the young man who did nothing to mask his curiosity. Involuntarily, almost as if in need of refreshing her image, Jay's eyes drifted back to the picture he had kept hidden for more than thirty-five years. The photograph showed a young woman standing in front of a large garret window, softly backlit from below by the opalescent lights shining up from Sheridan Square below. She was wrapped in a white sheath dress and had struck a slightly suggestive pose. Her light brown hair cascaded down over her left shoulder, her body was angled slightly to the right. The camera seemed to have devoured her extraordinary figure with an almost animalistic prurience. Her face was turned toward the picture-taker, aglow with a smile that he believed then, as he believed now, reflected the love she felt for him. If only time could have been frozen like the photograph, he thought. But of course, the very moment the light from the flash dissipated into the night, the clock resumed ticking, bringing with it the labyrinth of twists and turns - the incidental events - that had brought him to this moment in time. *Why did I decide to bring her picture with me?* he asked himself. He could find no answer.

"And where is she now?" the young man inquired as he watched Jay put the picture carefully back into a folder and insert it in his briefcase.

"Interesting you should ask. Oh," he said looking out the window, "I think we're about to land. "Nice talking with you." he smiled at the young man and said no more.

MAY 1957

1

Joanna

The first time Jay Carraway saw Joanna he knew that he would love her for the rest of his life. Despite the improbable odds of spending a lifetime with this woman, he nonetheless knew what he knew at that moment to be true.

Minutes before he had found himself somewhat befuddled and ready to make an exit from the job interview when, after several questions about his knowledge of mid-town Manhattan, the office manager announced, "Ad-Film is looking for another gopher."

Gopher? Did she say gopher? he asked himself. *What does a rodent have to do with this job?* Jay just nodded inconclusively doing his best not to let his face reveal that he had no idea what the tall, reasonably attractive woman with hair piled high on her head was talking about.

"You'll go-fer coffee, go-fer pickups at the film lab, go-fer deliveries to the ad agencies. Ok?"

Go-fer! The light came on. *Go-fer this! Go-fer that! This is not exactly the job I'd been hoping for,* he thought, *but—well, everybody has to start someplace.*

"My name is Vivian Abato and you'll be working for me," she said as they began a quick tour of the office. As they passed through the reception area, she introduced the receptionist who was busy taking a phone message. "This is Joanna Olenska. Joanna, this is Jay Carraway."

The receptionist glanced up and gave him a distracted, perfunctory nod. It was her eyes that he noticed first. They were large, magnetically compelling eyes—the source of fantasies. She parted her light brown hair in the middle and let it cascade down the sides of her face in soft waves that ended below her shoulders. Her nose had a slight upturn accenting a perfect, inviting mouth. He would, for as long as he could visualize their first meeting, remember her face as an extraordinary combination of remarkable events

Jay became aware that she had the quizzical look of someone who suspects that they are about to be subjected to a critical appraisal. He turned away quickly in an effort to mask the embarrassment at having over-stared his welcome. When he glanced back at her, it appeared to him that she had taken refuge behind a wall of indifference.

While Jay's attention had been fastened on Joanna, Vivian was doing her best to explain how go-fers were to determine the permissible mode of transportation on any given pick-up or delivery. "We mark it *'Rush'* to impress the client, but as far as you're concerned, 'rush' doesn't mean what it says. What it means is that you walk or take a bus or subway. You don't spend money on a taxi. *"Hot"* on a package or envelope means you *grow wings and fly*—or, failing that, take a taxi, as long as the destination is more than ten blocks, or eight on rainy days."

Vivian might as well have been speaking Chinese for all that Jay heard, much less absorbed, so obsessive had become his desire to savor the woman behind the reception desk. Whatever was being said on the other end of the phone was clearly irritating her. He began to wonder what it would take to induce the porcelain veneer to crack and produce a smile. Jay found himself hoping that Vivian might be called away for a few minutes so that he would have an opportunity to cross the bridge of her apparent disinterest.

The elevator door opened and five well-dressed men emptied themselves into the reception area. The youngest among them walked over to Joanna and informed her that they were from J. Walter Thompson and had arrived for the 9:30 screening of a new Ford Fairlane commercial. Immediately, Vivian abandoned the tour and turned her attention to the five men greeting them with the assurance that they were going *to love* the finished version. Jay watched as one of the five slipped away from the group and returned to the reception desk. The man spoke to Joanna in a hushed voice that Jay could not hear. From the mildly salacious grin on his face, it appeared as if he were launching an assault designed to penetrate Joanna's wall of passive detachment. The words were barely out of the man's mouth when he reacted as if he'd been bounced off a stone wall. *Whoa!* Jay thought. *You don't mess with her.* As the agency man retreated, Jay suppressed the impulse to yell *Attagirl!*

Once the five agency visitors had been ushered into the screening room, Vivian turned her attention back to Jay. She indicated the mail room as their next stop, but before they left the reception area, he managed to catch Joanna's eye. "Nice to meet you," Jay said, nodding his head slightly. She smiled at him briefly in an ambiguous sort of way, but said nothing as she turned to answer that phone. In that instant, Jay Carraway became invisible.

Jay arrived early for his second day, intent on making himself a known quantity to Miss Joanna Olenska. As he got off the elevator, he discovered that her attributes were not limited to her face. She was standing by a sideboard, setting up coffee and cups. Jay guessed her to be about five foot seven or eight. She was wearing a light blue sweater that seemed to take inanimate pleasure in bringing a soft accent to her more-than-ample breasts. Her nicely sculptured ankles rose dramatically to taut, well-formed calves, which, after giving way to subtle knees, led to thighs playing peek-a-boo through the slit in her skirt. Suddenly he found that love and lust were in competition. "I'm Jay Carraway," he said, doing his best not to let his eyes wander unleashed around her incredible body.

"I know. Vivian introduced us yesterday."

Of course she did. I must sound like an idiot, he said to himself.

Joanna picked up a small package, wrapped in brown paper with a "hot" label on it. "You'd better get going with this."

As Jay took the package from her, he tried to think of something clever to say—something pithy that would signal that he was much more than his go-fer job title implied. But before he could speak, her phone started to ring and the elevator door opened expelling a bevy of Ad-Film employees, instantly engulfing her in the discordant din of voices, each demanding her immediate attention.

* * *

As he became more of a fixture at Ad-Film, Jay found time to observe the phalanx of salesmen/producers who appeared to spend their time alternately talking on the phone, going to lunch, regaling one another with their business conquests and hitting on the secretaries. They were, he decided, like male dogs constantly sniffing rear ends in search of any bitch in heat. Everything in their conversations with their clients, with their peers, with the office staff was laced with sexual innuendo. The offices which they inhabited had been labeled by the women of Ad-Film as *'Stud Row. The Home of Grand Delusions.'* Jay assumed that Joanna, stunning as she was, must have been under a constant sniffing assault from the nattily attired dog-men from stud row. He wondered why she had not been plucked from her perch at the reception desk and claimed by one of the studs in the back as their secretary.

"Think about it, the very thing which draws the office *yakapuks* to her also prevents them from daring to give her a desk back here with us." The observation came from John Baskham, an Ad-Film producer. John was a balding man of fifty with a large mustache and heavy glasses who seemed to have had a briar pipe implanted permanently into the side of his mouth. Baskham's job was to call on his agency clients and bid on the production of new commercials. Victory came each time he returned from the streets with a story-board in hand. Jay realized from the first day he slipped into his office to introduce himself that John considered himself both different from and superior to the other producers who worked at Ad-Film. Baskham had shown an early interest in Jay, asking about his aspirations, viewing his two NYU films, offering advice and, in the process, granting him a level of friendship which he was stingy about dispensing to most of the other people in the company.

"How would one of the producers explain someone like Joanna to his wife?" John left the question floating as he relit his pipe. "Tell me dear," he said elevating his voice to a falsetto, "does she sit on your lap and take dictation? Does she *have* to wear those tight skirts? Does she *have* to look like that? No, Jay, through no fault of her own she is the kind of woman who inspires assumptions and those assumptions, once planted in the mind of a wife, are nearly impossible to dislodge."

Baskham leaned back in his chair putting some distance between himself and his desk. "The way I figure it, there's been a tacit agreement to keep her on display in the reception area ... isolated, yet available to be appreciated by arriving clients or ogled by the yakapuks on the way to the men's room."

* * *

Jay seized upon every excuse to create opportunities for him to pass through the reception area - despite the fact that Marty Oppenheimer, the Ad-Film owner, had decreed it to be off-limits to go-fers except when absolutely necessary. They, the lowest of rodents in a production company, they who ran the city streets with film cans under their arms, were notified to limit their comings and goings to the back hall. Nevertheless, Jay was willing to risk the owner's wrath, even if it meant immediate dismissal; such was the irresistible allure of Miss Joanna Olenska.

Slowly, Jay managed to establish a marginal level of conversational rapport with her. Clearly, he was so far down the office food chain that she had exempted him from the ranks of office sniffers who seemed relentless in their efforts to penetrate the oral karate that Joanna used to fend off their advances. Jay decided the dog-men were really masochists who somehow enjoyed being on the end of her verbal emasculation. Joanna was nothing short of masterful in her handling of the more aggressive sniffers. She reminded him of a knight, who when accosted by an opponent, emerges from the castle wielding her words like a broad sword and, with one stroke, cuts the adversary off at the knees.

The first time Jay saw her in action she was waiting for the elevator with one of the sniffers. "When are you going to let me get to know the *real* you, Joanna?" His come-on lacked originality, but her response did not.

"Tuesday."

"What?" The surprise in his voice revealed that it was not the answer he'd expected.

"Next Tuesday. I'll call your wife so we can all go out to dinner and get to know the real me." Whack. Right at the knees.

Another time Jay witnessed Joanna's physical ability to deal with unwanted advances. He was passing a door leading to the reception area just as one of the sniffers laid an uninvited hand on her behind. Slowly she slid her hand over his and, in a move that Jay later discovered she learned in a self-defense class, twisted his hand backwards inflicting instant pain causing the man to buckle at the knees. "How do you think that hand is going to look in a cast, Mickey?"

"Jesus Joanna!" the pain evident in his voice. "What t'hell's got into you?"

"Certainly, not you," she said hotly.

* * *

The first time Jay managed to have an extended conversation with Joanna, he had returned from a delivery and picked up a sandwich to take back to the office. He walked into the lunchroom at just before two and found her on a break, sitting alone, reading a newspaper and having a cup of coffee. Almost from the first day Jay sensed that she seemed intent on surrounding herself with a protective shell, a barrier to prevent anyone from getting too close.

"Hi," he said.

"Late lunch?" she asked indifferently.

"I was over on the West Side and couldn't get a taxi. I don't know where they all are today." He put a dime in the soda vending machine, removed the bottle, then sat down at a table next to hers. As he unwrapped his sandwich, he realized Joanna had been staring at him with a quizzical, almost judicial look. "I sense a question," he said.

"You sensed right."

"Ask away."

"What are you doing here?"

Jay knew what she meant by 'here,' but decided to feign ignorance. "Well, I thought I was eating my lunch."

"You know what I mean. I'm talking about Ad-Film. Look at you. A sport coat and tie. Creases in your pants. Shined shoes. You don't look like a go-fer."

"And I don't much like being one."

"Which brings me back to my question: What are you doing at Ad-Film?"

"I'm a little embarrassed to admit this, but I was told that if I wanted to become a film director, I'd have to start at the bottom and work my way up. So here I am ... at the bottom." He added, with emphasis, "The *very* bottom."

A smile crept over her face, followed by a quiet, unguarded laugh.

"A sorry stop on the way to the top." They were both laughing now. "Seriously, though, I'm hoping that it'll give me a chance to meet some people, make some connections and maybe learn a few things."

"Like?"

"Like how you get from way down here to way up there. I figure other guys have done it, so why not me?"

"So, is making movies something you've always wanted to do?"

"Pretty much. When I was about twelve, my father gave me a motion picture camera. He decided I needed a hobby. It was a Bell & Howell Imo, the kind they shot combat pictures with during the war. I made epic films with that camera. Every time I saw a movie that I really liked, I'd recruit my friends to be the actors and shoot my own version. I know my parents thought that one day I'd grow up and lose interest in making movie epics in the back yard and, you know, get serious about a real career. I fooled 'em. I didn't."

"Didn't what? Grow up or get serious?"

"Either one."

She looked at him with a bemused smile, as if wondering what manner of being was seated at the next table. After a long moment she said, "You're funny, you know?"

"Funny strange or funny *funny*?" he asked cautiously.

"Just good funny," she said, with a sincerity that sent Jay's heart racing.

"Jay! I got a 'Hot!'" The screech came from Vivian somewhere down the hall.

"My master's, or more accurately, my mistress' voice," he said, wrapping up what was left of his sandwich and pushing back his chair. "Funny, huh?" he said, smiling at Joanna as he backed out of the lunchroom.

"Good funny," she repeated, returning the smile.

2
Arabella's Rules

"If my old man were worth a zillion dollars—"

"Actually, he's worth just a little less," Jay said, correcting his friend.

"Whatever. If my old man were as rich as yours and planned to one day give me half the family business, I think I might have thought twice about telling him to 'stuff it.'"

"I never told him to 'stuff it.'"

"But you said 'no,' right?"

"I said I wanted to give this a try. I worked for my father for a couple years before I went to graduate school and I can tell you that it's not what I want to do for the rest of my life." Jay tightened his grip on the silver grab pole to steady himself as the subway car lurched first to one side and then the other, its metal wheels sending an ear-piercing squeal through the car.

"I don't know, Carraway," Anson Fuller said, shaking his head, "to walk away from an enormous house in Greenwich and a cushy job with a guaranteed multi-million future to be a friggin' Cecil B. Demille wannabe is a little crazy if you ask me."

"Hey, mark me certifiable and lock me up."

"Might have to do just that."

Anson laughed. "What the hell, every family needs a black sheep." Then, in a more serious tone, "I imagine things got a little tense when you told your father that you were chuckin' the family business."

"It really got bad when I told my mother."

"I'm sure she wasn't too happy to learn that the masters degree in economics you were supposed to be getting at NYU turned out to be two years of film production courses."

"You're totally irresponsible!" Jay said, mimicking his mother. " Do you have any idea of how this makes us look with our friends? Why can't you be like your brother? Do you enjoy being a constant source of consternation?"

"Consternation. Is that anything like constipation?"

"In my mother's case, it tends to have the same effect." Jay Carraway nodded toward the subway doors as they opened. "This is your stop, right?"

"Right." Anson said, leading the way onto the platform.

As they climbed the steps to the street Anson asked, "So, how did you leave it with your father?"

"Better than you might think. He was pretty cool. Naturally, he was disappointed. After my mother left the room we had a long talk. Finally, he said that if this was what I wanted to do, I should give it a shot. But he made it clear that I had to do it on my own."

"Translation: No dinero from the family treasury for lunch money."

"No dinero," Jay echoed. "Just what I had in my own bank account. Which is not bottomless."

"You know, I've always considered you one of my best friends because you were rich. Now that you've been tossed out on the street without a penny to your name, I may have to look for a new friend."

"I still have enough to buy us a beer."

"In that case, I won't start looking until tomorrow."

***

Jay and Anson shared a couple of beers and then ordered a pizza and a bottle of wine. "I don't know man," Anson said pouring the last of the wine into his glass, "if I had your money and your looks, I'd say to hell with working and just lay back tell the women to line up and take a number."

"Yeah, right. That'd be a short line." Jay looked around as if preparing to reveal a secret. "To tell you the truth, there's only one woman I'd want in my line."

"And who might that be?"

"A woman I met at the office."

"And are we on our way to first base with this lady?"

"First base? Not exactly. Actually, I'm barely up to bat. But, I gotta tell you, I have feeling—a very definite feeling that …" He cut himself off, deciding he'd said enough, for the time being, about Miss Joanna Olenska. "Well, as they say in the Saturday afternoon serials, this story to be continued. Hopefully."

At ten, the wine having begun to work its will, they made their way north on West End Avenue, past the endless rows of heavy, brown, prewar buildings, toward 85th Street. Jay said, "Tell me again about this guy whose apartment I'm commandeering."

"Eddy Valerian. He's a jazz musician who's on tour with some group in London and points east. He'll be gone for at least a month, maybe more. As I told you, he gave me the key and said I could use it if any of my crazy friends needed a place to sack out."

"So what happens if he should come back unexpectedly? Like in a couple days?"

"Don't worry, he won't. If he does, I'll ship you back to the Dixie hotel."

"I'll sleep on a park bench first. I'm not sure which was worse in that place, the hookers or the cockroaches."

"Whatsa matter, you don't like insects?" Anson teetered slightly and grabbed the stair rail to steady himself. "Next time, we've got to buy better wine," he said groaning. He fumbled in his pocket, then handed Jay the key to Valerian's apartment. "Excuse me while I go upstairs and get sick."

The musician's apartment looked like a handball court with its bare wooden floor, flat white walls and white ceiling, into which someone had stored and then forgotten, various pieces of inconsequential furniture. There was a double bed, a desk, a sagging sofa that looked as if some *one* or some *thing* possessing great weight had spent considerable time in the middle. Next to the wall, near the door, a badly painted yellow wooden table with two chairs was intended, he supposed, to serve as his dining table. A door near the far corner led to a walk-in kitchen that Jay found was stacked with dirty dishes, clearly left unattended for weeks. Four large, blow-up prints of jazz musicians had been hung on the walls, apparently with no sense of plan or purpose. One wall, opposite the bed, showed dozens of random round black marks that looked as if the tenant had, in fact, used the room for a handball court.

Jay unpacked his bags and turned on the TV, doing his best to adjust the rabbit ears so that he could clear the electronic snow from the picture. It was hopeless. He finally gave up and, giving in to the after-effects of the cheap wine, dropped into the bed.

It was well after midnight when he was awakened by the sound of someone fumbling to insert a key into the door lock. Jay bolted into a sitting position. The door opened a crack and the grimy yellow light from the hall fixture slashed into the room.

"Eddy?" It was a small female voice.

The door swung open revealing a silhouetted figure.

"He's not here." Jay made sure that his response sounded sharp and potentially threatening.

He could see a hand feeling its way along the wall toward the light switch and then flicking it on. For an instant, the light blinded him, but as his eyes adjusted, he found himself staring up at a very thin young woman with boyishly cut brown hair. She was dressed in a sleeveless loose-hanging blouse and baggy pants. Her eyes were big and curiously apathetic, showing no sign of surprise or concern at finding herself confronted with a man who clearly was not the Eddy she had been seeking. Around her neck, an enormous snail shell was suspended by a leather thong. A flower appeared to be *growing* out of the shell.

"Who the fuck-n-hell are you?" There was a dispassion in her voice that Jay found totally incongruous with her choice of expletives.

"I'm Jay."

"Where's Eddy?"

"If you mean the Eddy who lives in this apartment, he's in London, I think. His friend, Anson Fuller, who lives upstairs, said I could stay here while I'm looking for a place of my own."

She made a short grunting sound that seemed to indicate she would not require further explanation. As she closed the door, she announced, "My name is Arabella. That's all. No last name. I've decided just to use one name from now on. Eddy lets me sleep here sometimes when it's too late for me to go home. We're friends. Just friends. Nothing more. I like his music." With that, she began to undress.

It occurred to Jay that nothing in his limited experience had prepared him for this.

She dropped her skirt and unbuttoned her blouse and in a matter of seconds, she was standing across the room from him wearing only a bright green bra and forest green panties. On her feet she was wearing green shoes that came to long thin points which curled back over her toes. All she had to do, he thought, was sprout gossamer wings and she could have passed for Tinkerbelle.

"My boyfriend and I have a place in Queens. He's a waiter. I'm into calligraphy. What about you?"

Lacking any other recourse, he replied, "I just got a job with a TV commercial production company."

"Which one?"

"Ad-Film. Ever hear of it?"

"Yeah, I know somebody there."

"Who?"

"An asshole!"

From Jay's limited exposure to the Ad-Film staff, he concluded that her description might apply to any of the several salesmen. "Does the 'asshole' have a name?"

"Dick Head," she responded. "Anything in the fridge to eat?" She stepped into the tiny kitchen and opened the refrigerator door. From her face and demeanor, Jay guessed that she was twenty-two or three, but her body looked more like that of a pubescent teenager. She had small nubs for breasts and her figure seemed devoid of all but the slightest suggestion of curves. Finding nothing to her liking in the refrigerator, Arabella walked over to the wall switch and, just before she turned it off, said, "I like to sleep on the left side." Her tone remained flat, without color or emphasis, almost as if she were explaining how to find the nearest subway station. "You've got a nice face. You look like a good guy. Are you a good guy?"

"I guess so, depending on your definition of 'good.'"

"By good, I mean you understand what I mean when I say that I'm not into screwing guys I've just met. So, for us to make this work tonight, you just have to keep your hands to yourself and we'll be friends. Those are the Arabella's Rules. *Vous comprenez?*" She seemed to assume that his response was in the affirmative, so she turned off the light, crossed the room and slipped into the bed.

A streetlight outside the apartment window cast enough light into the room for Jay to see that she was still wearing her Looney-tune footwear. "Shoes?" he said pointing to her feet.

"Almost forgot," she said, kicking them off and sending the shoes flying one after the other into random parts of the room.

What kind of nut case was this? he wondered. He considered getting up and relocating himself on the couch, but by now, the residual effect of the wine had taken hold, leaving him with a pronounced hammering in his head and the certainty that it had swelled to twice its normal size.

"I hope you don't mind if I cuddle a little," she said. "I like to feel a body next to mine when I sleep. It gives me a sense of security." With that, she rolled over, wiggled her back into his mid-section and said no more.

His last thought, before succumbing to sleep, was that either he should be taking precautions against the possibility of her being some kind of a diabolical killer who preyed on unsuspecting young men, or that she fully expected him to test the limits of *Arabella's Rules*. It made no difference; he was incapable of pursing either option. When he awoke, sometime after eight, her side of the bed was vacant. He began to wonder if his visitor had been a hallucination brought on by the last glass of Chianti. It hadn't. Next to him on the pillow, he found her snail shell with the flower and a note.

Thanks for being a good guy. Here's a present from me to you.
Don't over-water the flower.
                    Love, Arabella

"Oh, so you spent the night with Arabella?" Anson couldn't help but laugh when he heard the story. "A real nut case. Eddy never knows when she's going to show up. Don't worry; she's harmless. Word has it her father is some rich guy who lives on Fifth Avenue and she's rebelling. Chances are, you'll never see her again."

As it turned out, she showed up about the same hour, three days later. Again, Jay was awakened by a key fumbling in the lock. He sprang off the bed and took the four steps necessary to put him at the door.

"Is that you, Arabella?"

"You still here, Jay?" she asked, stepping inside.

"Still here."

"This is Yoshiro," she said, gesturing to a small Japanese man, who nodded as he entered and took off his shoes. His pointy face and big brown eyes reminded Jay of a chipmunk. "My boyfriend and I broke up and now I'm living with Yoshiro. He's from Japan and doesn't speak much English. He can sleep on the couch. Keep in mind that Arabella's Rules are still in effect."

Little more was said as Yoshiro curled up, fetal-style, on the couch. Arabella took her place on the left side of the bed. She snuggled her back into Jay's mid-section and then suddenly turned to him, as though he had just violated the house rules. "I just remembered, you work for Ad-Film, right?"

"Right."

"Do me a favor?' she asked.

"Sure. What?"

"I'll tell you in the morning," she said and went to sleep.

As before, when he awoke, she was gone. He was relieved to discover she had taken Yoshiro with her. Once again, she'd left him a note on the pillow.

Don't expect to see me anymore. Yoshiro and I are going to Japan. About the favor: If you meet Marty at Ad-Film, give him a message for me. Tell him Arabella said for him to go fuck himself.

Have a nice life!
Sayōnara, Arabella.

Marty? Ad Films Marty? he wondered.

3
Deli Date

A distracted waiter in a stained white apron, shouting something to another waiter over his shoulder, arrived with their orders. He looked at the plates. "Special? Chicken salad plate?"

"Chicken is hers. Special is mine," Jay said.

Lunch with Joanna at a crowded deli on Lexington Avenue was not how Jay had imagined their first date, if it could be called that. In an impulsive moment he'd asked if he could buy her lunch fully expecting her to turn him down. To his surprise she seemed happy to accept on the condition that they split the check.

"How long have you worked for Ad-Film?" he asked.

"A little too long, almost four months. I'm actually just a temp. I got the job with the understanding that I'm out of there when something better comes along."

"And what might that 'something' be?"

She ducked the question "It might be 'something' we can talk about another time." Joanna picked up a French fry and before she popped it into her mouth she asked, "Where are you from? You're not a New Yorker."

"Grew up in Greenwich."

"Village?"

"Connecticut."

"My, my. The high rent district. I guess you're an exception."

"An exception to what?"

"I thought everyone in Greenwich was rich and dull." There was drollness to her tease.

"You thought correctly," Jay said, assuming a pompous air." We are all very rich and dreadfully dull. We spend our days at the club, go to church on Sunday, we hardly ever mistreat our servants, you'll never hear us curse and we do our best not to get our girl friends pregnant before they graduate from Miss Porters prep school."

"What?" she laughed.

"Actually, I lied. We do curse now and then." He laughed with her.

"The kid from Greenwich has a sense of humor," she said appreciatively.

"Hey, you said I was funny. So count on me to be a laugh-a-minute."

"Tell me, speaking of prep school, is it true that after prep school everyone in Greenwich goes to Yale?" She was clearly enjoying needling him.

"Everyone but me. Too dumb for prep school and too wild for Yale."

"Somehow, it's hard for me to buy 'dumb,' but I may accept 'wild' once I get to know you better," she said, smiling. "Do you have brothers and sisters?"

"Older brother. Younger sister. And you?"

"Just me," she answered quickly and then bounced the conversation back to him. "What do they do?"

"My brother is in business with my father and my sister is still in college. Ok," he said straightening up in his chair and adopting a resolute tone, "you now know about all there is to know about me ..."

She cut him off, *"This* is all there is? I guess the book on Jay Carraway is a very thin volume."

"You're right. It's a *very* thin and a very uninteresting volume. So let's talk about something more interesting, such as what Miss Joanna Olenska does when she's not temping as a receptionist."

"When I'm not temping as a receptionist, I'm temping as a secretary. I'm a whiz at shorthand and I can type a hundred twenty words a minute."

"I'm impressed. Now, when you're not taking short hand or typing, what do you do?"

"You may not find it all that interesting."

"Let me be the judge of that."

Joanna hesitated, as though looking for the necessary resolve to step out of her shell–to leave her armor behind at the bulwark and talk about herself. "Well, beneath this underappreciated, hopefully very temporary temp, I'm a singer, a dancer and a generally an out-of-work actress who has performed with a long list of very unusual co-stars."

"Such as?

"Well, I've sung to a car, danced with a refrigerator, played a scene with a talking gorilla suit and had a close personal relationship with a diesel truck, to say nothing of sharing the stage with a bunch of TVs, dishwashers, Avon Ladies and a stack of car tires."

Jay choked back a laugh. "What kind of shows have you been in?"

"Industrial shows."

"Industrial shows?" he echoed, asking for clarification.

"They're a meal ticket for a lot of aspiring actors. When a company, like Ford or GM, for example, introduces a new car to their dealers, they call in a theatrical production company to create what looks and even sounds a lot like a Broadway musical. Singers, dancers, actors, sets ... the whole nine yards. The only difference is that, in an industrial, the *car* is the star."

"Is the money good?"

"More than I make at Ad-Film. The problem is that it's very irregular. You might get four to six weeks with a show then nothing for months. But when you're working, the pay not only covers the rent, but also gives you a little extra for those times when you're, as we say, between jobs. One benefit is that you never know when you might work with someone who has connections with a Broadway producer."

"Have you ever been on Broadway?"

"Off-Broadway a few times. My most recent debacle was a show back in January at the Bowery Lane."

"I take it the show didn't run very long."

"Well, let's put it this way. The producer saved a lot of money by holding the opening night and closing night party at the same time."

"Must have been some party."

"Like a wake. On the positive side, I've been in a couple of musical revues that ran for six weeks. Unfortunately, I've spent most of my time on stage doing my best to look excited about whatever the client's product happens to be."

"So what's next?"

"I got a call back for a revival of *Born Yesterday.* Maybe I'll get lucky. Then I've got a couple go-sees lined up."

"Go-sees?"

"Casting calls. It's a great way to have your ego adjusted."

"As in?"

"Assaulted. Beat up. Stomped on. They don't call it a cattle call for nothing. If you're an actor, a cattle call most always ends up as a personal slaughter."

It was as though Jay had unknowingly opened a valve and the flood of words poured out—probably, he thought, for the first time in a long time. "I take it casting calls are not a lot of fun."

"No, not a lot. They're usually held in some rehearsal studio and the first thing they tell you is to wait out in a hallway with a million other out-of-work actors. After a couple hours of inhaling stale smoke and listening to everyone bitch about this or that, you're called in and given two minutes in front of a half-dozen people sitting behind a table: the producer, director, the client and who knows who else."

"And then...?"

"Then they ask you to read from a terrible script extolling the virtues of a station wagon, or whatever it is the show is about. You sing four bars of whatever song you've prepared and show them you know how to dance. When you finish, they start to whisper with each other and then the producer says something like, 'Thanks for coming in, but we're looking for someone taller, or shorter or don't call us, we'll call you, leave the script and don't let the door hit you as you leave.'"

"Not exactly a great business for a fragile ego."

"You've got to love rejection," she said sarcastically. "If you can't handle being beat up by people you've never met, you aren't going to make it."

"No business like show business, right?"

"Trouble is, you tend to fool yourself into thinking that eventually you'll get a break. Maybe you'll get a part, even a small part, in a Broadway show. You find yourself dreaming that maybe you'll understudy the lead and the lead will get sick and you'll get your chance to show people just how good you really are." Then, with a short self-deprecating laugh, she said, "The reality, of course, is that most actresses find themselves waiting tables, sitting in a typing pool or playing the part of a receptionist at places like Ad-Film." Joanna's gaze drifted toward the window and out onto Lexington Avenue. Jay was left to wonder if she was regretting having opened up to him. Finally, she turned back to him and said in a quiet, pleasant sort of way, "You know, it bothers me a little that I find you so easy to talk to."

"It bothers you? Why? I certainly like talking to you."

"It's just that a lot of guys ..." she decided not to finish the thought and changed the subject. "So where are you living here in the city?"

"Well, while I look for something to rent, I'm staying up on West End Avenue in what I guess you might call a communal crash pad."

"A communal crash pad?" Her expression indicated she was looking for an explanation.

He then proceeded to tell her about his two nights sharing a bed with Arabella and the arrival of Yoshiro.

"Arabella's Rules," she laughed. "I love it. A totally unknown woman jumps into your bed and expects you to obey her rules." She paused and gave him a doubting look. "And did you?"

"If you had seen Arabella, you wouldn't be asking me that question."

"You mean girls wearing snail shells with flowers growing out of them are not your type?"

"Definitely not my type," he assured her.

Joanna glanced at her watch. "We should to be getting back."

They split the check, despite his attempt to handle the transaction himself and left the deli. As they walked up Lexington Avenue to 52nd Street, she dominated the conversation. The subjects were unrelated, stream-of-consciousness observations and random comments on the stores they passed, people at the office and whatever seemed to come to mind. What was important to Jay was that she did most, if not all, of the talking confirming that, somehow, he had managed to penetrate her protective veneer—at least a little.

4
HERDING CATS

J ay walked into John Baskham's office and handed him a large envelope. "Storyboards from Jordan, Day and Green."

"The Tasti-Feast commercial, right?" Baskham was asking for confirmation.

"Right. A blueprint for a disaster."

"What makes you say that?"

"I took a look at the boards on the way back from the agency. I don't know who dreamed up this commercial, but they clearly don't know much about cats. Believe me, my sister had six at one time, so I know from cats. Anyway, if I'm reading that right," he said pointing to the envelope, "the woman puts down a bowl of Tasti-Feast and all of a sudden nearly a hundred cats appear from every direction making a dash for the food."

"And …?

"Well, unless the director is Dr. Doolittle and can talk to the animals, the cats are not about to line up like it shows in the storyboard and take their turn at Tasti-Feast bowl. What you're going to have is one hell of a catfight."

Baskham smiled. "Should make for a very interesting shoot."

"I gather you're not concerned."

"Nope. Not my problem. This commercial is the personal baby of the agency's creative director who, in my humble opinion, ranks as one of the premier yakapuks of all time. He's going to direct the spot himself because our guys—how did he put it?—'Don't know how to handle pussy.'"

"And he does?"

"The point is, we're not shooting pussy, we're shooting cats. And you're right, it could be a disaster. You wanna come watch?"

"Sure!" Jay said enthusiastically. "But I don't think Vivian will let me out of here."

"Leave that to me. The crew call is for eight Thursday morning at our 54th Street sound stage."

***

Jay arrived at the studio just as the crew was beginning to light the set—what there was of it. The commercial was to be shot against a totally white background. The stage floor and the walls of the cyc had been painted white to create a sense of infinity. In the middle of the stage, the prop man had hung a window frame. Below it, he had placed a stove, refrigerator, sink, counter area and two stools, to suggest a kitchen.

The storyboard called for a woman to enter carrying a bowl with the words Tasti-Feast on the side. She was to set the bowl on the counter and, as she filled it with Tasti-Feast say, "We decided to conduct a Tasti-Feast taste test. In this bowl, Tasti-Feast. A wonderful blend of fish and meat." At that point, the camera was to reveal five other bowls placed in a neat row on the floor. She was to go on to say, "In these bowls, five competitive brands. Let's see which cat food discerning cats like yours prefer."

At that point, she was to set down the Tasti-Feast bowl with the competitive brands and suddenly, out of nowhere, a hundred cats rush from every direction and make a beeline for the Tasti-

Feast. Once the cats had selected the sponsor's brand over the competitors', the actress was to say: "There you have it, proof that discerning cats prefer Tasti-Feast."

At nine, Jay watched the animal handlers arrive on the stage with twenty cages of cats that appeared to be anything but happy about their upcoming participation in the commercial.

"Are those the fuckin' cats?" Jay turned toward the foghorn-like voice, which belonged to Jackson Korman, the man Baskham had pointed out as the creative director from Jordan, Day and Green. He was exceedingly short, but very wide and walked like a wounded duck. His face seemed to be locked in perpetual sneer.

"All 101," the animal handler answered.

"They're hungry, right?" Korman looked at the cages as he put the question to the animal handler.

"Really hungry. Haven't fed them a thing since yesterday."

"Good. I want those little fuckers ravenous."

The animal handler turned to Korman. "There's only one thing; being as hungry as they are, there's a good chance they're going to eat everything you set out for them. Including the competitors' food."

"No chance. I've put so much disgusting shit in the brand 'X' cat food that the smell will have them tossing up fur balls before they get within two feet those bowls."

"But that isn't exactly a fair comparison, is it?" the handler asked.

"Fair? Who's talkin' fair? I'll tell you what's fair. What's fair is that the fucking cats eat the Tasti-Feast and we end up with a great commercial. All you have to do is turn those cats loose when I give you the cue."

At nine-thirty, a large contingent of sycophants and minor functionaries arrived from Jordan, Day and Green, along with

Tom Martin, the brand manager from Tasti-Feast. The agency people immediately descended like locusts on the breakfast spread that the catering service had set up in the rear of the studio. It looked to Jay as if none of them had eaten in weeks.

"Hungry group, aren't they?" Baskham said to Jay.

"Almost as hungry as those cats," Jay replied.

"G'morning, John," Tom Martin said as he stuck out his hand to Baskham. "Is this going to work?" he asked, nodding toward the set.

"Korman says it is."

"I didn't ask him, I asked you."

"I'll let you know in a couple of hours."

"In a couple of hours, I won't need to ask."

Jay turned his attention to the set, where Korman was directing the camera crews where to place the five cameras he'd ordered to cover the action. At least, Jay thought, Korman recognized that he wasn't going to be able to get more than one or two takes of the cats rushing onto the set.

"I don't think they had that many cameras to shoot the chariot race in Ben Hur," Baskham said.

"I've got a feeling this is going to be a one take shot," Jay added.

Korman stood in the middle of the set and shouted. "Listen up, everybody. I'm going to shoot the last scene first, so we can get those cats the hell out of here. Put the cages where I told you," he said to the animal handler, "and have your guys ready to let 'em loose." He then turned to the prop man and said, "Give the bowl of Tasti-Feast to what's-her-face." He pointed toward the woman who was to deliver the lines.

"Maybe I should wear a nametag!" the actress shot back clearly offended that the director had forgotten her name. "It's Angela."

"Angela," he repeated with a shrug. "Ok. Pay attention. On action, you take the cat food and set it down at the end of that line of competitive bowls and start calling for the cats. Give me a 'Here kitty, kitty.' That will be the cue for the animal guys to open the cages."

The handler and his assistants placed the cat cages around the perimeter of the set, out of camera range. The makeup lady made a quick, last-minute touch-up on Angela's hair, while Korman called for the lights. "Ok, let's get ready to roll film," he shouted.

The actress took her place on the set and Korman turned to the cat handler and his assistants. "You guys ready?"

"Ready."

"Ok, you know your line, right, sweetheart?"

"The name is Angela and I'm not you're sweetheart!"

"We'll talk about that later," Korman's salacious grin made it clear that his retort was for the benefit of his ego and the amusement of the crew. "Stand by and … action!"

The actress looked up at one of the cameras and said, "Let's see which cat food discerning cats like yours prefer." She knelt down on one knee, placed the Tasti-Feast bowl in line with the competitive brands and called, "Here kitty, kitty!"

Korman pointed to the handler. "Cue the cats."

The cage doors opened and the cats dashed out of the cages like convicts during a prison break. Jay watched as a virtual tidal wave of felines surged across the white floor from all directions toward the kitchen set and the bowls of food. As Korman had planned, they avoided the tainted competitors' food and made a rush to the Tasti-Feast.

"Too many cats, too little food," Jay whispered to Baskham.

It was mayhem. A catfight to end all catfights broke out almost at once. Each cat was trying to get to the solitary bowl of Tasti-Feast. The cats treated the kneeling actress as nothing more than a barrier between them and the cat food, a barrier to be pushed, climbed on, slipped under and scratched aside. After failing in an effort to stand up, she toppled back onto her fanny and began to scream. "Get these fucking cats off me! Get them off! Get me out of here!"

"Cut!" Korman yelled.

"Now that would make a hell of a commercial," Jay said, doing his best not to laugh. "Nobody, I mean *nobody*, would forget it."

"Dr. Doolittle he ain't?" Baskham added fully enjoying the mayhem.

The actress screamed obscenities as the cats continued to fight for a chance at the Tasti-Feast.

"I think somebody'd better help her," Jay said, volunteering for the job. He hurried onto the white stage floor, made his way through the ravenous cats and literally picked up the actress and carried her out of the melee to the edge of the set.

As he put her down, she spat, "I hate cats! I hate 'em! Look what they did to me!" She showed Jay her scratched arms. "I'm calling my agent!" she screamed at Korman as she stalked off toward the dressing room.

"Get those fuckers back in the cages!" Korman yelled. He ran over to the animal handler, who was attempting to corral a couple of cats and jerked him around, shouting into his face. "What the hell are you doing? Those cats were out of control! This is not what I asked for! Now, you get them reset for another take! We got to make some adjustments, cause this ain't' going to work." Korman turned his back on the handler and walked off the set, calling for a conference with his agency minions.

Martin looked at Baskham, "Unless we figure out some way to save this thing, I'm gonna catch a lot of crap from my boss. I don't know, maybe we should think about calling it a day and going back to the drawing board."

"Your call."

"First, I'm going to have a little chat with our creative genius."

Jay watched as Martin crossed the stage to where Korman was pacing back and front in front of his staff. Baskham turned to Jay, hardly able to control his amusement. "I can't wait to see how Korman deals with this."

"Set up for take two," Korman shouted. "We're going to try it again. Maybe they won't be as hungry this time."

"Well, there's your answer," Jay said. "It appears he hasn't learned much about cats."

"I think we're going to need a Plan B," Baskham said.

"Can I suggest one?"

"You have an idea?"

"It's something I was thinking about last night. I drew it up, just for the heck of it." He pulled a piece of paper from his shirt pocket and began to unfold it. "It's a lot different from what the storyboard calls for, but I think it makes the same point about the product." He laid the piece of paper in front of Baskham.

"It looks like a maze."

"That's what it is. Sides are about a foot high. And in the center," he said, pointing to a square area in the middle of the maze, "we put the Tasti-Feast. Then we put one cat on the outside of the maze in front of the entrance. We turn the cat loose and let him run through the maze, looking exactly like he knows where he's going, until he finds his way to the food. You could shoot it from several different angles, like we're covering a sporting event. You've got five cameras, so each should give the editor a lot of options. Anyway, when the cat gets to the center, the actress, or whoever's voice you use, says, "Smart cats always find their way to Tasti-Feast."

Baskham said nothing as he digested the concept, then simply, "I love it. It's great. One question: Will a cat run the maze?"

"I think so. If he's hungry enough."

"Let's ask the animal handler."

He called the animal handler over and showed him Jay's drawing.

"Yeah, I can get a cat to do that. I'd need about a half hour to get him trained. Do you plan to do it in one shot or a series of cuts?"

"I think it would be more effective if we did it in cuts," Jay said.

"Then it's no problem. Worst case, we'll pull a bag of catnip on a string in front of him just out of camera frame."

"Good," Baskham said. "Let's run this by Martin."

"Tom!" Baskham called to the brand manager who was standing off to the side of the set talking to Korman. "Tom, can you come here a minute? I want to show you something."

Martin left Korman, crossed the set and sat down next to Baskham. "This is Jay Carraway," Baskham said, nodding toward Jay, who stood behind him, looking over Baskham's shoulder. "He's one of our brighter young guys and he's come up an idea that I think you ought to look at."

Five minutes later, Martin called for Korman to join them and showed him Jay's concept.

"No, no," Korman said, tossing up his hands to indicate he'd been personally offended that anyone would dare offer an alternative to his creativity. "That's all wrong. Sends the wrong message. I don't like it." Then he looked at Jay and spat out derisively, "Who the hell is this kid to tell me how to make my commercial?"

"*My* commercial," Martin said quietly, but firmly, correcting Korman. "I know this is somewhat of a departure from the storyboard, but I'd really like you to give this some thought. It's simple, it's clean, it's visually interesting and the message is essentially the same as yours."

"Tom, let me be very clear about this," Korman said in a condescending, gratuitous tone. "It's a shitty idea. I'm the creative director on this account and I don't like it and that's all there is to it. I'm not going to shoot a cat running in some fucking maze."

"Well, you may be the creative director, but I'm the client," Martin said sternly. "And if you're not going to direct this commercial, then we'll find someone who will."

"You're not serious?" his challenge was tinged with the suspicion that Martin just might be serious.

"Oh, but I am. Further, I think its best that you and your staff take the rest of the day off. I'll let John Baskham and his people handle this."

"Wait a minute!" Korman said, looking for a retreat. "We need to talk."

"I'm done talking. You might tell Mr. Jordan or Mr. Day or Mr. Green to give me a call when one of them gets a chance."

Korman's face turned red and Jay thought he looked as if he was about to unload on Tom Martin. Jay decided he must have thought better of dumping his vitriol on the client, because he stalked off the stage, muttering something under his breath.

"Can you find someone to take over, John?" Martin asked.

"John," Jay said, "I can direct this. There's really nothing to direct. We've got five cameras here, so we can cover the action five ways to Sunday."

"You know the union says we're supposed to only use Director's Guild members. Do you belong to the DGA?"

"No," Jay said, his face falling

"So who's to know? Get out there and make this thing happen."

***

At just after five, they called it a wrap. Tom Martin walked up to Jay and Baskham, smiling. "For my part, it's been a very good day all around. Let me know when I can come see the rough cut."

"Will do," John said.

"Now I'm going to find myself the nearest bar."

Not ten minutes later, Marty Oppenheimer burst into the studio, spotted Baskham and let loose. The small blue veins in his cheeks stood out like the blue lines on a road map. "What in the fuck is going on here? I got a call from Jackson Korman. He is pissed as hell." Marty began to jab his finger at Baskham's chest, stopping just short of touching him. "Korman says that we ... actually *you*, Baskham . . . fucked him over with his client. That you went ahead and shot some fucking piece of shit that had nothing to do with his storyboard. I want to know what the fuck happened."

Jay found himself involuntarily taking a step back, but Baskham just folded his arms and listened calmly, touching his face now and then to remove the flying spittle that seemed to punctuate Marty's tirade like exclamation marks.

"Do you want to hear what happened or do you just want to yell at me?"

Oppenheimer shot back, "I want to know what happened."

Baskham proceeded to tell him about the cat melee and how the client was about to cancel the shoot when Jay came up with an idea that Martin loved. "Korman threw a hissy fit and said he wouldn't shoot the new version. So, Martin told him to take a hike. The scenic guys built us a maze and we shot Jay's version. Martin loved it."

"Jay? Jay? Who the fuck is Jay?"

Jay stepped forward. "I guess that would be me."

"Are you with the agency, or 'Tasti-Feast?"

"I'm with Ad-Film."

"You work for me?" Oppenheimer was taken aback. "When the hell did we hire you?"

"About a month ago."

"I've never seen you in the office."

"That's because I'm usually out on deliveries or pick-ups."

Oppenheimer turned his back on Jay. With a look of total disbelief, he asked Baskham, "Is he telling me he's one of our go-fers?"

"Yeah," said Baskham, finding it difficult not to laugh. "That's what he's telling you."

"Jesus H. Christ! Since when did our go-fers start writing commercials? Shit! Did Korman know who the hell he was?"

"All he knew was that Jay was with me and he had a better idea."

"God damn it! He had no business butting in."

"But Korman's concept was ridiculous. It was never going to work. You should have seen the fiasco. And Martin told me he would have caught a lot of shit if he'd come back with something that looked like the Revenge of the Vampire Cats. Marty, the truth is, Jay saved the client's ass. I'm sorry if Korman had his delicate creative ego offended. He's a first-class asshole and you know it."

"Get this straight, Baskham. We're in business to provide a production service, not to fuck over some half-assed creative director and to embarrass the shit out of him so that he looks like the dumb fuck that you and I know he is. If the shoot fucks up because the concept stinks and the client decides to call it a day, that's not our problem. They still have to pay us for the shoot."

"Marty, hear what I'm telling you. Tom Martin owes us now. You can bet your sweet bippy that we're going to shoot every one of his Tasti-Feast commercials. His business is locked-up for us now."

"Now you hear what I'm telling you," Oppenheimer said, right in Baskham's face. "How many cat food commercials do you think they're going to shoot every year? I'll tell you how many. One! And that one grosses us about fifty grand. On the other hand, Jackson Korman and his ad agency represent about one million dollars of business for us each year. Now you tell me, who's more important to this company? I can't believe you screwed Korman."

"I didn't! It was Martin who made the decision to go with the new commercial."

"Maybe, but you're the one he's pissed at."

"Me? Why isn't Korman pissed at Martin?"

"Because Martin is his client and we are the production company and Korman can shit on us but he can't shit on his client. Now, listen to me carefully: I want you to get a hold of Korman and apologize like you really fuckin' mean it. I don't care if that means you have to kiss his bare ass in Macy's window. You make goddamn sure we don't lose any of his agency's business. Do you hear what I'm saying? Get it done!"

Marty started to walk toward the door then turned back to Jay. "And what the hell are you doing on the set anyway? I don't pay my go-fers to flake off and watch us shoot commercials." With that, he turned and hurried toward the door.

Then, loud enough so only Baskham could hear, Jay said, "And it was nice meeting you too, Mr. Oppenheimer." He turned to Baskham. "Should I start looking for another job?"

Baskham shook his head. "No. I've known Marty for ten years. By Monday, somebody else will be at the top of his shit list. But, just to be on the safe side, call in sick tomorrow. I'll clear it with Vivian."

"Out of sight, out of mind?"

"Won't hurt for you to be among the missing for a day."

"So what are you going to do? About Korman, I mean?"

"I thought I might go over to Macy's and check out their windows."

***

Jay did as Baskham had advised. He called in sick and used the day to start looking for an apartment to rent. The following morning, Jay got in early, hoping that a delivery would take him well away from the office and Marty Oppenheimer. As he passed through the reception area, he felt someone take his arm. It was Joanna.

"Come with me," she said in a hushed voice. "You've got to tell me what happened the other day on the set." She steered him back to the empty lunchroom. "I understand the studio was overrun with cats."

"It was a disaster."

"John Baskham told me you came up with a great idea for a different commercial and the client bought it and that you actually directed it."

"Wasn't much to direct, actually. We just pointed the cameras at a hungry cat and let it find the food."

"Don't knock it. A directing credit is a directing credit," she said. "Is it true that Jackson Korman threw a fit?"

"Let's just say that his ego sustained a lot of damage when he got tossed off the set."

"Good. Couldn't have happen to a more deserving asshole."

Jay was a little surprised at the vindictive tone and her choice of adjectives. "I take it he's not one of your favorite people?"

"You take it right. All it took was one trip alone in an elevator with that man for me to think seriously about carrying a club. He is definitely on my 'avoid at all costs' list. Right above Derrick Owens."

"Who's Derrick Owens?"

"He's the director of the *Born Yesterday* revival."

"Oh, I meant to ask, how did the callback go?"

"I can have the part."

"That's great."

"Not great. I can have the part if I agree to *special* rehearsals in the director's apartment. I told him what he could do with the part."

"Good for you. I'm sorry it didn't work out."

"Don't be. As it turns out, there was no money in it for the cast. 'But consider the experience,' Owen told me. I decided I didn't need that kind of experience."

"I guess all the creeps in the world aren't limited to guys who wear ties. It's got to be frustrating putting all that time and effort in, only to have some lowlife pull that kind of crap."

"You get used to it. Or maybe you just get numb," she said turning her attention back to the coffee.

Jay saw a fleeting shadow cross her face. It looked like resignation seated on sadness. Despite her protest to the contrary, he sensed that she had not 'gotten used to it' at all.

"You know what you need?" he said impulsively. "You need to get away from it all for a little while. What if you and I were to set sail for the Lake Isle of Innisfree this Saturday?"

She wheeled around and confronted him with a short laugh. "Where? What are you talking about?"

"Metaphorically speaking and with all due respect to poet William Butler Yeats, the Lake Isle I propose taking you to is in Central Park. Why don't I pick you up Saturday afternoon and carry you off in my personal subway car? Then, with picnic basket in hand, I will lead you to the Boat House, where we'll rent a rowboat. I will then demonstrate my skill as an oarsman and take you to a special place I know ... my Lake Isle. We will dine on cheese and wine and whatever else I can find at a deli.

We'll listen to the concert in the park and talk about things other than casting calls, off-Broadway directors, ravenous cats and Jackson Korman."

Joanna gave him a quizzical look as if she was trying to determine what was behind the invitation. Then she said, playfully, "Are you asking me to trust you to row us across a pond to some remote island in Central Park, where you'll ply me with wine and cheese while we listen to music?"

"That's what I'm asking. And as far as trusting me: Fagitaboutit! When I take beautiful women on boat rides to remote islands, I'm very untrustworthy. But aside from that, I am inviting you to spend Saturday with me in the park."

"Invitation accepted."

"Great. I'll be knocking on your door at 3:30."

Jay poured himself a cup of coffee. He could feel her eyes on him, as though she were trying to discern who this person was that had just promised her a trip to Innisfree. When he'd finished stirring in the cream and sugar, he picked up the cup and found Joanna still looking at him with a somewhat perplexed, quizzical stare.

"What?" he said feeling a little self-conscious.

There was softness in her voice that he had not heard before. "Are you for real, Jay Carraway?"

"I like to think so," he said simply. It was, he thought later, a perfect exit line, delivered just before several Ad-Film employees in search of coffee wandered into the kitchen. When they saw Jay, the questions began to fly about Tasti-Feast, Korman and the great cat debacle.

The cats had made him a legend.

5
Saturday in the Park with Joanna

Jay spent midday Saturday piecing together a picnic of fried chicken, potato salad, carrot sticks, pickle wedges, chips and dip, three different cheeses, several kinds of fruit and two very good bottles of red wine. He bought a checkered tablecloth, napkins and, at a secondhand shop, purchased some silverware, plates, two ornately decorated wine glasses and two candleholders that he felt would give their outing a more elegant flare.

He arrived in front of her apartment on Sheridan Square just before three thirty. Her apartment was in one of two brownstones wedged in between tired-looking apartment buildings. Jay guessed that it must have been a single family home during some period in Village history. Now, as evidenced by the bank of mailboxes imbedded in the vestibule wall, the five-floor walk-up was home to eight tenants. He read Olenska on one of the boxes. At three-thirty he pushed the buzzer next to 4B.

Her voice came back over the intercom. "Is that you, Jay?"

"Your subway car awaits."

"Be right down." Minutes later he heard a door close at the top of the stairwell and footsteps bounding down the stairs. Joanna was wearing a blue blouse and khaki Bermuda shorts. She'd pulled her hair back in a ponytail and there was, Jay believed, an expectant glow on her face.

She greeted him with broad smile. "Hiya. Great day for a picnic."

"I ordered it special, just for you," he said. *Damn, she's gorgeous*, he thought. *I wonder if I look as wobbly on the outside as I feel on the inside?*

They rode the subway up to West 72nd Street, crossed over Central Park West and took the first entrance into the park. Sunlight found its way through trees animated by the whims of an occasional breeze, creating a dappled tapestry on the ground. They descended the broad staircase to the terrace surrounding the Bethesda fountain, its Angel of the Waters statue standing above the umbrella-shaped pattern of water that flowed over the sides. Beyond the terrace was the large pond which, on the maps of the park, is simply called The Lake.

They walked past couples out for an afternoon stroll engaged in their private conversations; artists working to capture the fountain on their canvases; and, occasionally, a solitary figure, encamped on one of the benches communing with unseen listeners. Once past the fountain they took the pathway that led to the boathouse. The young man in the red T-shirt staffing the rental shack actually appeared pleased to have someone looking to rent a rowboat.

"Here, let me hold the boat while you get in," Jay said pulling the boat hard against the dock with one hand while holding out the other to help her. "Sit in the back. That way you can watch me row and check out my style," he said laughing. Joanna carefully stepped into the boat and made her way to the back. Jay placed the picnic basket in the bow and then sat down between the oars.

"Do you know how to row this thing?" she asked, trying to look concerned.

"Does Mickey Mantle know how to hit a baseball? You're about to see the benefit of eight years in summer camp."

"Summer camp? You went to summer camp?"

"Yes," Jay said locking his lower jaw, "every boy in Greenwich who aspires to row his own boat goes to summer camp."

Jay put the oars in the locks and turned the bow into the lake. It was immediately obvious that he knew what he was doing.

"I'm impressed."

"If Ad-Film fires me maybe I can get a job here."

"How is it that a Greenwich boy like you knows so much about Central Park?"

"My Aunt Isabel used to have an apartment just over there." He nodded toward Central Park West. "My sister and I visited a lot."

The afternoon turned even softer and the breeze abated leaving the lake a mirror in a green frame. There were remarkably few rowboats on The Lake for a summer afternoon. Joanna repositioned herself on one of the seat pillows and lay back staring at the sky. She dropped her hand over the side letting her fingers draw squiggly lines in the water which trailed momentarily behind the boat before they disappeared.

Jay turned the boat around a small neck of land jutting out from an area known as The Ramble and set his course for the Bow Bridge, the ornate arch that separates the two halves of the lake. A couple on the bridge, resting on their bicycles, watched them approach.

"I hear music," Joanna said.

"It's a concert at the Naumberg Band Shell, I think."

"Sounds familiar. *In the still of the night* ..." She sang softly as an almost unconscious response to hearing the music. She completed the first verse, started on the second and then suddenly stopped.

"Don't stop," Jay pleaded.

"I'll scare the fish."

"Not with that voice you won't. They'll hop into the boat just to hear you."

"Cole Porter is one of my favorites. Did you hire them to play that song for me?" she teased.

"Cost me a week's salary," he replied.

"I do like men who know how to spend money," she said with exaggerated earnest.

Jay beached the boat in front of the small island beyond the Bow Bridge. Together they laid out the checkered tablecloth and set out the food. He poured them both a glass of wine, then pulled the candelabra from the picnic basket and set it in the center of the cloth. "We'll light the candles later."

"A nice touch, Mr. Carraway."

The music from the band shell across the lake floated over the Bethesda Fountain and drifted softly toward them.

"Do you know the words?"

"I do." she said confidently.

"So sing. Consider it a command performance for your lowly go-fer."

Joanna waited for the refrain, then began to sing. *"So taunt me and hurt me ..."*

As Jay listened to the last line—*So in love with you, my love, am I*—he said to himself, *Sing that as if you mean it, just for me and*

I will be happy to die on the spot. "You're good. *Very* good, I should add. Have you always liked to sing?"

"Ever since I can remember. My mother played the piano when I was a little girl. She used to play and I'd sing, or we'd sing together. She was actually a frustrated actress, but her parents put the kibosh on a singing career and made her marry my father. I really never knew him all that well."

"Why was that?" he asked, then immediately worried that he sounded like he was prying.

She did not hesitate to answer, so his concern seemed unfounded. "He died in a construction accident when I was about four. Then my mother died when I was eight."

The realization that she'd been an orphan left him wondering how to respond. He did the best he could. "That's rough."

"For the next couple of years I lived with my Aunt Edna. She had an apartment over in Brooklyn Heights. Not exactly a happy situation. She didn't like children and I didn't like her. So when I was about ten she shipped me off to St. Madeleine's in Flatbush."

"What's St. Madeleine's?"

"It was an orphanage, a convent and a girls' school. I think it's been replaced with an apartment building now."

"How long were you there?"

"Until I escaped from high school. They called it graduation, but I called it a jailbreak. We were both happy to get me out of there. I wasn't exactly what you'd call a model inmate. Excuse me, *student*." Her voice was tinged with sarcasm. "Another girl and I used to climb out our windows after curfew and ride the subway into the city. It got to the point where the sisters took turns standing guard beneath our window. Let's just say the nuns didn't like us all that much. When they'd whip out their rulers and give us a whack I had the feeling that they were punishing us not for whatever we'd done, but for having lost our parents."

"I've heard stories about nuns with rulers," he said.

"The first year or so I was very lonely. Cried a lot." She drifted away from him for a moment and then came back on the crest of a short, protective laugh. "I remember we had a radio in our common room and they let us listen to shows like Ozzie and Harriet. I used to pretend that I was the little girl they didn't have. You pretend a lot in an orphanage. Eventually, you learn to live with your loneliness and sometimes even escape from it."

How sad it must have been, he thought, for a little girl to have been so alone in the world. Her life in the orphanage was so far removed from his that he began to wonder what she would think if she knew how he had grown up. He was quite sure he could never have survived a childhood like hers. It was all he could do to subdue the urge to take her in his arms and protect from her past. She must have sensed he was searching for something to say.

"I know this sounds like I'm ready to cry in my beer," she said looking down at her glass, "or wine, to be more exact. But I'm not. That's all history and mostly filed away." Then, as if to be sure she'd made her point, she added, "I'm not looking for pity or anything."

She had clearly mastered the ability to stuff escaped emotions back in their private place He wondered if he might have inadvertently opened a window she would have preferred to keep closed. As he reached for the bottle of wine to refill his glass, he became aware that she was staring at him with a quizzical look. .

"What is it about you that makes me talk so much? I haven't told anybody about St. Madeleine's for years. If ever."

"Hey, sometimes it's nice to talk to someone you know you can trust."

"I do trust you, Jay. I hardly know you, but I really feel … well …," she groped for the right word, "safe."

"Good. I want you to."

Their eyes met and Jay felt as if time had been momentarily suspended. *Stop the clock,* he thought.

She broke off first. "Are we going to eat, or are you just going to keep talking at me?" she asked playfully. For the next few minutes, the conversation focused on the items Jay had chosen for their picnic. "This is wonderful, Jay. However, are you aware that you've brought enough food for six people?"

"I like to be prepared."

"For what?"

"Well, who knows if some rowboat full of people might find their way to our island and need food?"

The music from the band shell continued to drift over them.

"I sang that once," she said.

"What?"

"What they're playing. It's called, *What is This Thing Called Love?* It was the first song I ever sang at an audition."

"What were you auditioning for?"

"Don't remember. There have been so many auditions since then, they've all become a blur."

"Have you always wanted to be in the theater?"

"No. It never really occurred to me. After I left St Madeleine's, I lived for a short time at the Barbizon. You know, the hotel on 63rd for women only. I had taken a shorthand and typing course, so I got a job at an ad agency in the steno and typing pool. To me, the fact that I was actually getting a paycheck ... well, I figured that was about as far as I'd ever go. Never having had any money I thought I'd died and gone to heaven. Of course, I was always out of money two days before payday."

"Anyway, when I left the agency, I sort of drifted for a little while. Then I met this girl who had theater connections. She got me a part in an off-off really off-Broadway play. The stage was in a vacant storefront down on Lafayette Street."

"What kind of part was it?"

"Not much of one. Just a few lines. The only one I remember was 'Is someone missing their underwear?'"

"Not exactly Shakespeare."

"And it went downhill from there. The show closed before they finished the third act." She laughed.

" Closed in the third act?"

"Not really. It seemed like that. Short as it was, I learned a lot during the rehearsals and the cast was a lot of fun. I had a great time. I knew then that's what I wanted to do. Of course, I wanted to do it on a little bigger stage and get paid. So, as the story goes, I joined the ranks of the thousands of unemployed actors who inhabit Manhattan, each convinced they'll make it to Broadway. So far I haven't gotten past Sixth Avenue."

"What's on Sixth Avenue?"

"Not much," she laughed. "Just a couple of companies that produce industrial shows."

Jay emptied the first bottle into her glass and opened a second. "Have you ever thought about doing something else?"

She smiled wistfully at him. "You mean, have I ever thought that maybe I should stop kidding myself and get a real job?"

Jay quickly tried to backtrack. "No, no, I didn't mean …"

She cut him off. "It's ok. It's a good question and one that I've been asking myself a lot lately. The problem with this business is that it's so easy to seduce yourself into wasting a lot of years."

"I know it's none of my business, but I'm surprised that some guy hasn't snatched you up and carried you off."

The question seemed to catch her off guard and she turned her head toward the lake as if to buy time to consider whether or not to answer. After a moment, as though replaying an unhappy memory, she began to shake her head. Slowly a wistful smile crept across her face. Without turning back to Jay she began, "It almost happened once. When I was twenty-four, I fell in love with Henry Day Thompson the Third. He wanted to, as he put it, rescue me from New York and carry me off to his parent's estate in the Hamptons. Unfortunately, I didn't quite measure up to the woman Mrs. Henry Day Thornton the Second had in mind for her son. She was so sophisticated that her bottom lip never moved when she talked. I'm not sure what bothered her more: that I was Polish, that I was from Brooklyn, that I wanted to be an actress, or that I lacked proper parentage. I'll never forget when Henry announced that we were going to get married. We were standing on her back porch having afternoon tea. From the look on her face, you'd have thought the septic tank had backed up."

"Obviously, it never happened."

"No," she said turning back to Jay, as it turned out, Henry's mother had never cut his umbilical cord. I don't think the three of us would have lasted very long sleeping in the same bed. Since Henry, there have been a number of *possibles*, but so far no real *probables*, if you know what I mean. Mr. Right just hasn't come along as yet."

Then I'll change my last name to 'Right,' Jay was tempted to say, but stopped himself short.

"Let's just say that when it comes to the men in my life, I've made a lot of mistakes. More than I care to think about."

"You're not against marriage, though?"

"No, of course not. There's nothing in the world I want more than to get married and have a family. That's very important to me. Someday I'd like to have a house. It doesn't have to be a big house, just a nice house in a nice neighborhood with maybe a garden and a husband who ..." She let whatever she was going to add drift off.

"Hey, why not? That's the American dream, isn't it?"

"But most of all," she said with an intensity he had not seen before, "I've realized that before I can be someone to somebody else, I have to be someone to *me*. Do you understand what I'm saying?"

Jay nodded.

"I have to prove to myself that I can *do* something with my life, that I can *be* somebody. And it doesn't have to be in the theater. I just want to do something, *anything,* that I can point to with a little pride. I know it sounds corny, but I need to find me." Her eyes searched his face in what Jay interpreted as quiet desperation, "It's hard for me to admit this, but for years I've just been drifting taking each day as it comes. Running as fast as

I can, but going nowhere." She lowered her eyes and shook her head. "I guess I'm having a pre-thirty life crisis."

All Jay could think about was how fast he was falling in love with this woman. How much he wanted to be with her, to protect her, to help her find the *me* she was looking for.

"I'm searching for something, Jay. And what makes it hard is that I not only don't know where to look, but I'm not sure what it is I'm looking for."

"For whatever it's worth, Joanna, I'm real good at helping people find things."

There was wistfulness in her smile and she did that searching thing with her eyes that had a way of rendering inoperative large numbers of his brain cells.

"I'll bet you are."

For the remainder of the evening, the music of Porter and Gershwin provided a musical underscore. After packing up the remainder of the food they lay back on the blanket and watched the evening light paint the sky with streaks of red and gold as though the sun was reluctant to give up the day.

"It's wonderful how the sound from the orchestra just seems to slip across the lake," Joanna said.

"Like a harmonic mist."

"Oh, I like that. Nicely said."

Then with a flourish he added, "If only we could but set sail upon the euphonic wave, it would carry us to Elysian Fields."

"Who said that?"

"What?"

"What you just said."

Jay was confused. "Ah … I think I just said it."

"I mean, is that a quote from somebody?"

"No. I just made it up."

"You do have a way with words, Mr. Carraway."

He wondered if maybe he had overdone it with the poetic prose. "Words may be the only thing I have a way with—other than rowboats, of course."

She stared at him with tender curiosity. "You know, I've decided that my go-fer is for real."

That's a step in the right direction, he said to himself.

She looked out at The Lake and echoed his words. "'If we could but set sail upon the euphonic wave, it would carry us to Elysian Fields.' Sounds like it ought to be a lyric in a song." She pondered the thought and then turned to Jay, "What are Elysian Fields? I'm afraid my St. Madeline education never got into mythology. The nuns preferred we focus on catechism."

"In Greek mythology the Elysian Fields were believed to be a land of perfect happiness. To get there you had to travel to the ends of the earth. Central Park isn't exactly the ends of the earth, but, from where I sit tonight, it's pretty close."

"Do you come up with quotable quotes like that all the time?"

"Only when the inspiration is right."

"You know what you are?" She didn't wait for him to answer. "You're a romantic. This is like out of a movie. A trip across the lake, a picnic, wine, music, a beautiful evening and a trip to Elysian Fields. This is not exactly my usual kind of date."

"Well, I like to think I'm not your usual kind of guy."

"No, you aren't. Do you seduce all your women like this?"

"Only a select few. A *very* select few." The words were no sooner out of his mouth than he wondered if she realized his bravado boast was in jest. The amused look on her face and her response told him that she did.

"A girl could get used to this kind of treatment."

"I'd like to be the guy who helps you get used to it."

Suddenly, the sky above them erupted with fireworks.

"Somebody must be celebrating something," she said.

"I arranged for those. I mean if I can arrange to have a beautiful day, wonderful music at the band shell, why not fireworks?"

"There goes another week's salary."

"More like two weeks."

When the last firework died into the night, Jay rowed them back to the boathouse. As he offered his hand to help her out, she looked up at him and said, "Mr. Carraway, you really know how to entertain a girl. I'm not sure how to say thank you for today."

As she stepped onto the dock, the top of her blouse parted slightly, revealing the roundness of her breasts. He was tempted to respond with a rather obvious suggestion as to how she might thank him. But that, he realized, would sound exactly like something she might expect to hear from an office sniffer. He opted instead on a decidedly non-sniffer line: "Joanna, just having you with me is thanks enough."

The look on her face told him it was a good decision.

**

It was after eleven when they got back to Sheridan Square. The only thing he thought about was how much he wanted only to be with her and how he longed to hold her—not in lust, but in love.

She searched for her key. "Jay, today was so very special. I can't tell you how much I enjoyed it. I know one thing for sure, I've found a real friend."

He wasn't prepared for that. Immediately he wanted to shout, *No, you've found a real lover. I'm not like the other sniffers from the office. I'm different. I love you.* He said none of that because before he could gather himself she delivered a line that deflated his ego faster than a pinprick on a birthday balloon.

"You're sweet Jay. You're like having a brother."

He could feel his ego drop into his shoes. *A brother?* "How did I get elected brother? I was running for ..." He was about to say "boyfriend" but quickly decided that sounded too juvenile. 'Lover' would certainly sound too aggressive. He searched for other words, but managed to find none more suitable. "I was hoping that you and I ..."

Joanna didn't wait for him to find other words. "Jay, how old are you?" Her tone sounded far too analytical, even parental, to suit Jay. "Twenty-three? Twenty-four?"

"I'll be twenty-six in October."

"That makes me four years older than you."

"In the context of the universe, that's not even a microsecond."

"Maybe. But earthbound people don't measure time in microseconds."

"So what do a few years difference in age have to do with how people feel about each other? And when you think about it, if I was 29 and you were 25, we wouldn't even be talking about age." He did his best to sound as if he believed his logic was irrefutable.

"It's just that in a relationship men are supposed to be older."

"Says who? What rule book is that in?"

"None that I know of," she admitted.

"So there you are. Case closed. Now that the age thing is no longer an issue, I'd really appreciate your thinking of me as something other than your brother. I want to be a lot more than that to you. A *whole* lot more."

Her winsome smile conveyed the possibility of concession, but her words said otherwise. "I might like that, but then what would I do for a brother?" Her eyes teased him, saying everything, yet promising nothing. "Good night," she said, "and thank you again for today." She gave him a quick kiss on the cheek and disappeared up the stairs.

As he left the brownstone and headed for the subway, he wasn't sure if what he felt was deflation, confusion, elation or some combination of all three. Whatever, he took his frustration out on some hapless man who cuddled his brown bag-covered bottle as he dozed on a bench near the subway entrance. "A brother? How could she think of me as a brother?"

The inebriated man on the bench did not appear inclined to offer an answer.

6
A Call to Mother

It was not out of necessity, but from some dim sense of obligation that he occasionally called his mother. As he waited on the phone, he could hear the maid's voice calling: "Mrs. Carraway, it's your son, Jay." For the last fifteen years, conversations with his mother had never been temperate affairs. For the first six years of his life, he would see his mother only once or twice a day. Usually, it was in the late afternoon, when his French nanny would present him to his mother in the library.

His mother would stroke his head, much as she might a pet dog and inquire about what he and "nurse" had done that day. To irritate her, he would answer in French—which he had learned from his nanny—knowing full well that his mother had not a clue as to what he was telling her. Then, as if by some private sign, the nanny would remove him from the room and feed him his diner. By age seven, Jay had shed the nanny and become an acceptable addition to his parent's dining table. Even at that early age, he and his mother seemed perpetually at odds. She lived by some relic of a turn-of-the-century social code. Any divergence from that code was, to her, totally unacceptable. He was born, he decided, to go through life as a code breaker, if for no other reason than to continually test his mother's resolve. The respect that his father demanded he pay to his mother could in no way be confused with traditional filial love.

His mother came to the phone and greeted her son with a tart, "Well, have you come to your senses yet?"

"No, Mother and no chance of that anytime soon. I just called to see how you and Dad are."

"We saw your friend Anson last weekend and he told us you got a job?"

"That I did."

"But as a delivery boy? I can't believe that a son of mine, with all your education and all your advantages, has ended up as a delivery boy."

"I don't plan to *end up* as a delivery boy, Mother." He resisted the temptation to rebut the "delivery boy" label and to counter by telling how he had earned his first directing credit on the Tasti-Feast commercial. Jay was not about to give her an opportunity to deride what he considered progress. Instead, he changed the subject. "How are Dad and Scott?"

"Your father and brother are as you left them. Disappointed in your decision, but otherwise doing fine." Then, as an afterthought, she added, "You'll have to come see their new boat."

"They bought another boat? Sail or power?"

"A sail boat, of course."

"How long?

"I don't know. It's ... very long. Now, to more important matters. I'm glad you called, because I was about to engage a detective agency to see if they could find your phone number."

"That would have been difficult, because I don't have one yet. I'm calling from Ad-Film."

"Ad-Film?"

"This is where I work."

She pressed on. "The reason I wanted to talk with you is to ask if you'd be so kind as to grace us with your presence on Saturday, June 25th. It's the first polo match at Conyers farm and I plan to have a lawn party for some of our friends afterwards."

Jay was tempted to respond with an immediate decline, but instead asked, "Is Scott playing?"

"Of course. He's got two new polo ponies that he's dying to ride."

"Ok. I'll try to come out." Then quickly he injected. "Can I bring a friend?

"A friend? What kind of friend?"

"A *friend* kind of friend. She's a woman I work with."

"A woman you work with?" his mother echoed, in a tone that carried an unasked question.

"Well, her job at Ad-Film is just temporary—she's between jobs, you might say. She's an actress and since actors and actresses don't work all the time, she fills in with temp jobs."

"Ummm. Temporary jobs? Don't you think that's a bit unusual? I've met Helen Hayes and Mary Martin and they certainly —at least to the best of my knowledge—never take temporary jobs between plays."

"She's not quite in that league yet. But forget all that. The main reason I want to bring her is because she happens to be someone that I've become very fond of."

"Well, keep in mind that Brooke Whitney will be at the party and I know how much she's looking forward to seeing you."

"Mother, please. Let's not start going 'round and 'round on Brooke. No matter how much you try to promote her to me, it's not going to happen between us. She's a very nice girl. She's an old friend. Always has been and always will be. But it's a 'no' when it comes to anything between us."

There was a great deal his mother did not understand about "No." When she made up her mind that something should be as she wanted it to be, she would plot, scheme, cajole, scream, pout, pursue and do whatever else was required until it happened. If that didn't work, she was not above doing exactly what she was told she must not, could not and definitely should not do.

"Well, who is this woman you're bringing from work?" The word *work* seemed to pass through her lips like someone spitting out a sour grape. "Is she ... how do I say it? Is she going to fit in with our friends?"

Jay understood exactly what his mother was implying. Breeding was uppermost in her assessment of her children's friends and, far more importantly, a major factor when considering whom they chose as a spouse. Immediately, Jay jumped on the defensive. Now, as so many times in the past, he would find perverse pleasure in purposely irritating his mother. "I think she'll fit in, although I have to admit she is a little different."

"In what way ... a little different?'"

"Well, she's kind of small."

"By small you mean ...?"

"She's kind of short, like a dwarf. And I'd appreciate it if you not serve pork or ham. She's Jewish." Jay knew that, as far as his mother was concerned, Jews were most defiantly not considered socially acceptable at any of her affairs. "And when you see her, don't ask where she got the tan. Everyone from the Belgian Congo has that color skin."

"You're not serious!" It was a command more than a question.

"No, Mother, I'm not serious. She is a very beautiful woman that I happen to like very much. My only concern about bringing her to the house is that she'll be bored silly by some of your tight-ass friends"

"There is no call for you to be so crude. I can see what this so-called job of yours has done to your manners and your language. What's this woman's name?"

"Joanna."

"And does she have a last name?"

"Olenska.

"That doesn't sound very American."

"It's not. But she is," he said curtly, suppressing an immediate desire just to hang up.

"Have you met her parents? Are they our kind of people?"

"Do you mean is their blood blue?" He did not wait for her response. "Mother, this is 1957, not 1907. People aren't judged by their pedigrees anymore."

"You needn't get angry, I was just wondering."

He cut her off. "Her parents died when she was very young."

"Good heavens! She's an orphan?"

With a tinge of sarcasm, he retorted, "Around the office, she's known as Little Orphan Annie."

Eleanor Carraway totally ignored his last comment. "Will the two of you be staying the night?"

Jay saw another opportunity to tweak his mother.

"No, we have to get back. She goes to Mass at 6 AM."

"She's a Catholic?" Catholics were second only to Jews when it came to those who never made her invitation list.

There was a long, exasperated sigh on the other end of the phone. "You are impossible, Jay. I don't know how you could be a son of mine."

"Maybe I'm not. Maybe they gave you the wrong baby at the hospital."

"You were born at home."

"Then I must be yours. Gotta go," he said. "I have to make some pizza deliveries," and hung up.

7
The Office Party

During the summer months, Marty Oppenheimer hosted frequent cocktail parties for his current and would-be clients. The event was held in the formal garden that Oppenheimer had created on the roof of the office building. There were those who claimed that an entire marble forest had to be cut down in order to create the elaborate walkways, fountains and the small, intimate, gazebo-like pavilions and dramatic sculptures that decorated his roof garden.

Marty expected, or rather, insisted, that all his female employees—at least the ones who looked good in cocktail dresses—attend his parties so that their comely shapes could provide animate decoration. To be sure that the women outnumbered the male guests, he further stocked his parties with handpicked models whose physical attributes met his personal criteria and whose desire to meet people who might put them in a commercial negated Oppenheimer's need to pay them for their time.

The go-fers were on call as well. Their assignment, as Jay and the two other go-fers saw it, was to make asses of themselves in public. Marty had supplied them with white coats and pants—a uniform not unlike that worn by Good Humor men—which he had trimmed with a heavy red piping along all the seams. To complete the costume, he had ordered red and white striped caps, which, as one of the go-fers described, made them look like refugee soda jerks from the 1930s. Their assignment was to mill about during the party, carrying long handled whisk brooms and butler dust pans, sweeping up cigarette butts, used cocktail napkins and other bits of flotsam and jetsam that might make their way onto the floor from the hands, plates and mouths of the guests.

Jay found it bad enough that his path to success had to detour though this mortifying valley of personal denigration, but that paled compared to the humiliation of having Joanna see him in this ridiculous uniform, sweeping up the leavings of advertising agency yakapuks.

He decided his best chance for saving face was to make it a point to do his milling and sweeping as far from Joanna as possible. Since it was a big roof and there would be more than two hundred people drinking and devouring food, he reasoned that it would not be all that difficult to avoid her, so long as she stayed generally in one place.

For most of the party, his strategy worked. Joanna seemed content to remain on one side of the garden. It was really only a matter of time before he was overcome by a rampant curiosity born of vigorous jealousy. Midway through the evening, Jay decided that he wanted to see if, as he'd suspected, she had attracted the attention of *guest sniffers*. He found a place behind a marble column, out of her line of view. His suspicions were confirmed. The extraordinary body in the black cocktail dress had drawn a crowd of Brooks Brothers suits, young men with important agency titles and even more impressive images of themselves. They had come to impress her with how important they were in the ongoing quest to prevent acid indigestion and tooth decay and to alleviate mass suffering from headaches, dry skin and foot itch. These were the master persuaders and it appeared to Jay that they were using all their persuasive talents on Joanna, who listened, smiled, laughed on cue and seemed to be enjoying the attention.

Jay, of course, was dying. And it didn't help when Marty Oppenheimer himself, breaking all protocol, suddenly materialized behind him. "What the hell are you doing? Why aren't you sweeping? Hey, are you the guy I met on the Tasti-Feast set with Baskham?"

Jay was about to respond when something—or, more likely, someone—diverted Marty's attention, giving Jay the opportunity to escape any further confrontation.

As the party began to thin out, Jay found himself drawn back to his earlier vantage point. The agency sniffers, who had been pressing their attentions on Joanna, had given way to Jackson Korman. Jay noticed that he was slowly, but irrevocably, backing Joanna into a corner, making a tactful escape nearly impossible. She was clearly having a problem dealing with his hands, which seemed to be on a major exploratory mission. She attempted to slide past him, but his hands found her buttocks and stopped her. He began to pull her toward him, pressing her breasts into his chest. She tried to push him away, but he managed to trap her arms under his so she could only squirm in protest.

Jay looked around, expecting that someone would come to her aid, but the guests were all so absorbed in their own conversations that no one seemed to notice the struggle going on in the corner. It took only five quick steps to bring him to Korman's back. He brought his open hand down hard on Korman's shoulder. Korman spun around, looking directly into Jay's chest. He glanced up. "What the hell? What are you doing?"

"I think the lady would prefer that you keep your hands to yourself."

"It's you!" he spat. "The fucking cat boy genius." Korman stepped back, looked him up and down and smirked, "I see Marty has promoted you to Bozo the Clown."

Jay's anger was bubbling just below the surface. His jaw tightened. "No, I've elected myself the trash man. I take out the trash and you're my first assignment." He took an intimidating step closer to Korman.

"Get the fuck out of my face, asshole." Korman turned his back on Jay and reached for Joanna's arm. "Joanna, let's get the hell out of here."

Joanna recoiled and pulled away.

In a quick deft move, Jay grabbed Korman's left arm and twisted it behind his back in a hammerlock. Korman let out a yelp. "High school wresting," Jay said in Korman's ear. "Basic move."

"Jay, don't hurt him," Joanna urged, alarmed at the impending violence.

Jay looked at her and, with a quick toss of his head, motioned for her to move to some other part of the roof. Once she had disappeared into the crowd, Jay released Korman, who immediately tried to take a swing at Jay's head. Jay blocked Korman' right hand with his left arm and delivered a solid punch to his jaw. Korman stumbled backward, making a frantic attempt to maintain his balance. It proved to be impossible.

"Boxing. Princeton." Jay said to the creative director at his feet.

By this time, the confrontation had drawn spectators, whose reactions offered a mixed review of his performance varying from shocked to bemused to even overt approval. Two of Korman's agency lackeys rushed over, looking first at their fallen leader and then at Jay. They appeared confused and unable to decide what to do. Korman made the decision for them. "Help me up, Goddamit!"

Jay decided that this might be a good time to affect a discreet exit.

"What the hell is going on here?" Marty Oppenheimer had witnessed Jay's punch and rushed to Korman's side. He shouted at Jay, "Where do you get off punching my guests? Are you nuts?"

Korman moaned as he put this hand to his jaw, checking for loose teeth. "You'd better fire that son-of-bitch or look for a new client."

Jay thought about trying to explain to Oppenheimer his side of the story. But, given what he'd witnessed on the Tasti-Feast set the week before, he realized that any attempt to explain would be futile.

"You're fired. Get the hell out of my sight!" The blue lines on Marty's face seemed to be turning red. He turned his attention back to Korman, who was rubbing the arm that Jay had held in a hammerlock.

"I think he fuckin' broke my arm!" Korman wailed.

As Jay made his way through the mostly speechless crowd, he noticed that some of the office staff and guests were grinning. Several of the Ad-Film employees actually clapped him on the shoulder whispering their approval.

"What happened?" It was John Baskham.

Jay glanced back and nodded toward Korman who was sitting next to Oppenheimer rubbing his jaw. "We had a creative disagreement which I settled in a rather ungentlemanly way. Oppenheimer has suggested that I start looking for other employment."

"He fired you?"

"He fired me," Jay confirmed

"I'd love to hear the details. Call me tomorrow," Baskham said.

Jay found a door, opened it and started down the steps. As soon as it slammed behind him, he realized that this was not the stairway to the lobby. At the bottom of the stairwell, he found himself in front of a door marked "Private." *Where the hell am I?* he wondered. As he debated whether to return to the roof or ignore the private sign, he heard a voice at the top of the stairs.

"Where the hell do you think you're going?" Marty shouted.

The decision had been made for him. Jay turned the handle, gave the door a push and found himself standing in the middle of Marty Oppenheimer's office. "Good choice," he mumbled sarcastically. "Of all the exits, I had to pick this one."

Marty slammed through the door. "You're fucking fired!"

"I heard you the first time. But you should know that bastard was nearly raping one of your employees."

"On the roof? In front of two hundred people? What are you, delusional?"

"His hands were all over her."

"So fuckin' what? That's none of your goddamn business! Now get the hell out of my office before I call the cops." He plopped down in his chair and swiveled it so that his back was to Jay.

As Jay headed for the door that would lead him out of Marty's office, he caught a glimpse of a large, framed photograph of a young woman, sitting on one of Marty's bookshelves. She had a petulant, rebellious expression, as if daring anyone to like the picture. *That looks like ... is it?* he asked himself. *Yes, it's*

Arabella ... or her double. It has to be Arabella. Who else would be wearing a snail shell with a flower growing out of it?

Marty spun around and saw him staring at Arabella's picture. "What the hell are you looking at?"

"Is this Arabella?"

"What of it?

"Your daughter?

"Are you one of her fuckin' boyfriends?"

"No, I'm not one of her fuckin' boyfriends. Her boyfriend's name is Yoshiro. The last time I saw her, she said they were going to Japan."

"Japan? She went to Japan? With some guy named Yoshiro?" He was incredulous. "That stupid little bitch!" He jumped up out of his chair, grabbed the picture out of Jay's hand and looked at it with parental disgust.

Now Jay understood who Arabella was talking about when she said she knew *an asshole* at Ad-Film. He could not help but wonder why any father would display such a terrible picture of his daughter. Maybe Marty had it framed to remind him of how much Arabella disliked him. Or maybe it was Marty who disliked her. Then he remembered the note Arabella had left on his pillow, explaining the favor she wanted him to do for her.

"Your daughter said that if I ever met you, I was to deliver a message."

"A message? From Arabella?" Marty asked, his anger having remained in full boil. "What message?"

8
Arabella's Rules Redux

The following day, Jay and Anson arrived home at the same time. "Haven't seen you in a couple days. How's it going?" Anson asked, as he followed Jay into the apartment building.

"Well, other than getting fired, it's going great."

"You got fired?"

"If you buy me dinner tonight, I'll give you a blow-by-blow."

"Deal. Pizza?"

"Sounds good. How goes it with you?"

"Market was up. All is right with the world. Only one problem."

"What's that?"

"I heard from Eddy today."

"Eddy?"

"You know, the Eddy Valerian who lives here when you don't?"

"Yeah."

"Two weeks from now he does and you don't. That's when I expect him back. But don't worry, we'll find you something."

"Just when it was beginning to feel like home," Jay with mock sincerity.

Anson started up the stairs to his apartment. "Give me an hour, ok?"

"Yeah, knock on the door when you're ready."

Jay put on some music, changed into his gym shorts and spent the next half hour abusing his body with a set of free weights that he'd found in the closet. Tired, sweaty and wondering if he'd pulled a shoulder muscle, he sat at the desk and began to look through the apartment rental ads in the evening paper.

The knock was early.

"I thought you said an hour?" he said opening the door.

"Hi, Jay ."

"Joanna!" Only Arabella would have surprised him more.

"Can I come in?" She was carrying a large grocery bag.

"Of course," he said while scrambling to find a towel to put over his sweaty shoulders.

"If you're wondering how I got in without ringing your buzzer, I came in with one of the other tenants."

"Yeah, we have a high level of security in this building. What brings you to the West Side?"

"I was on my way home and thought I'd stop in."

"Joanna," Jay said in a droll tone, "you may have forgotten, but you live in the West Village and this isn't exactly on your way home."

"Maybe, but I like to take different routes. Plus, you don't have a phone, so I couldn't call. Then I remembered that your address must be in the employee file."

"Unfortunately, I just learned that I won't be living here much longer. The guy whose apartment this is will be coming back."

"Well, if you haven't got other plans tonight, I'd like to make you dinner. Consider it a thank you for the other day at the party."

"I'm afraid I got a little carried away. But the son-of-a-bitch was ... well ..."

"He was drunk, obnoxious and very strong. I've had to deal with some pretty aggressive guys in my life, but no one who was that physical. Anyway, as a thank you for the rescue, I'd like to make dinner to say how sorry I am that Marty fired you."

"As it turns it, it might be for the best."

"How?"

"The good news is that John Baskham said he had a job lead for me. A friend of his owns a production company. Apparently, the guy needs a production manager and John's going to recommend me."

"I'll keep my fingers crossed. Now, point me to the stove and let me show you what a culinary wizard I'm not."

"This way to my sorry excuse for a kitchen," he said leading the way to the six-by-four foot walk-in. "I'm afraid it's a bit of a mess. Cook's night off, you know. Maybe I should just take you out to dinner."

"No, I've bought all the groceries and I'm cooking."

"I'll just jump in the shower and get changed and then you can tell me what I can do to help."

"You can start by getting lost and letting me handle things."

"The least I can do is open a bottle of wine to keep you company while I clean up." Jay grabbed a bottle and inserted the corkscrew. As he removed the cork, he watched, with no little embarrassment, as she began to bring some order to the mess he'd left in the kitchen.

"Hey, Jay," said Anson, his voice preceding his body through the door. "Are we going to ... ?" Anson never finished the question. He heard the noise in the kitchen and moved to where he could see into the walk-in. "Is that her?" He asked Jay without ever taking his eyes off Joanna.

"If by 'her' you mean the woman I was telling you about, yes. Joanna," he said, "this is my friend, Anson. He's the one who arranged for me to use this apartment."

She stepped out the kitchen, wiped her hands on a dish towel and offered Anson her hand.

"Jay said you were drop-dead gorgeous, but that was an understatement."

She glanced at Jay and then, to his surprise, actually blushed.

"Don't hold back, Anson, just say what you feel."

"Sorry," Anson said apologetically to Joanna. "Now you know why they call me Mr. Suave."

"I'm fixing dinner, would you like to join us?" she offered.

Jay caught Anson's eyes, daring him to accept. "No, no," Anson sputtered, "I'm going to meet some people and ... Hey, it was nice meeting you. Maybe we can all go out sometime."

"Sure. Nice meeting you too, Anson"

After he left, Joanna beat her way back into the kitchen, past the pile of dirty dishes, as Jay took refuge in the shower. Several minutes later, he emerged in khakis and a polo shirt.

Jay barely recognized the kitchen. "So that's what was under all those pots and dishes."

"Amazing, isn't it?" she asked, clearly pleased with the transformation.

As Joanna busied herself with the meal preparation, Jay decided this would be as good a time as any to tell her about his mother's picnic on the 25th. "How would you like to see how the other half lives?"

"The other half?"

"Actually, how the other half of the top one percent lives."

"What are you talking about?"

"Ever been to a polo match?"

"No."

"Well, there's a polo match in Greenwich. My brother plays polo. Afterwards, my mother is having a lawn party for about five thousand of her closest friends. I told her that I'd like to bring a friend."

"Five thousand?"

"I exaggerate."

"So I assumed."

"More like a couple hundred."

"Far more intimate."

"I guess I should warn you that you'll have to meet my family."

"And...?"

"Well, they're sort of an eclectic group."

"Meaning?"

"Some you'll like. Some you won't. You'll like my brother, but hate his wife. My sister has no sense of reality, but she's very sweet. There's nothing not to like about her. My father's a dynamo in the boardroom, but is reduced to a coat rack at home when my mother's around. You might like him, you might not. And my mother?" He took a deep breath and sighed. "Let's just say that the last time we had any meaningful connection was just before they cut the umbilical cord."

"So what's she going to say when her prodigal son comes home dragging this refuge from Brooklyn?"

"I'm more concerned about what you're going to say when you meet her?" Jay thought for a moment, "You know, as I think about it, this is going to be sort of like a trip to the zoo. You're going to see all kinds of strange and mutant social animals. If you should decide to cancel out...."

"Not a chance. This will give me a chance to see the real Jay Carraway in his natural habitat," she teased.

"No, no," he said throwing up his hands in defense. "You saw the real Jay Carraway in the park."

"Good," she said simply turning back to her dinner preparations. "You want to help?" she asked, holding up a head of lettuce.

"Sure, what would you like me to do?"

"Wash the lettuce."

Jay took the head of romaine and looked at it quizzically. "You want me to *wash* the lettuce?"

"Yes," she said.

"With soap and water?" he asked doing his best to look serious.

She snatched the lettuce back from him in a playful sort of way and began to peel off leaves and rinse them under the faucet. "You haven't had a lot of experience in the kitchen, have you?"

"In North Greenwich," he said in his Greenwich voice, "we have *people* who do that kind of thing."

Minutes later Joanna had their dinner on the small wooden table.

"So what do you think?' she asked after he'd sampled her efforts.

"I think it's terrific."

She looked at him as if she doubted his sincerity.

"No, I mean it. It's very good. Where did you learn to cook?"

"Out of a book."

"Out of a book?"

"I think it was called *101 Ways Disguise Hamburger,* or something like that."

"No cooking courses at St Madeline's, I guess."

"They didn't even teach the cooks to cook."

"Probably too busy instructing you on how to be a good Catholic."

"I'm afraid they didn't do too well in that regard."

"I take it you're no longer a Catholic."

"I guess not. We sort of had to part company."

"Why?"

She sighed deeply and averted her eyes. "It's a long story and not one I really care to talk about."

Jay immediately realized that the answer to "Why" was locked behind a bolted door. He was not about to ask her for the key. "Then let's talk about something else."

"Let's talk about you."

"Haven't we done that already?"

"Not really. I mean, I know you want to be a director, that you can row a boat, create great quotes and dazzle a girl on a picnic. But you haven't told me anything about your personal life."

"Like what?"

"I have to assume that a good looking guy like you has a string of girlfriends waiting for him up there in Greenwich."

He shook his head. "Right now, the waiting line is very short."

She pretended to be shocked by his answer. "What are you telling me? That you don't like girls?"

"Girls are for boys, my dear," he said adopting his Humphrey Bogart persona. "I prefer ....women."

"And what do you prefer in women?"

Jay found himself tempted to say that everything he preferred was sitting across the table from him. *Too aggressive*, he decided and opted to deflect the question with humor. "I prefer women who ... well, women who bathe regularly, have most of their teeth, speak English and ..."

"No, I'm serious," she said, cutting him off. "What do you look for in a woman?"

Jay realized that she really wanted to know. As he thought about his answer, it occurred to him that she had given him an opportunity to begin convincing her to move him out of the brother category. "Ok," he said, pretending that he was willing, but mildly reluctant, to give in to her request. "I'm looking for a woman that I can talk to openly and honestly—pour out my feelings—and know that what I say will always be safe with her. I'm looking for a woman who wants to share things like dreams, hopes, a life ... even something as ordinary as a beautiful sunset in the park. A woman who can say more to me with the simple touch of her hand than other people could say in a thousand spoken words. A woman who will never have any doubt that I love her more than anyone else in the world."

"I hope you find her," she said softly as her hand made its way slowly across the table in search of his.

Their fingers were just inches apart when the apartment door blew open. "Hey, guys!" Anson's shout seemed to be the force that propelled him into the room. "If you're through with dinner, are you interested in going bowling?"

The man's timing is unbelievable. I'm going to kill him tomorrow. Maybe yet tonight. Jay glanced over at Joanna, who was shaking her head in disbelief and choking back a laugh.

"Maybe I should ask Anson what he's looking for in a woman."

"Don't think so. The man has bizarre tastes."

"I'm not interrupting anything, am I?" Anson asked.

"No, no, not at all," Jay said opening his arms with an expansive gesture. "We were just wishing that someone would magically appear to do the dishes. And who walks in? Anson, the dish-washing genie." Jay turned away from Joanna and gave Anson a look that said, 'Please disintegrate...now!.'

Anson got the message. "Excuse me while I do an about face." Anson whirled around on his heels and headed back for the door. "Dishes are not this genie's thing. I'm a paper plate man. See ya!" And with that, he left.

"I guess that leaves me as the dish-washing genie," she said, picking up their plates.

"Oh, no it doesn't," he said and held up his hands in protest. "You did the cooking, so I'll do the dishes."

As Jay cleared the table, Joanna began to wander around the apartment, taking the measure of its primary resident. "Well, this Eddy whatever-his-name-is likes music, that's for sure," she said, inspecting the pictures on the wall.

"That's what he is," Jay said, "a musician."

Her tour brought her to the desk next to the bed, where she found a typewriter and a stack of papers. The top page bore the title *Maria of Avenue A*. "What this?"

"What?"

"This," she said, holding up the pages.

"Oh, that's a story about a little girl that I used in the documentary I shot while I was at NYU."

"Can I read this?"

"Sure. Keep in mind that it needs some editing."

While Jay washed and dried the dishes, Joanna curled up on his bed with his story. When she finished she said, "It's beautiful. Absolutely tears your heart out. What are you going to do with this?"

"I don't know," he said drying the last of the dishes. "Submit it to a magazine maybe. I'm not sure yet."

"I'm impressed. You have a writing gift—you really do."

Jay, who was not much practiced when it came to accepting compliments, shrugged it off with. "The jury is still out on that, but, I'm glad you liked it."

Joanna slid off the bed joined him in the kitchen as he found a home in the cabinet above the stove for the last of the dishes. "You know, you're quite a surprise. Writer, cat director, dishwasher and the biggest surprise of all: you're a defender of women." She chuckled briefly and then became serious. "Jay, I want you to know that in my whole life, no one has ever stood up for me like you did the other day. It meant more than I can say." She laid her hand on his arm.

If he'd been a block of ice, the look on her face would have instantly converted him to a puddle.

She looked at her watch. "I think I better get going."

"You plan on taking the subway?"

"Cabs are a little rich for me right now."

"Then I'm going with you. The defender of women is not about to let you ride the subway alone at this hour."

"You really don't have to."

"But I want to," he said.

"Thanks," she said, in a way that told him she was grateful for his offer.

They left the apartment and walked through the lobby. Jay opened the front door to a cold gust of rain-drenched wind.

"Do you have an umbrella?" Joanna asked.

"I did, but I don't. Left it someplace."

"Maybe it will let up in a few minutes."

"This looks like it's here to stay for a while."

"Do you think we can run for it?" she asked.

"We'd get soaked. And it's a cold rain. We'd probably both end up with pneumonia."

Joanna looked at her watch. "It's getting late."

"You can stay here tonight, if you like."

Joanna looked out at the rain. "It's not going to stop."

"Not any time soon, anyway." He renewed the offer. "You can have the bed; I'll sleep on the couch."

"No," she insisted. "If I'm to stay, you take the bed and I'll take the couch."

"The couch is really uncomfortable unless your body is shaped like a 'U' ... and it's a big bed."

She thought about it, then smiled and asked, "Arabella's Rules?"

He could not suppress a laugh. "OK, Arabella's Rules."

Later, as Jay lay next to the beautiful woman sleeping in his bed, he found that her perfume and proximity made the prospect of getting any sleep very slim. Occasionally, during the night not always accidently - his hand found her shoulder or his leg touched hers. Each time, it only added to his frustration. *Why in hell did I ever tell her about Arabella's Rules?*

9
A Thousand Years from Now

Baskham suggested Jay meet him at Ad-Films West 60th Street editing rooms so they could screen the final cut of the Tasti-Feast spot. When the lights came up, Baskham said, "Looks great, don't ya think? Client loves it. It really delivers the message. I'll get you a couple of 16mm copies for your demo reel."

"It's going to be a pretty short demo reel."

"You have to start with number one sometimes. By the way, you've become a legend at Ad-Film. A lot of people enjoyed seeing you flatten that turkey."

"It cost me my job, but between you and me, it was worth it."

"The son-of-a-bitch had it coming."

"So what are you working on this week?"

"Well, my mission this week is to save the average housewife from suffering the ultimate humiliation of having to tell her husband that she cannot remove the dirty ring around his collar. You gotta wonder what in the hell he's doing to get his white shirts so dirty? We shot one spot that looks like mama is married to a coal miner."

"Do coal miners wear white shirts?"

"This one did, anyway." John leaned over and dipped his pipe into his tobacco pouch, took it out and began to tamp the tobacco into the bowl. A smile crossed his face as he turned to Jay . "Every once in a while, I imagine someone a thousand years from now digging up our civilization and all they find are the commercials. They figure out how to screen them and come to the conclusion that we were a race of incompetent, bumbling husbands married to women who had a fetish for detergents and achieved orgasms over the softness of their toilet paper. Then, when they get around to writing the bottom line on us, the future scholars will conclude that while, as a civilization, we lacked any signs of intellectual substance, we were certainly very clean."

Jay laughed. "You've nailed it."

"Right now, the tough part of this business is working for Marty. He takes the fun out of it. It might be time for me to move on. Who knows? Maybe one day I'll tell him to stuff it and set up my own shop."

"Have you ever thought seriously about that?"

"Actually, I have. But to jump out of here, I'd need an account or two. You can't start a production company if you haven't got a couple of clients in hand to pay the bills."

"I bet you could get the Tasti-Feast spots."

"Possibly. But I'd also like to do more than just commercials."

"Like what."

"Corporate image films. Maybe some documentaries. Sales films. That kind of thing. It might happen."

"For your sake, I hope it does."

"We'll see. Now, let's talk about you. It could be that your getting fired was a godsend. As I told you, a guy I know owns a small production company. It's called Film Arts. His name is Elliott Pierce. He's probably one of the best directors in this business. His personal life is a little screwed up and he can get a little out of control, budget-wise, when he's on a shoot. But he comes back with great footage. Right now, he's paying the bills doing commercials, but he told me he's getting ready to do a feature."

"He's doing a feature?"

"I guess it's in the works. He said something about tying up the rights to a book. But that's down the road. He's still looking for a production manager. I told him I knew a bright young guy with a lot of talent who was a fast learner and not afraid of hard work. He said you sounded like his kind of guy."

"Great."

"I have to warn you, however, the downside of working with Elliott can sometimes be like nailing Jell-O to a wall. The upside is that it could be a hell of a learning experience. And hey, maybe if he does the feature, you'll get to work on that."

Damn, a feature, Jay thought. "When can I go see this guy?"

"He's out of town for a couple weeks, but if you can tread water until then ..."

"Not a problem. It'll give me a chance to look for someplace to live."

10
Sheridan Square

"I've found you an apartment," Joanna announced. "It's not great, but it's cheap and it's furnished ... kind of."

"By 'kind of'... you mean?"

"It's about as bad as the place you're in right now," she said, enjoying the comparison.

"Where is it?"

"In my building. The fifth floor. That's a lot of stairs, so I don't know if that will work for you."

In your building. He heard the voice in his head say. *To be in your building, I won't need stairs. I'll just fly up to the fifth floor.* "It will be good exercise," he said. "And if it's got a bed, a chair and a kitchen, who could ask for anything more?"

"Well, it's got a little more than that. I looked at it today. It's a studio, sort of like an artist's garret. In fact, an artist was renting it. I hardly ever saw him. Kept really strange hours. According to my landlord, the guy hasn't paid his rent in three months and nobody knows where he is. So, if you like it, it's yours."

The price and the proximity to Joanna—in reverse order—made it an instant sale, sight unseen. Two days later, he moved in.

As Joanna had described, the studio apartment consisted of a single large room with a small bathroom and a recessed kitchen. The furnishings were sparse, generally threadbare and stained, but adequate. What immediately appealed to Jay, other than the $67.50 a month rent, was the large, six-by-eight canted window that looked as if it had been imported directly from the Left Bank in Paris. Mullions divided it into sixteen different panes. The view from the window was over the Village rooftops, looking north toward mid-town, where buildings rose like carelessly placed building blocks. It was, Jay thought, as if he were seeing the city for the first time with its promise of endless fascination, endless opportunity, endless questions. The streets and the square below him—which was actually in the form of a triangle—had all the color and ambiance of an O. Henry short story.

"You know," Jay said to the landlord, "since this place looks like a Parisian garret, I went out and bought an easel, some paints and brushes."

"What are you going to do with 'em?" His tone was almost accusatory.

Jay read him as a humorless man and decided to have a little fun. "I plan to paint beautiful women draped only in diaphanous material."

"I don't permit no tenants to use their apartments for sex-related purposes."

"I'll keep that in mind," he said, barely able to contain a laugh.

Several hours later, Jay answered a knock on his door.

"I heard the music from the second floor on up," Joanna said

"I didn't realize it was that loud," he said, turning down the volume on his record player.

"I see you're all moved in. Furniture's a little ratty, isn't it?"

"I like to think of it as having character."

She walked over to the garret window. "What a great view! You can see all the way uptown." She turned around and gave the apartment a quick inspection. "I like this little garret of yours. Easel, paints, a little wine, music. What is that?" she said indicating the music. "It's beautiful."

"Puccini's La Bohème. It's one of my favorite operas."

"I've never been to an opera."

"Then I shall take you," he said with a gallant flourish. "Next time it's at the Met."

"Give da broad a dose of culture, right?"

"You got it."

"Did Baskham's job lead turn out?" she asked.

"We'll see. I have an interview next week. The company is called Film Arts. Ever hear of them?"

"No, but that doesn't mean anything. There are hundreds of production companies in New York." She pointed toward his easel. "Writer, director, rescuer and now artist? Are there any talents that you lack, Mr. Carraway?"

"None," he said with a comic flair.

"Can I look?" she asked, indicating the canvas.

"Right now it's not much of anything other than something to wipe my brushes on. Between you and me, that might be the limit of my artistic ability."

"I'm sure you're just being modest."

"No. Truthful.

"Would you like to paint me?"

"Sure," he lied, confident that she wasn't serious and knowing full well that he couldn't paint her fingernails.

"I'd like to have you paint me in the nude ... now," she said with a playfully seductive look that would have derailed a train. Slowly, tantalizingly, she began to unbutton her blouse.

"What?" Jay felt his heart jump into his throat. *My god*, he thought. *She's going to take off her clothes and expect me to paint her.*

"Then again," she said, looking at him askance and buttoning her blouse, "maybe this isn't a good idea. I'd get goose bumps and you might lose control and ... well, who knows where that would lead?"

"Who knows? Maybe we should find out," he said with a bit of male bluster.

She studied him long enough to cause him to wonder if there was something wrong with his face, or if his mouth bore some residue of the milk he'd had earlier. Under the scrutiny of her stare, his bravado began to wilt and the facade of male swagger melted like butter left too long on the stove. "Why do I feel at such a disadvantage here? Did I grow another head and not notice?"

"I'm sorry," she said, smiling. "I just like looking at you."

He was all but helpless at that point.

"The reason I came up was to see if you'd like to join me for dinner in my apartment, to celebrate."

Celebrate what?"

"Two things. I no longer work for Ad-Film."

"They didn't let you go because of ..."

"No," she said, cutting him off. "I resigned because I got an Industrial. It's with a Home Show. I'll be singing a duet with a musical refrigerator. We travel to four cities."

"That's great. Congratulations!" he said. "But ... you said there were two things."

"Well, the second is not something that I'm really all that anxious to celebrate. Thirty is not my favorite number."

"Thirty?"

"Today is my birthday."

"Today?" he lit up with surprise. "It's your birthday? Why didn't you tell me? You made dinner for me the other night and now I'm going to make dinner for you. Only I suggest we do it in your apartment, because the landlord hasn't turned on the gas up here as yet."

"I didn't think you knew how to cook."

"Don't worry, I'll let you wash the lettuce. But I can broil steaks and what I can't cook, I can buy at the deli."

With that, he bounded down the five flights and searched the street for a place to buy a cake and a bottle of champagne. He found steaks in the local market, the champagne in a shop around the corner and salad and potatoes in a deli. That accomplished, he looked for a present, but all he could find was a storybook doll in a toyshop. *A little silly maybe*, he thought, *but why not? At least it's a present.* He had the sales lady wrap it for him and put a bow on it. As he headed back toward Sheridan Square, he ducked into a flower shop, purchased a dozen roses and hastily wrote a card.

***

After they had finished dinner, Jay presented the cake and sang an acapella version of "Happy Birthday." Then he gave her the present.

"This is so exciting," she said, holding the box in her lap, reluctant to unwrap it.

"Open it," he urged.

"In a minute. The longer you wait to open a gift, the longer you get to wonder what it is."

"As you're wondering, keep in mind that this is a sort of last-minute desperation gift. You didn't give me a lot of shopping time. So if it's not exactly the mink coat I had in mind ..."

"Then you'll just have to exchange it," she chided with mock indignation.

Her expectant expression was that of a little girl at a birthday party and Jay wondered if there had been all that many birthday parties as she grew up. She opened the box lid, gently pulled away the paper tissue and lifted out the doll. The small card tied around the doll's left arm identified her as Cinderella. Joanna stared at the doll and said nothing for a long time. Jay began having doubts about his gift. He had thought she'd get a kick out of it. But now he was concerned that she might be wondering what kind of nitwit would give a thirty-year-old woman a doll. He began to look for an excuse, "As I said, I would have bought a mink, but being a little short of time and cash ..."

Joanna shook her head. "I'd rather have this," she said pensively. It was apparent to Jay that, for some reason, the doll had begun to topple a line of emotional dominoes. It had clearly touched her, but he wasn't sure why.

"You couldn't have picked a more perfect birthday present," she said quietly. Then she opened another window on her past. "The day I was to leave my aunt's house for St. Madeleine's, I went to my bedroom, packed all my dolls and waited for the sister who was to pick me up. Sister Francis had the most wonderful face and I remember thinking as she came up the stairs in her long white habit that she looked like an angel floating up to me. I took her into my room and showed her all the boxes I'd packed.

She looked at them for the longest time, then she sat down with me on my bed and explained that there wouldn't be room for all my things in the orphanage."

"That had to hurt."

Joanna nodded and then sighed. "Not only me. As I think back, I realize that it almost broke her heart when she told me I'd have to choose just those dolls that were most special to me. She said I could take three, but the rest had to stay behind. It was so hard to choose, because I loved them all. Finally, I decided on my Raggedy Ann and the teddy bear that my father had given me before he died. For the third, I took a doll with a missing eye because I felt sorry for her and knew that nobody would want her if I left her behind."

She paused, collecting her thoughts. "Then I picked up the Cinderella doll that my mother had given me for my seventh birthday. She was special, too. I made her a secret promise, one that Sister Francis couldn't hear. 'I'll be coming back for you,' I whispered." Joanna looked up at Jay, the tears welling in her eyes. "You have no idea what it means to me to keep that promise after all these years."

For the first time, Jay fully understood what he had suspected since the night in Central Park; deep inside Joanna, there were wounds that had never healed. This woman, who could cut the office sniffers down with a single verbal karate chop, was far more vulnerable than she ever permitted anyone to know. She had, however, just let Jay know. Joanna showed no embarrassment, no shame in having him see her searching for vestiges of a childhood that had been taken away from her. It was as if she was showing him her most fragile possession, confident that he would handle it carefully. Finally, she put the past back in its private place and looked up at him with a bright smile. "I just love it. You must have a sixth sense about me. She's just beautiful."

"I guess all she needs is for the prince to find her shoe."

Joanna gave Jay a playful look and, in her most seductive voice, said, "Tell me, Jay —if I leave my slipper in your apartment, will you knock on all the doors in the building until you find that it fits me?"

Jay nodded. "Except I wouldn't bother knocking on any door but this one."

Joanna placed the doll in the center of the table, using the little metal bracket that made it possible for Cinderella to stand on her own. "Thank you, Jay ," she said leaning over and giving him a kiss on the cheek. "I think this has been just about the best birthday I've ever had."

Jay suddenly realized that he'd forgotten something. "The roses. I forgot that I composed a little poem to go along with them. He reached in his pocket and handed it to her."

"A poem? You *are* prolific."

"Well, it's not going to win any prizes. I didn't have much time to think about it while the lady was wrapping up your roses. But, the sentiment is there. I mean, it says what I want it to say."

She opened the envelope and read it aloud.

I love the girl on the floor below,
She means more to me than she can know,
One day I'll knock on door 4B
And ask her to spend her life with me.
Happy Birthday.
The guy from the floor above.

She did not lift her eyes from the card, but read it again, this time to herself.

As Jay watched her, waiting for a reaction, what he felt was no longer a passion stemming from just a physical attraction; it had become something deeper, maybe primordial and intrinsic to the ordained scheme of things. Or, he wondered, could this be simply the magnetism of opposites, its only logic to be found in the calculus of human physics? Whatever, for him it was real.

"Thank you, Jay. One day, I may be ready for that knock on my door."

"I'm in love with you, Joanna."

There was a moment while she weighed her words. "You're special to me, Jay. More than you know. Believe me when I tell you, there's no one I'd rather be with than you. But let's go slow … at least for a little while longer. There's so much you don't know about me. So, so much. I don't want to disappoint you." Her eyes asked for his acquiescence and there was no way he was going to deny her.

He leaned across the table, holding out his hand to her and nodding his acceptance. "I don't think it would be possible for you to disappoint me. Maybe the other way around. We'll go slow … but not too slow, please. Keep in mind that right above your head there's a guy who loves you very much."

"I know and it makes me very happy," she said, taking his hand and squeezing it.

By the time Jay said good night and went back upstairs to his apartment, he realized the transformation was complete. The fascination that had gripped him the first day at Ad-Film had evolved to different plane. True, he still lusted for the body, but now he was hopelessly in love with the person.

As yet, it remained a solo act.

11
The Other Half

"How long a ride is it to Greenwich?" she asked as they stepped off the platform at Grand Central and into the rail car.

"About twenty-five minutes."

"Are you sure we're dressed OK?" Joanna was wearing Bermuda shorts and a sweater and Jay was in khakis and a polo shirt.

"We're going to a picnic. Looks like we're dressed for a picnic to me."

As the train left the tunnel under Park Avenue and rumbled through Harlem, Jay said, "I'm beginning to have second thoughts about taking you home. I'm not sure how to prepare you for this."

"You think I need to be prepared? Why?"

"Well, a lot of my parent's friends live on a different planet. Most of them have little attachment to reality. Their money allows them to lead insular lives. It's like they live on a private island so they can be very selective as to whom they accept. The women think only about the next social event or getting their kids into the right schools and then marrying them off to someone from the right family."

"They sound a lot like Mrs. Henry Day Thornton."

"Probably the same mold. For the men, making money—more than they could ever need has come down to a competition.

Their bank accounts are a way of keeping score. If you don't have a lot of money, you're not a player. And if you not a player, you're not going to get invited to the island."

In her most exaggerated Brooklynese, Joanna said, "Hey, ya shur yuz bringin' home a goil from Brooklyn is gonna be cool wid dem swells? Dey may not let yas inda dour wid me."

"You know, I just escaped from all that so I'm beginning to wonder why am I going back? I have an idea, why don't we just stay on the train and get off at Westport and go to the beach?"

"No way. I want to see how the other half of the top one percent lives. As you said, I should think of this like a visit to the zoo. I love zoos. And I promise not to touch the animals."

"Don't try to feed 'em either. They bite."

***

They took a taxi from the Greenwich station and headed north. As they crossed Putnam Avenue, Jay pointed to a large building set well back off the street. "Over there," he said, "is the headquarters of Carraway International. I worked there for almost two years, running errands for my father and brother. It was a lot like what I did at Ad-film, except that they paid even less."

Fifteen minutes later after crossing over the Merritt Parkway they turned off North Avenue and passed through a large iron gate. Over the gate were the words: "Deerfield Park."

"What's Deerfield Park?"

"That's the name my mother has given our property."

"It must be pretty big if it has a name."

"Either that or my mother wants you to think it's pretty big."

The taxi rolled down a long, tree-lined driveway. The majestic oaks formed a leafy tunnel. The driveway lead them onto a large, cobblestone courtyard that was embraced on either side by the grand wings of the house. It had been built in 1894 as a smaller version of the Grand Trianon at Versailles. The architect chose to refine the French original into more manageable H-shaped structure that preserved many of the neo-classical exterior details. The near-white terra cotta tiles that covered the exterior were bright and clean, having fended off the discoloration of time. On either side of the courtyard, large, circular fountains sent streams of water into the air that fell back into large, circular cement pools. The taxi pulled up in front of the massive front door and Jay paid the sum on the meter, plus a tip.

"I didn't know places like this existed in America," Joanna said as she stepped out.

"There are those who would tell you that North Greenwich isn't in America."

"And this is your house?" Joanna said, making no attempt to hide her awe.

"No, not mine. It belongs to my father."

"But you grew up here."

"True. But then, I didn't exactly have any other option. Although I was sent off to camp so often I began to think my mother might have been hinting at something."

"This place is unbelievable. It's like a castle. Those fountains are beautiful. Can I ask you a question?"

"Do I have to answer it?"

"Yes."

"OK, ask."

"Why, when you could live in a place like this and ... and ... well, commute to the city, why would you want to live in a 5th floor walk-up?"

He looked at her as if he couldn't believe she didn't know. "Because of who lives on the 4th floor."

"No, really," she insisted.

"Really?" he was serious now. "Because inside those walls you're not permitted to be what *you* want to be, only what *they* want you to be. Guess what? What they wanted was not what I wanted. For me, this house is not my home anymore, just a place to visit now and then."

"A lot of people would say you're crazy to give up all this."

"A lot of people can say whatever they want, as far as I'm concerned."

"Jay!" The voice came from a pert young woman in a flowing white frock who was running out the front door. She didn't stop until she had jumped up and thrown her arms around him. "Oh, I miss you, I miss you, I miss you so much!"

As she let go and slid back to the ground, Jay said, "Joanna, this in my little sister, Cornelia Carraway, who prefers to be called by her initials, Ceci."

"Hi," she said, shaking Joanna's hand enthusiastically. "Mother says you're an actress and a singer. Is that true?" Then, without waiting for answer, "It has to be true. Anyone who looks like you has to be an actress or a model or something."

"Or *something*, might be more like it."

Ceci either didn't hear or care to question Joanna's response. Instead, she took several steps backward and looked at the two of them, shaking her head. "You can't be serious, dressed like that. Where are your clothes?"

"Our clothes?" Jay asked

"Didn't Mother tell you? The picnic is summer-casual formal."

"Summer-casual formal? What did she mean by that?"

"Coats and ties for the men and Mother has asked—which is to say, she has insisted—that all the women wear white or pastel dresses."

"She never said anything about what Joanna and I were to wear. Not a word. I guess she'll either have to take us as we are or we'll just go back to the City."

"Mother will not be happy with you, Jay ," she said, her voice full of warning.

"When is she ever happy with me?"

"If she sees you at her party like that, she will just ... you know, give birth to kittens." She turned to Joanna to offer an explanation. "Our mother," she said with emphasis and a touch of disgust, "is so difficult when it comes to things like this. Everyone has to conform. Do what she says or she, well ..." She shrugged.

"Will throw a fit," Jay said.

"It's usually easier and a lot less hassle just to do what she says. But, as far as getting you dressed, there's no problem. Jay, you've got plenty of sports coats and slacks upstairs in your room. She looked Joanna up and down. "Joanna and I are about the same size and I've got tons and tons of dresses you can borrow."

"I wouldn't want to impose," Joanna said.

"You're not imposing. There are dresses up there I've never had on. Somebody has just got to wear them, at least once, before they're out of style."

"Yes, Joanna," Jay said in mock seriousness. "You wouldn't want all of Ceci's dresses to be sent to the Salvation Army having never been worn at least once."

Ceci rocked her head back and forth as her way of accenting how perturbed she was at her brother's mockery. "Jay you are such a … such a … there must be a word to describe you, but I can't think of one."

"I'll think of one for you," Jay volunteered.

Ceci ignored him. "Come with me, Joanna. I'll take you up to my room," she said latching onto her arm.

"Wow," Ceci said expansively, but sincerely, as she escorted Joanna up the front steps. "What I wouldn't give to go through life looking like you."

Jay put on a shirt, tie, white pants and a blue blazer and quickly came down the sweeping staircase that emptied into the grand entrance foyer. As no one else seemed to be around, he walked into the library—his father's favorite room. It was, by any measure, a grand and imposing room, exuding a male dominance that was generally lacking from the rest of the house. Bound books, both the classics and non-fiction works, lined the wall; many volumes were behind glass cabinet doors. The carved woodwork and ceiling moldings all appeared to be and were, imported from Europe by the architect. The bureau plaque tables were of 18th century vintage. The heavy leather chairs and sofas, centered on the massive fireplace, seemed to invite the company of men with their cigars and pipes to talk about the current state of affairs.

Jay liked this room and, as a boy, he liked to retreat here. His mother had, for some reason, tacitly relegated it to his father and only on rare occasions deigned to join him there for family consuls. For that reason, Jay found it an ideal place to listen in secret to radio shows like Intersanctum, Lights Out, the Green Hornet, Gun Smoke and other radio serials, which his mother had declared unfit for young boys.

"Jay," Ceci whispered as she opened the library door and poked her head inside. "Wait 'till you see Joanna. She's right out of a magazine."

Ceci turned back to the foyer and called to Joanna, "In here."

Joanna entered the room and it was immediately clear that the dress had found a home. It was a white sheath with a scooped neckline that showed just a hint of what lay below. The dress seemed to enjoy accenting her narrow waist and only reluctantly let the eye be interrupted with a silk bow that bloomed in a simple tie at her hips. On her head, Ceci had placed a large-brimmed, straw hat accented with a pink ribbon.

"I feel like Cinderella," Joanna said, clearly enthralled with Ceci's dress.

"Except instead of going to a ball, you're going to a polo match and a picnic. I'll be right back," Ceci said and hurried out into the foyer.

"Cinderella never looked so good."

"Even her shoes fit me," Joanna said, holding out a foot. "Jay, I've never seen so many clothes in my life, except in a store. Her closet is bigger than my apartment and it's full of dozens and dozens of dresses and sweaters, slacks and ... I couldn't begin to count the shoes."

"I'll let you in on a family secret: Ceci was born with a congenital condition that has turned her into a shopaholic. The first words out of my sister's mouth when she learned to talk were 'charge it.' If it weren't for her, God knows how many New York boutiques would have to close."

Ceci stuck her head in the room. "Polo anyone? The car's waiting for us out front."

They arrived just before the third of six chukkers was beginning. As they made their way along the sidelines through the crowd of elegantly dressed spectators, Jay was aware that Joanna had suddenly become a magnet for appreciative glances from the men and critical assessments from the women. She was, it seemed to Jay, attracting more attention than the polo match.

Jay pointed to one of the horses as it thundered by. "See that horse out there with the number 1 on it?" he pointed

"Yes."

"That's my brother, Scott." As if on cue, Scott's horse broke free from the pack. At a full gallop he leaned to the right and swung his mallet striking the ball and sending it flying in a low, arching curve toward the opponents' goal. Two strokes more and his team had another score.

"How do they stay in the saddle riding that fast with one hand on a mallet?"

"It's not easy."

"Ok, time to turn her loose and let me have her." It was Ceci. "I want to introduce her to some of my friends. Don't worry Jay, I'll bring her back." Then to Joanna, "this will give me a chance to get to know you better."

As Ceci took her arm and escorted her away, Joanna glanced back at Jay as if to ask, what should I do?

His expression indicated that resisting his sister would be fruitless.

"Hello, stranger." The voice came from a petite young woman in a yellow dress. The light blue hat nicely framed Brooke Whitney's face and blond hair. She had, as always, a sunny personality and a warm glow that greatly enhanced a pleasant, but not remarkable face. Her reserved appearance, the demure dress and the white gloves seem to suggest that she would never provide potential suitors with the stuff of erotic fantasies. Yet, she was the kind of woman that could more than hold up her end of a conversation on myriad subjects. She was what Jay described to friends as a sweet, considerate, intelligent girl.

"Hey, Brooke. It's been a while. All done with school?"

"Graduated last month."

"So what are you going to do with yourself?"

"Well first, I have to do the *mother thing*," she said, making no effort to suppress her dread at the prospect.

"The mother thing?"

"I don't mean to sound unappreciative. I mean, it will be fun, I guess. When my mother graduated from college back in the twenties, her mother took her on a grand tour of Europe. So she decided that we should do the same. Frankly, I don't know what we're going to see than I haven't seen already. But she's like your mother; you don't say 'No' if you want to maintain peace in the family."

"I understand completely," he said. "When you come back, what then?"

"Well, I might teach. But Daddy would like me to work at his foundation."

"Foundation?"

"It gives money to organizations that work with children from broken homes. Kids that have been mistreated, maybe even abandoned. I like the idea of helping people. Of course, a teacher can do that as well. I'll try to decide while I'm gone."

"Well, you've always been into that kind of thing. I mean, you've always been concerned for others and that's good. World needs more people like you."

Brooke seemed a little embarrassed by Jay's praise. She tended to be the kind of person who gave compliments rather than received them.

From the time he was in his teens, his mother had decided that Brooke Whitney would make him an ideal wife. "The match would be perfect," she had said more than once. "She comes from such a prominent family. Her mother can trace her roots back to Charles the V of France"—as if that was a major consideration in picking a proper mate. Jay imagined that Brooke's mother had probably made similar comments. Jay was fond of Brooke Whitney, but much in the same way he was fond of his sister. Romantic involvement had never been a consideration.

"Ceci tells me that you're living in New York and directing films."

"Living there, yes. But directing films ... ah ... not yet. One day, hopefully."

"I remember when we were kids and you had that camera and you made those films with us. Who knew that one day you'd want to do it for real?"

"Well, certainly not my parents. They'd like me to pursue a more *responsible* career." He verbally underlined "responsible."

"My advice is to do what makes you happy."

"I couldn't agree more."

"Brooke!" the voice came from somewhere off to the left.

"Mother," Brooke said, identifying the voice to Jay . "I guess we're leaving. We had to say 'no' to your mother's picnic invitation because Daddy had scheduled something else. Promise me that we'll have a chance to catch up when I get back from Europe."

"Sounds good," he said, his indefinite response letting the promise drift quietly away. "Have a good time on 'the tour.'"

"I'll do my best. See you," she said. And then, like a tardy schoolgirl, she hurried off in the direction of her mother's voice.

***

The match was well into the fifth chukker when Ceci reappeared with Joanna. "I'm bringing her back before she gets kidnapped. Joanna draws men like honey draws flies. Nobody watches the polo match when she's around."

Ceci rattled on about how she just loved Joanna and how they had talked to her brother as he was changing horses for the next chukker. Jay noticed that three men he had not seen in years decided to excuse themselves from their dates and come over to renew his acquaintance. As they approached, their true agenda was instantly obvious. As soon as Jay introduced Joanna, the three fell over themselves trying to impress her. It wasn't long before the three abandoned women walked up, looking as if they fully intended to mug Joanna and forcibly drag off their wandering men.

"Jay, it's been ever so long," gushed the one in the pink dress.

"Yes, where are you keeping yourself?" asked the one in the blue dress, in a tone that reeked of a lack of interest in hearing an answer.

"Aren't you going to introduce us to your ... friend?" the woman in yellow asked as she gave Joanna a head-to-toe inspection.

Like some local society militia, the women were priming their weapons, ready to drive off or lay low this social interloper. Jay considered excusing Joanna and himself, but he knew running from the assault he suspected was coming would be a mistake. "Excuse me," he said politely, "this is Joanna Olenska. And this is ..."

Before he could announce their names, the blue dress sent the first verbal volley across Joanna's bow. "Olenska. Are you Russian or something?"

"Or something," she responded and then added, "It's Polish."

Immediately, Jay sensed Joanna's radar was picking up that this was not to be just a friendly exchange of inane pleasantries. She began to strap on her armor and sharpen her broad sword.

The blue dress was loading her musket. "Polish? Are you from Poland?"

'Brooklyn."

"But she lives in Manhattan now," Jay injected.

"Brooklyn!" echoed the yellow dress, ignoring Jay. "I don't believe any of us have *ever* been to Brooklyn." Her emphasis was the same as if she had announced that she had never been to Mars.

"I'm not even sure I even know where Brooklyn is," said the pink dress, appearing slightly amazed to have come face to face with an actual Brooklyn native. "Does anybody here know someone who lives in Brooklyn?" She glanced around at the growing gaggle of ogling men, seemingly assured that no one would admit to knowing someone from Brooklyn.

"Oh, come now," Joanna said, feigning surprise. "I can't imagine that even up here in Greenwich you haven't heard of our Duke."

"Your Duke?" pink dress echoed.

"Yes. We call him 'The Duke of Flatbush.' He's a long time resident of Brooklyn."

"A Duke lives in Brooklyn?" blue dress asked incredulous.

"Oh yes. Lives there. Plays there. Does most everything there," Joanna said as though shocked that none had ever heard of this pillar of Brooklyn royalty.

The three men began to smile and smirk, clearly eager to assume their roles as spectators at what promised to become a first class skirmish.

"Have you ever met him?" the yellow dress asked.

Jay could hardly contain himself. *Joanna is going to chop them up*, he thought.

"Met him? Well, in truth, we don't usually run in the same circle."

"What's circle does he run in?"

"The one that goes from home to first, to second to third and back to home."

The male onlookers burst into nearly uncontrollable laughter.

The man standing next to the blue dress blurted out an unsolicited congratulations. "Very good, Joanna. You really had 'em going."

The three women did little to hide their growing pique at having been made the butt of Joanna's joke. The scorching looks they gave their dates not only incinerated their laughter, but also promised to wreak irreparable physical damage.

"I don't get it," the blue dress said, exposing herself to ridicule.

"Duke Snider plays centerfield for the Brooklyn Dodgers," the man next to yellow dress explained.

The three girls looked totally befuddled. Clearly, it was going to take a more concentrated barrage to drive off this foe.

"I suppose, then, if your Duke plays baseball, he doesn't play polo," said the yellow dress.

"Well, it's true that he doesn't play polo, but he does play *at* the Polo Grounds from time to time."

The spectators made no effort to muffle their guffaws.

The girl in pink had no idea what Joanna was talking about and decided on a different attack. "Do you ride?"

"Of course. Doesn't everybody?"

"In New York? You ride in New York?" the pink dress asked.

"I ride the number 6 on the IRT Subway line almost every day."

More smirks and chuckles.

The second girl, doing her best to regain the high ground, lifted her chin in a haughty manner as though ready to balance something on it. "Well, I ride *horses*," she said, emphasizing the word 'horses,' "and I hunt."

"Oh, I hunt, too," Joanna said sweetly. "I hunt for work all the time." Laughter continued to frolic among the men, only adding to the growing vexation shared by the three women.

Seeking to salvage the encounter and deliver at least one embarrassing blow, the blue dress said, "I've always thought of Brooklyn as so ... so plebeian. I mean I've never heard of a debutante party there. I presume you never came out?"

"Oh, but I did," Joanna said sweetly. I came out of reform school in '52 and rehabilitation in 1955." The laughter rolled up and over the three girls. The assault repelled, they beat a hasty retreat.

"I love this girl," said one of the escorts, gaining instant agreement from the other men.

"I could love her even more," said another.

"And now, if you'll excuse us?" Jay said as he took Joanna and Ceci by the arms and led them away. As they left, he thought he actually heard some applause.

"I'm sorry," Joanna said quietly to Jay and Ceci. "I let them get to me. I should have just ignored them. Did I embarrass you?"

"Embarrass me? Hell no. You gave them exactly what they deserved."

"I agree," Ceci added. "I only feel sorry for their dates. They're going to catch hell from those girls."

"I'm not sure what I did to make them come at me like that."

"It was God that did it," Jay said. "He made you beautiful. In nature, the ugly always trys to compromise or destroy beauty."

"They weren't ugly," she protested.

"Well, next to you they were," Ceci offered.

"And they are certainly ugly on the inside," Jay said. "They wanted to embarrass you to make themselves look superior. Instead, you made them look ridiculous. You hit them right square in their elitist egos. They're just empty girdles, if you ask me."

"If they'd acted like that to me," Ceci said, "I would have just cried and run away. I wish I could have done what you did." Ceci turned to Jay and blurted, "Jay, your Joanna is terrific. Why don't you marry her so we can be sisters?"

"Now, there's an idea," Jay said, looking directly at Joanna.

***

The car dropped them back at the house. They passed through the foyer and stepped out on the rear terrace. In front of them, the formal gardens appeared to have sprouted well over two hundred guests. Round tables, positioned at various spots on the terrace and along the garden walks, seemed to sag under the weight of the enormous display of food and drink. Trays of champagne, balanced on the hands of black-tie waiters, floated among the guests as if programmed to follow some preordained orbit. Vacuous gusts of laughter erupted now and again as vocal confirmation that the guests were, indeed, enjoying themselves.

"Joanna, this is my father," Jay said as Wilfred Carraway approached. He was a tall, distinguished-looking man with pepper-grey hair. "Dad, this is Joanna Olenska."

Wilfred Carraway smiled and held out his hand. "I'm glad you could join us. We did well weather-wise, I think," he said looking up at the sky as if checking for uninvited clouds.

"Perfect weather," she said.

"Did you enjoy the polo match?"

"I did. It's the first time I've ever seen one. I can't believe those horses. The way they stop and turn and take off at full speed."

"They're a special breed. Wonderful animals."

"I love your gardens. I've never seen anything quite like this. It must take a lot of work to keep it like this."

His father smiled and looked out at the beds of flowers, the pergola draped with roses and the fountains playing discreetly in the several ponds that sat among the flower beds. "Amazing what you can do with a half dozen gardeners and an unlimited budget. Between you and me, this is my wife's thing. And frankly, she's let it get totally out of control. In four months, it will all be dead and brown and then nine months later, we start all over again. Aside from that, I'm glad you like it."

"Given that my garden is just three flowerpots in the window, this is pretty special."

"You live in the City?

"Same building as Jay ."

"Good. Then I'm counting on you to see that my prodigal son behaves." At that point, one of the servants approached Wilfred Carraway and whispered something in his ear. "Excuse, will you? A minor crisis with the waiters requires some attention. It was very nice to meet you, Joanna. Please enjoy yourself," he said and then followed the servant.

Jay felt a slap on his shoulder. "Where have you been hiding this woman, brother? I almost fell off my horse when Ceci introduced us. If she's not in movies, she ought to be," he said, taking a quick inventory of the woman on Jay 's arm.

Joanna responded with an uncomfortable smile.

"What did you think of the match?" Scott asked.

"I just have one question. How do you hang on? I'm surprised no one fell off."

"It's against the rules to fall off," he joked. "Plus, it hurts, a *lot*. Especially if the other horses step on you."

The woman standing just behind and to Scott's right observed the conversation with a contemptuous interest. It was only when she cleared her throat in a purposeful way that Scott remembered she was there and made the introduction. "Oh, Joanna, this is my wife, Tolova."

Tolova held out a limp hand and said, "Very nice to meet you." Her greeting lacked even a trace of enthusiasm. "First time at Deerfield Park?"

"First time. It's really magnificent."

"How's the film business going, Jay ?" Scott asked.

"Keepin' at it."

"Good." That seemed to be all he needed to know about his brother's progress. Scott immediately turned his attention back to Joanna. "Say, this is going to be crazy here this afternoon. Won't be much time to talk. Why don't you guys come out with us on the boat? That'll give Tolova and me a chance to get to know you better."

"I thought you knew me already?" Jay said, acting deeply hurt.

"Not you, turkey." Suddenly, Scott grimaced in pain and his hands clutched at his stomach.

"Are you ok?" Jay asked, showing his concern.

The pain subsided and Scott forced a thin smile. "Oooo. That hurt. Think I must have pulled a muscle or something. I'll be ok. Anyway, as I was saying, I'd like to take you and Joanna out for a sail. You'll love our boat, Jay ."

"Scott," Tolova said, in a tone that indicated she'd had enough of watching him ogle Joanna. "I think we should see to our guests." She took her husband's arm and began to lead him away.

"Catch you later," Scott said, taking one last look at Joanna. "Movies. Definitely should be in the movies."

Jay gave Joanna his arm and they walked into the garden along the crushed white marble pathways, past bed after bed of flowers. Jay greeted the people he knew and nodded to others. They stopped at various tables to sample the over abundance of hor d'oeuvres and helped themselves when a waiter presented a tray of champagne.

After a while, Joanna whispered to Jay, "Why do I feel that everyone is staring at us?"

"Because they are," Jay said. "They want to see what the prodigal son has brought home."

"And this, I presume, is Joanna." His mother's voice passed over them like an indifferent breeze. She was wearing a bright red dress and a large red hat that appeared to be sprouting a flower garden to rival the one they were standing in. Her hair was silver grey and sculpted, sprayed, teased and styled. The perfectly formed curls and waves looked more like a wig than real hair. She was tall, about Joanna's height, but very thin, having long since subscribed to the axiom that a woman can never be too rich or too thin.

"Mother, I'd like you to meet Joanna Olenska."

"It's nice to meet you, Mrs. Carraway," Joanna said warmly.

"Somehow I imagined you'd be blonde." Her tone was coolly analytical as her eyes made a quick appraisal. "Jay has always tended to prefer blonds."

"Mother, you have no idea what I have *tended to prefer.*"

His mother, as was often the case when engaged in a disagreement, ignored his rebuttal. "Of course, you will be staying tonight." It was a statement, not a question. "I'll have Melarosa fix a room for you in the guesthouse." The comment was intended for Joanna, but directed at Jay.

Jay sensed that his mother had made up her mind—probably immediately after their phone conversation—that Joanna was to be dispensed with as soon as possible. He noticed she was doing her best to avoid eye contact with Joanna, as if by refusing to look at her, Joanna might conveniently evaporate. Jay was tempted to say something, but for Joanna's sake, he decided not to risk an embarrassing confrontation. He forced a smile and said, "That won't be necessary, Mother, Joanna has to be on a 6:30 AM train for Philadelphia tomorrow."

"6:30? Philadelphia? On Sunday? Whatever for?"

"I'm in a show and we have a rehearsal Sunday afternoon."

"You're in a show ... on a Sunday?" She sounded like a proponent of Blue Laws.

"Just a rehearsal."

"Oh, yes, I believe Jay did say something about your being an actress."

"And a singer," Jay added.

"Do you sing in your show?"

"A little."

"Something I might know?"

"I'm afraid not. The song is about the features and benefits of a Westinghouse refrigerator." She laughed a little self-consciously.

The expression on his mother's face might well have accompanied the discovery that a vagrant had just dropped into her garden. "A refrigerator? You sing a song about a refrigerator? Never heard of such a thing."

Jay came to the rescue. "Mother, there are a lot of things you've never heard of. I'll explain it to you at some other time."

"I'm sure I will be incredibly fascinated to learn why people sing about refrigerators," she said, making no effort to conceal her total lack of interest in the subject. Turning to Joanna she said pointedly, "I'm sorry you can't stay tonight. I'll have James call you a taxi."

"Mother, I'll be taking her home," Jay said sharply.

"Oh, Jay, dear," she said, with suspect motherly disappointment oozing from every pore. "Do you really need to return to New York tonight? I'd planned to have you join us for Sunday dinner. I've invited the Whitneys."

"Give them my regrets." Jay was teetering on the edge of saying something that he knew he would regret. "Now, if you'll excuse us, Joanna and I are going to take a walk down by the pond."

"Nice meeting you," Joanna said as Jay took her arm and left his mother standing alone.

As they walked away, Jay took a quick glance back at his mother. Her peeved expression said she did not appreciate having been so abruptly dismissed.

Joanna looked up at him and said quietly, "Didn't Ceci say your mother wanted everyone to wear white or pastel?"

Jay laughed somewhat derisively. "You noticed her fire engine red dress, did you? That's my mother's way of making sure she remains the center of attention at her own parties. It's like she's daring anyone not to notice her."

"I don't think your mother likes me very much."

"Truth is, most people don't like *her* very much. If she didn't live in this house, host extravagant parties, claim some remote relation to the Astors and use her money to control every major social function in Greenwich, she'd have no friends at all. Money will buy you friends—or at least people who will pretend to be your friends. Without it, nobody would put up with her arrogant, snobbish, condescending personality."

"Are you sure you're not being a little hard on her?"

"Well, maybe." There was a whimsical tone in his concession. "Let me put it another way: once you get beneath her self-absorbed, obstinate personality, her myopic outlook on life and her manipulative and overbearing nature you'll find," he paused, "a nearly anorexic woman."

"She is very thin, isn't she?"

"Very." As they approached the pond that nestled itself well below the garden, Jay suggested they sit down on a bench. "This is where I used to come to think. And, in truth, to escape now and then."

"How do your brother and sister get along with your mother?"

"My brother ignores her and my sister does what's she's told. At least up to now. My father, on the other hand ... well, I guess you could say that he's found some way of dealing with her."

"Your father seemed very nice."

"One-on-one, he is. When she's with him, he's different. I think it's because my mother is holding him hostage."

"Hostage? What do you mean?"

"Well, my father is the fifth generation of Carraways to run the family business. His father, unfortunately, had made some pretty bad decisions just before World War I. The business was in real financial trouble. So—and this is a dark family secret—to get the financing my grandfather needed to save the company, he made what I guess you'd have to call a *deal* with my mother's family."

"Marriage for money?"

"Exactly. And in subtle and not-so-subtle ways, my mother never lets him forget it."

"Not exactly the basis for a happy marriage, is it?"

"I think that's why my father travels a lot. Speaking of travel, if's we're going to catch the 7:10 train, we'd better get changed and get out of here."

They found Ceci, who said that she'd have the chauffeur bring the car to the front courtyard. Then she took Joanna went up stairs to change back into her clothes. Jay quickly went up to his room, changed and came back downstairs where he found his mother standing in the foyer. She gestured for him to follow her into his father's library.

"I need to talk you about that girl, Jay ."

"I presume you mean Joanna?" Jay said, preparing for an acerbic critique.

"I don't know what your relationship is with her, but she seems ... well, very mature. How old is she?"

"Thirty. Why?"

"You're not yet twenty-six. That's quite an age difference."

"What does that have to do with anything?"

"Well, any girl who is that much older could have certain motives."

"What are you talking about?"

"I hope you are not so naive as not to believe that this woman could—and notice I did say *could* —be a gold digger. You wouldn't be the first young man to get trapped by a woman like that."

"Mother! For Christ sakes!" he shot back. "That's a goddamn insult! You're talking about a woman that I'm very, *very* fond of and I don't appreciate your accusing her of being a gold digger—which, I can tell you, she is most certainly not!"

Now her temper began to show. "I am just trying to open your eyes. What do you think that this woman—this orphan from Brooklyn—must be thinking when she sees all this?" She broadly indicated the house with a sweep of her hand. "You come from a great deal of money, which makes you a major catch. She would not be the first woman to ... well, to trap a rich man into marriage."

"Mother, I'm going to pretend that we are not having this conversation. Because you don't know what you're talking about."

"On that, you are very wrong! I have our family's interests to consider. I do not want us to find ourselves in the same fix as the Wellingtons. When their daughter took up with some fellow they knew nothing about, Abigail Wellington had the good sense to hire a detective to check him out. What they found was nothing short of scandalous. God knows what kind of devastation the man could have done to the family's reputation."

Jay did nothing to hide his growing rancor. "What do you want to do? Hire a detective to follow Joanna around? Hey, maybe you'll find that she's a secret shoplifter or a woman of ill repute in her spare time. Does she look like any of that? For God's sake, Mother, I don't know what gets into you at times."

"All I'm saying is that if you continue to have an interest in this girl, we should know more about her background. The last thing I will do is sit by quietly while a child of mine entertains the idea of marrying someone who is not properly suited to bear the Carraway name. You will not disgrace this family!"

"Oh, so you prefer that I marry some airhead like Tolova. Dumb as a stone and a pompous bitch besides. But she's acceptable, because she's from a proper family."

"What's wrong with marrying someone from your own class? What possibly could you have in common with a Joanna Olenska?" she spit her name off her tongue. "Brooklyn and North Greenwich are at opposite ends of the world."

"Mother, listen to me carefully," he said through gritted teeth. "This is my life and you have got nothing ... zero ... nada ... to say about it. And don't threaten to disinherit me. I know you and Dad control the trust. But, if necessary, I'll be happy to disinherit myself!"

"You are being totally irrational. I don't know why we cannot have a civil conversation. I find your impertinence and insolence most distasteful. Please remember that you are addressing your mother!"

"I am very aware of that. That's why I don't want to say things that we'll both regret. So let me make one thing clear before I put an end to this conversation. I happen to love Joanna and it may well be that one day, she'll consent to marry me. When that happens, you're going to have to get used to the idea of grandchildren with red blood rather than blue. So, if you think you can force me to break off my relationship with Joanna ... well, as they say in Brooklyn, fahgeddaboutit." He leaned over and gave his mother a dutiful peck on the cheek and said, "I have to go. We have a train to catch." Ignoring her icy gaze, he turned away and bounded upstairs to rescue Joanna from his sister.

No rescue was needed. Joanna had changed back into her Bermudas and sweater and was walking down the hall with Ceci toward the stairs.

Ceci grabbed his arm. "Jay, Joanna is just super. She's promised to sing for me sometime. Please, please promise to bring her back."

"Why don't we bring you into the city instead? We'll introduce you to the other Greenwich—the Village."

"Oh, I'd love that!"

"We'll give you a first-class tour," Joanna said.

"When Joanna gets back, I'll give you a call."

"I consider that promise."

As Jay and Joanna left the house and started down the front stairs toward the waiting limousine, Joanna said, "I feel like Cinderella after the ball, having been put back into my rags."

"Well, you're not exactly dressed in rags. However, I want you to know that I did find your glass.slipper and I'll be knocking on your door soon."

"Goodbye, Joanna," Ceci called as Jay and Joanna got into the waiting car. "I'm going to hold you to your promise to show me the Village."

"Hey, I never break a promise," Jay said.

"And thank you again for the use of your dress."

"You were so beautiful in it that no one will ever be able to wear it again. I mean, no one, ever!" Ceci called.

As the car pulled out of the courtyard, Jay said, "Well, you've certainly won over my sister and brother."

"They were both very nice."

"But everybody else?" He paused. "I told you you'd feel like you were visiting a zoo."

"Actually, there were times when I felt more like a foreign exchange student from some distant country that they'd never heard of."

***

Sunday morning at 5:50AM, Jay knocked on Joanna's door. Your yellow limo is waiting to take us to Penn Station."

As they traveled up Eighth Avenue toward the station, she said, "How am I going to call you? You still don't have a phone."

"The phone company said someone would be around to put in a line this week. I can't believe no one in that apartment ever had a phone."

"If they said next week, it really means the week after."

"Tell you what. As soon as I get a number, I'll call Ad-Film and leave it with Vivian. Check in with her every couple of days."

"In the meantime, I'll write letters, she said."

He carried her bags to the gate and walked down to the platform with her. "I'm really going to miss you," he said.

"Me too," she said softly.

"So meeting my family yesterday hasn't turned you off on me?"

"I was thinking about your family and all those people at your home last night before I fell asleep. It's hard to imagine that you were ever a part of that. Because you're not like them and they certainly are nothing like the Jay I've come to know. My Jay takes me rowing in Central Park to the Isle of Innisfree. My Jay rescued me from a slimly ad agency creep. My Jay gave me a birthday party that was the best in my entire life. My Jay doesn't live in a big house in Greenwich; he lives one flight up in a garret with ratty furniture. That's my Jay, the one I've fallen in love with." She pressed her body into his and lifted her face up to give him the kind of kiss that matters, the kind that transcends words.

"Hey, Joanna. We're in the next car up," a voice was calling to her from further down the platform.

"No long goodbyes, or you'll miss the train," came another voice, well down the platform.

Joanna stepped back, her eyes never leaving his. "That's the cast and some of the crew," she explained, nodding toward the voices. "We're all on the same train."

She picked up her bag and began to back away, smiling. Her lips mouthing the words, "I love you."

Jay stood on the platform until the train pulled out. He felt as if his heart might jump right out of his chest. The euphoria he was experiencing had the effect of an opiate. His mind was reduced to a solitary thought: She loved him back!

It was no longer a solo act.

12
Elliott

J ay checked the address that John Baskham had given him. "Elliott Pierce, Film Arts, 15 East 48th Street." The building was old, probably built in the late 1800s. From the look of the lobby, it had once been a hotel or small apartment building. Jay checked the directory board and saw that Film Arts was on the fifth floor. He got off the elevator, followed the arrow indicating the entrance and stepped into the reception area of what had clearly been the front room of the living quarters. The last vestiges of the apartment's former glamour, the detailed moldings and the alabaster filigree on the ceiling, still managed to show through the many layers of white paint. The office was comprised of several large rooms, all of which appeared to be in a state of confusion and disarray. The wall to the left of the reception desk was covered with production stills.

Several men in sports coats and loose ties sat in director's chairs, deeply involved in animated phone conversations. The office was a cacophony of sounds, dominated by the clack of moviolas and the jabber of sound tracks running back and forth over sound heads. Phones rang incessantly. A woman in another room was laughing uncontrollably.

Jay looked for someone to tell that he'd come for his appointment, but no one appeared to be a likely candidate. He walked over to the wall opposite the main entrance, which held most of the pictures. In the middle was a large, colorful rendering of the classic Pierce Arrow automobile. Elliott Pierce? Pierce Arrow. Of course. He looked at a picture immediately to the right and saw a group of people in the desert gathered around a movie camera. Below was a picture of a man giving directions to the driver of a stock car. In another, the same man was kneeling and looking through the viewfinder of a camera. This has to be Elliott Pierce, Jay thought. He judged him to be in his thirties. Other pictures suggested that he was probably no more than five-ten and in excellent physical condition with light sandy hair and rugged good looks. Still another showed Pierce with two women—actresses Jay guessed—who looked as though they were waiting for him to decide upon which he would bestow his favor. It occurred to Jay that Mr. Elliott Pierce could have made a living working on either side of the camera, as director or as the model pitching the product.

Behind him in the reception area, Jay heard the office door open. He turned to see a very attractive woman walk in. An expressionless, skinny young woman, with long black hair and very pointed features appeared out of one of the other rooms and, barely looking at the woman, said to her, "You lost?"

Not exactly what Jay would have categorized as a friendly greeting. But then, from the disdainful attitude of the skinny woman with pointed features, it did not appear that *friendly* was one of her personality traits.

"This is Film Arts, isn't it?"

"That's what it says on the door."

"I was told that you're holding a casting session today."

"You're a day late."

"Oh," she said, clearly disappointed. Then, in an attempt to try to salvage the visit, she asked, "Would it be possible for me to at least meet Mr. Pierce?"

"He's busy."

"Can I leave my head sheet?" She opened her bag pulled out an eight-by-ten picture with her resume on the back.

"Whatever." The skinny woman with the pointed features said and took the head sheet from her. "I'll be sure to show it to Mr. Pierce."

Her promise did not sound at all convincing to Jay and his skepticism was born out almost immediately. She waited until the model left the office, then tossed the picture in the wastebasket.

Jay could not help but wonder how many times some receptionist had done the same to Joanna.

The skinny young woman with the pointed features looked at Jay with the same blank facial mask she had worn for the model. "Can I help you?" Her tone suggested she really had no interest in helping anyone.

"I have an appointment with Mr. Pierce."

"Your name?"

"Jay Carraway."

Without further comment, she turned around and, with diaphragm support that would have served her well in any opera house, screamed in the direction of the back rooms, "Elllllllyet! Someone's here to see ya."

From the reaction of those in the office, it appeared that she'd roused everyone's attention except "Elllllllyet's." The men on the phone glanced up with pained expressions, as if they'd suffered permanent damage to their inner ears. An older man stuck his head out of one of the editing rooms and said, "Jesus, Lucy. Do you have to do that? We have an intercom, you know."

"There's someone to see Ellyet," she said, repeating the obvious.

Jay waited for several minutes, feeling increasingly uncomfortable and rapidly convincing himself that there would be no job here. It was a waste of time. He wondered what he'd say to John. Finally, he saw the man shown in the pictures on the wall approaching from a hallway that led to the back offices. The photographs had been in black and white, but Elliott was in full color. He wore a bright red dress shirt and a deep navy tie. His face had the ruddy brown look that you'd expect on a man who spent a lot of time outdoors. He was, as Jay had guessed, just under six feet and compact. As he approached, Jay realized that Elliott Pierce didn't walk—he claimed space in a way that said "self-confidence." *God, he looks just like a director ought to look,* Jay thought.

"You must be Jay Carraway." Elliott Pierce extended his hand and gave him a welcoming look.

Jay stepped toward Elliott and shook his hand. "I appreciate your taking the time to interview me for the job."

"What interview? John Baskham already sold me on you. He says you'd make a good production assistant. That true?"

"Yes sir. Yes sir, I think I would. I'm not afraid of work."

"Good," Elliott said, looking up at him. Jay thought he sensed that Elliott didn't like having to look up at someone who was four to five inches taller. He was aware that some men are very sensitive about their height, or lack of it. Jay shifted his weight and slouched to make himself appear shorter.

"John tells me that you were a Phi Beta Kappa in college."

Jay nodded.

"A piece of advice: Keep that a secret from our clients. Advertising people get nervous when they have to deal with someone who has more than an 80 I.Q." Elliott's tone gave no hint of whether he was being serious or facetious, leaving Jay slightly off balance. Then, without missing a beat, he said, "Let me make some introductions." He gestured toward the dour young woman who had greeted him. She was just reemerging from the ladies room. "This is Lucy—she of the high-decibel voice—our Mary Sunshine. She, happily, does all those things everyone else refuses to do and she always does them with a smile. Don't you sweetheart?"

She gave Elliott a *please perform an unnatural act on yourself* kind of look and then faked a toothy grin.

"That gentleman making his way back to the editing room," he said, pointing to a slender, dark-haired man, "is Teddy O'Keefe, our number one editor. Best cutter in New York."

Teddy stopped, retreated and shook Jay's hand, welcoming him to the company. Then he disappeared back to where the moviolas were contributing to the din.

"And these two worthless-looking human beings," Elliott said, pointing to the two men who had been busy on the phones when he came in, "are salesmen. The bald one is Jack Harder and the funny-looking one is Billy Epstein. Guys, this is Jay Carraway. He's going to learn the commercial film business at my knee."

The two men nodded and, without getting up, made slight waving gestures to suffice in lieu of handshakes.

"Their job is to bring in storyboards so that we can make money. If they don't sell, we don't make money and they don't get paid. That's how simple this business is. Right, guys?"

"Right!" they echoed in near unison.

Elliott hardly took a breath. "You like cars?"

"Yeah. I love cars," Jay said.

"Good. One of the best things we do here is shoot cars." He turned to Jack and Billy. "Guys, do we shoot great cars?"

"Absolutely!" came back the enthusiastic response.

"We're the best goddamn car shooters in New York," said Jack.

"What we do, we do better than anyone else," Elliott added. "And if things go like I plan, they're going to be saying the same thing about the way I make features."

That was music to Jay's ears. He was definitely in the right place.

"You prove yourself and you'll be my right-hand guy."

Jay's head was whirling. This was just too good to be true.

"Ellyet," Lucy interrupted. "You got a call on two from Hillman."

Elliott excused himself and left the room to take a phone call. Jay knew that he'd found his mentor. This guy has it, Jay thought. The whole atmosphere of the place seemed to say *film and* he'd been dropped into the middle of it. Fantastic!

When Elliott returned, he pointed to a small desk in a windowless room just off the reception area, "You can make that your home, OK? Now, are you ready for your training program?"

"Sure," Jay said, sounding a little surprised.

"My training program is based on instant and full emersion. In other words, I toss you in the water and if you don't immediately start to swim, you sink and you're out of here. Now, there are just three things you have to remember. One: watch and listen. You'll learn a lot by just observing how things get done. Two: ask questions. If you're not sure of something or you don't know, ask. Everybody here is more than willing to answer any questions you have."

"I'm not afraid to ask questions," Jay said.

"Good. There's only one restriction. You get to ask only one really stupid question a day. Finally, number three: think. Show me you know how to use your head and your life here is going to be beautiful. One last thing you need to know. It's a secret that we never, ever repeat outside this office."

Jay bit. He was sure he was about to learn the ultimate secret of the commercial film business.

"You must promise not to let this leave this room."

"Yeah, I promise," Jay said, not sure what he should be preparing for.

"The secret is this: making TV commercials is not brain surgery. If it was, we'd all be looking for work."

Jack and Billy laughed. "See?" Elliott said, gesturing toward the two men. "They know! But our clients don't know and that's something we never, ever tell them. OK, end of training program. Get to work."

Elliott was not exaggerating; he dropped Jay into the middle of things and said "swim."

Jay's first assignment was to sit with the company's comptroller and business manager, Nathan Best and learn how Film Arts budgeted their productions. Nathan looked like a casting agent's idea of an accountant. He was a small man with terrible posture accented by a stomach that forced him to unfasten the bottom button on his suit coat. He was well past fifty, balding, wore heavy glasses and looked as though he had not only borne the weight of the world, but had been squashed by it. Nathan was a purposeful man who harbored a universal skepticism of all things except those that could be reduced to definitive numbers. At first, he appeared to resent the fact that he had to waste his time teaching some green kid the fine art of budgeting commercial productions. But Jay's enthusiasm and obvious intelligence, along with his confident respectfulness, soon won him over.

"Your toughest job," Nathan said, repeating what was clearly his mantra, "is to keep Elliott on budget. Once he's on location, he forgets that this is supposed to be a profit-making business. To him, everything is secondary to getting great shots. As a result, the clients get a lot more than they paid for and we end up eating the costs."

Another one of Jay's assignments was to set up casting sessions. While he and Elliott stood at their respective urinals in the men's room, Elliott taught him all he would need to know about casting calls. "It's simple. Just call the Oscard agency and ask for Fifi. You send her a copy of the storyboard, tell her when and where we want to see bodies and she'll take care of the rest." Elliott flushed the urinal and the lesson on how to set up casting calls was over.

13
I Am Going to Die

Aweek later, as Jay was about to leave the office, he felt Elliott's hand on his shoulder. "Tell me something. With all the hours you're putting in, you finding time to get laid?"

Jay grinned. "I'm hardly finding time to eat."

"Well, I can't get you laid, but I can do something about the eating part. Why don't you plan on coming home with me tomorrow night? My wife's cooking won't win any awards, but it will fill you up."

Jay was embarrassed. "I didn't even know you were married."

"I keep it a secret," he smiled. "Fifteen years, two kids, one dog."

"That's terrific," Jay said sincerely.

"We'll aim for the 5:48 train." He started back toward his office then turned, "Do you like to jog?"

"Yeah, sure," Jay lied.

"Bring your running stuff in tomorrow. We'll do a few miles together."

A few miles? As in *miles?*

***

Jay hated running—passionately. In fact, had he made a list of things he'd rather not do, *ever,* running just for the sake of running would be right up there near the top.

This is going to be god-awful, he thought. He glanced up at the zinc-grey sky. It was one of those mornings that you get sometimes in the Northeast when the calendar thinks it's April and the chilly wet wind becomes something for everyone to complain about. Jay hoped that Elliott might decide to cancel their run because of the weather. No such luck.

As Jay lumbered down the driveway after the loping, gazelle-like figure, he remembered the last time he'd gone running. It was during his sophomore year in college. He'd signed up for an around-the-campus race to prove to his fraternity brothers that he wasn't the physical disaster they claimed he was. His singular achievement that day was to humiliate himself by throwing up on the shoes of four other runners.

Now here he was, once again about to become the victim of his desire to prove something. What? That he was in terrible shape? "Of course I jog, doesn't everybody?" he'd answered when Elliott had asked him a second time. Upon reflection, he was embarrassed by his pomposity. He knew it would come back to haunt him. There was no way he could escape making an ass of himself.

Jay had no wind to speak of; he was more into sports where you chase a ball over very short distances. Jay knew that, even if he managed to run for at least a mile, eventually his spleen would put up one hell of a protest, giving him the distinct sensation of having been stuck in the side with a fork—from the inside.

He looked up ahead at the taut, solid frame of Elliott Pierce as he continued to increase the distance between them. His feet seemed barely to touch the ground. He made it appear effortless, as though he'd made some kind of devilish pact with gravity.

"Oh, God," Jay groaned, but softly enough so that Elliott wouldn't hear, "I think my lungs are going to collapse and I'm going to die." As they ran toward an intersection, Jay could see that the street to the right looked as if it went straight up a mountain. The one to the left was flat. *Take the one to the left*, he said silently, trying to telepathically impose his will—or more accurately, his desperation—on Elliott's mind.

Apparently, all the telepathic lines were busy. Elliott veered to the right and took off like a motorcycle at a hill climb. Jay was determined to keep the distance between them respectable, but that was before his knees turned to rubber. He looked down, fully expecting to see that some physical transformation had taken place. *I can't be this out of shape*, he groaned in silence. But the painful messages coming in from all over his body told him that he was.

Elliott had it in overdrive now and was showing his complete disdain for the steep incline. Jay couldn't believe it. Nobody who drank like Elliott should be able to run like that. Jay had seen him put away four martinis at lunch yesterday and he must have downed a half of bottle of scotch last night. *Tarzan has come to Mamaroneck, New York and is running loose in the streets.*

Got to make it to the top of the hill, he told himself, as he leaned forward and shortened his stride to a series of choppy little steps. "I thought it was against the law to build streets with fifty percent grades," he puffed, wondering whom he was talking to and why he was talking when it hurt so much. His body was now laboring under total protest. Even his pride was giving the whole thing some second thoughts. Finally, he plodded over the crest of the hill and there was Elliott. The sonofabitch was doing jumping jacks.

Oh, God, please God, if he asks me to do jumping jacks, just let me die quickly. He tried to get himself up on his toes to give the impression that he too had been relatively unaffected by the hill climb. No way. His feet slapped their way up to where Elliott was exercising.

"What's the matter, Stud?" Elliott asked. *Stud* had become Elliott's affectionate nickname for Jay. "Can't keep up with an old man? If you run any slower, they're going to pick you up for loitering. Come on, let's sprint this next block."

Jay began to wonder if Elliott had decided to run circles around him to prove that he was the superior being. But why? What was he trying to prove that Jay would not have readily and willingly conceded? He was nothing. Elliott owned the company. He was the director the clients asked for. He was the one who was going to do the feature. What did he have to prove by brutalizing Jay on the streets of Mamaroneck, New York?

Jay searched for a way to save face and a lie seemed like his best option. "Can't sprint," he said between gasps for air, with all the conviction he could muster. "Had this respiratory thing I picked up last year. Haven't been ... able to run ... for six months. Doctor's ... orders." He glanced at Elliott out of the corner of his eye. He was buying it.

"You should have said something," Elliott said, showing genuine concern. "Tell you what," he said, starting the jumping jacks again. "Up around the corner, there are two big boulders right next to the street. You can't miss them. They're right in front of a white colonial. Sit there and rest and I'll pick you up on the way back."

Jay nodded his agreement, hoping that his face would not reveal his elation at having been spared any further torture.

"By the way, keep your eyes on the house and I'll see if I can arrange for some stimulating entertainment while you're waiting."

"Entertainment? What kind of entertainment?"

"You'll see," he said, grinning. "Just keep your eyes on the house." Elliott turned, took two quick steps and was immediately into his steady, rhythmic stride.

Jay slowly walked up the street until he found the two big rocks. Per instructions, he chose one of the rocks and sat down facing the white colonial. As the cold from the rock began to creep into the cheeks of his behind, he decided Elliott had been putting him on.

And then he saw her. She was standing in the large, second-floor bay window. Long blond hair, somewhere in her thirties and totally naked. At first, he thought he was imagining things, but as he continued to stare, he saw that she was fondling herself. It was a show all right and Jay realized that he, the lone member of her audience, was seated atop the boulder in full view. His first impulse was to make a dash for the nearest tree, but he was frozen, mesmerized. *There's no way she hasn't seen me,* he thought, *but she doesn't seem to care.*

So this is the stimulating entertainment Elliott was talking about. He began to wonder if she did this every morning. The woman turned around, revealing her firm, round buttocks and rubbed herself seductively. *This is really right out of the Peyton Place novel,* he thought. He wondered if maybe she was the kind of woman who passed her favors around the neighborhood. There was no sign of her husband and Jay decided that she was probably divorced or something. She turned back to him, still caressing herself and pushing her body closer to the big pane of glass.

"That must be cold," he said to the image in the window.

It looked to Jay as if she were staring at him. Not just looking, *staring*. A smile formed on her lips. Slowly, she began to raise her right hand. *What is she doing? My God, she's giving me the finger.*

With that, she disappeared from the window. End of show. Jay could not begin to comprehend what would motivate a woman to display herself like that.

He slid off the rock as he heard Elliott's even stride bearing down on him—on his toes, no less. He didn't even seem winded.

"Get a little show this morning?" he asked, slowing down.

"Does that happen all the time?" Jay asked as he fell in beside Elliott, matching his stride.

"Just the mornings when her husband is out of town." Parenthetically, he added, "He travels a lot."

"Does she ever invite her audiences in for a more intimate review?"

Elliott just smiled and then, with what sounded like an expression of personal pride, he said, "Let's just say that I never miss an opportunity to service an account."

"Am I to take it you run around the streets in your shorts servicing the accounts of the ladies of Mamaroneck?" Jay was amused at the thought.

"I'm always available to make house calls," he responded with a touch of braggadocio, which he punctuated by sprinting ahead.

Jay laughed out loud. Elliott almost sounded like he meant it.

***

Back at Elliott's house, Jay showered, dressed and found that he had arrived in the kitchen before Elliott. "Good morning, Jay," Sherry said brightly. "Breakfast will be ready soon. Help yourself to the coffee."

Yesterday, as he and Elliott had ridden out from Grand Central on the train, Jay had tried to imagine the kind of woman Elliott might have married. He guessed she would be small, with an energy level that would match his. He also presumed that, because Elliott had the kind of face that could have appeared in any men's clothing ad, his wife would be attractive—probably *very* attractive. The woman that greeted him at the door was a cheerleader. She had short blond hair, bright blue eyes and a perky, almost too cute look about her that made it easy to imagine that, not too many years ago, she was prancing about on a basketball floor shouting "Go-team-go! Yet, at the same time, there was something fragile about her. It wasn't physical; it was more in her personality.

During dinner, the night before, she and Elliott sat at opposite ends of the table. Jay was on one side and the two children—who were remarkably well-behaved—sat on the other. Elliott seemed preoccupied and Sherry worked overtime to maintain the flow of conversation, connecting her thoughts with short, tension-laced bursts of forced laughter. Jay noticed that whenever they ventured into some area calling for an opinion, her eyes darted in Elliott's direction, as if she was fearful of contradiction, or perhaps looking for confirmation. He was not sure which. *She's trying too hard,* Jay thought and *Elliott's* not helping. Occasionally, Jay glanced over at Elliott, expecting him to participate in the conversation, but clearly his mind was somewhere else.

Before they'd finished the main course, Jay realized that, in this environment, Elliott was someone he'd never met. The meal stumbled on through dessert. Sherry excused the children, leaving the three adults in total silence. Jay tried to fill the void with innocuous comments about their kids, their house and the weather. His words seem to fall like rocks that no one wanted to pick up. Finally, Elliott offered him an escape with the suggestion that he retreat to the guest room and read the story treatment of a book that he was intent on turning into his first feature.

Jay had worried briefly that breakfast might be a repeat of dinner, but the residual pain of his morning jog with Elliott had made that a secondary concern. At Sherry's invitation, Jay poured himself a cup of coffee and sat down at the kitchen table. "I hope you like your eggs scrambled," Sherry said, looking directly at him. "I'm sorry, I forgot to ask. Elliott likes his scrambled."

"Scrambled is fine."

"Did you enjoy your run this morning?"

"Well, to tell you the truth, I'm not all that much into jogging,"

"Me either," she said. She appeared almost ashamed to admit it. "I'd rather sleep. I'm really not a morning person."

He fumbled with his fingers and studied his shoes as he tried to think of something to say. Instead, he found himself wondering what it was that had brought on this great sense of pity. The melancholy mist was pervasive and it created an oppressive grayness in the room matched only by the grayness of the day.

"Do you get to see Elliott direct very often?" Jay asked when the silence had become noticeably uncomfortable.

"Once in a while," she answered absently. "Actually, I think he prefers that I not come to the studio or join him on location.

He really doesn't like to mix his work with his family life, which is all right with me. I'm not all that comfortable with what he calls the 'agency-types.'"

"Some of them are pretty awful," Jay said. "If there's one thing I've learned, this is a very demanding business."

"Yes, it demands a lot. But then, it's not always easy for us, either. We eat alone here many nights. I'm not happy about it, but Elliott and I made our peace with his career a long time ago. My father wanted him to go into the family business in Boston."

"Which is?"

"Boat building."

"Big boats?"

"No, yachts. Sailboats. Daddy's done very well with his business and he hoped Elliott would join him. Elliott loves sailing, or at least he did when he had more time. My father had planned to give the business to my older brother. He was much older, actually. But he died in the war ..." her voice trailed off. For a moment, some forgotten, now recalled, pain showed in her eyes.

"Anyway," she resumed, "boat building wasn't for Elliott. He had chosen this life when he asked me to marry him, so I really have no right to complain. If directing car commercials makes him happy ..." again her voice trailed off.

Jay didn't like where this conversation was going. It didn't take a family therapist to see that there was a good deal of ache and conflict in the Pierce household. He decided to try to inject something positive into their conversation. "I guess you must be pretty excited about his feature?"

"Feature?"

"*Death of a Gran Prix Racer.* Elliott gave me the treatment to read last night."

She was silent for what seemed to be a long time. Then with what sounded like resignation said, "I hope if it happens it will make him happy."

Jay found that an unsettling reply. "Well, there are worse ways to make a living," he said, not so much in defense of Elliott's career, but as a feeble attempt to support his end of the conversation.

"Don't misunderstand me; I totally support what he's doing. I believe that a man has to do whatever it is that will make him happy. And if a woman truly loves her husband, then she's going to be happy, too."

Jay got the feeling that she was reading lines out of the book for *dutiful and supportive wives.*

"I know that if he were to drop everything and go into business with my father—no matter how much money he'd make—Elliott would be miserable. If he were miserable, then I would be, too." Then she added, plaintively, "I just hope ..."

"You just hope what?" Elliott asked, entering the kitchen.

"I just hope your eggs aren't cold," she said without looking at him. Sherry put their plates on the table and then joined them with a cup of coffee.

"Kids up yet?" Elliott asked perfunctorily.

"No school today. Teacher meetings. I thought I'd let them sleep in."

"I'll wake them on my way out."

"Busy day today?" she asked.

"Usual."

"Will you be home in time for dinner?"

"Ah, not sure. I'll give you a call. No, wait. Don't count on me unless I call before five."

"Oh," Sherry said, showing her disappointment. Then she changed the subject. "What do you want me to tell the people from that lawn care place?"

"Tell them to stuff it. It's a rip-off."

Their conversation rambled on about domestic matters and Jay got the impression that he was listening to two actors reading lines from some inconsequential soap opera He realized that not once during the entire breakfast did Elliott even so much as glance at Sherry. What they weren't saying was certainly a lot more revealing than what they were saying. Maybe they'd had a fight after he went to bed last night. Maybe Sherry had been pushing him to go into the boat business. Married people argue. So what's new? In any event, Jay decided it really was none of his business.

After breakfast, Jay went back to the guest room and picked up his bag, then came downstairs and found Sherry standing at the front door. Elliott was already backing the car out of the garage.

"Well, it was very nice having you here, Jay. It's seldom that I get to meet any of Elliott's associates. Please feel free to come back anytime," she said, leaning forward and giving him a light peck on the cheek.

"It was nice of you to have me. Everything was just terrific and you've really got a great house." As he walked toward the car, he glanced back and waved. The little cheerleader didn't look like she would be leading cheers that day.

He got into the car and Elliott backed into the street. "What'd you think?"

"About what?"

"About what?" Elliott echoed. "About *Death of a Gran Prix Racer*. Did you finish it?"

"About one a.m."

"And?"

"I loved it. It's got everything. That last scene, when Eddy Merrill knows he has the race won and then deliberately turns into the wall—that ending will tear 'em apart. It's a terrific story. You must really be anxious to get started."

"What would you think of Paul Newman as Eddy Merrill?"

"He'd be perfect. I mean, it's like the part was written for him. Do you think he'd do it?"

"I've got a feeling that when he sees the story treatment, he's going to want to talk."

"Have you sent it to him?"

"If I *sent* it to him, he'd probably never open the envelope. No, the only way to get a script in front of Paul Newman is to hand it to him. But not by just anybody. It has to be handed to him by the person he trusts most in the world."

"And that person is?" Jay waited for Elliott to fill in the blank.

"His agent. She's a woman and I'm told she reads everything before he does. If she likes it, it's all but a done deal."

"So how do you get it to her?"

"Sherry has a friend whose sister knows the agent. Sherry got her to agree to take it personally to his agent."

"That would be great!"

"Let me tell you something," Elliott said, "all Newman has to say is 'I like the story, I want to see the screenplay' and we've got it made. I could have my pick of the best screenwriters in

Hollywood. In fact, I wouldn't be surprised if Newman asked to pick his own writer. Maybe he'd even want to co-produce."

"Well, here's hoping."

"Just one thing; I put down ten percent for the option on the book. Now I've got to give them the rest or lose it."

"How much are you talking about?"

"A lot. A *whole* lot. And I don't have it right now. But thanks to a Mr. Sigmund Hillman, I will have it in the next two weeks."

"Who's Sigmund Hillman?"

"Stud, he doesn't know it yet, but he's about to become my personal benefactor."

As they crossed the Triboro Bridge into the City, Jay found himself wondering to what he owed his incredible luck—to have both Joanna and Elliott in his life at the same time.

14
A User

"It's taken the phone company two weeks to get a guy up here and it must have taken him all of five minutes to install the line," Jay said. "Now that I can finally talk to you, there's something I'd like to know: Have you been spending a lot of time with my competition?"

"Your competition?" Joanna's response made it clear that she had no idea what he was talking about.

"Yeah, that refrigerator you're singing with every day. Considering how long you've been on the road with that thing, I was getting worried ... well, you know ..."

"It's pretty attractive. I mean, can you offer me a freezer, a vegetable crisper, rotating shelves and a cold-water dispenser?"

"Clearly, I'm outclassed. So how's it going?"

"Client's happy. But I'm getting a little punchy with this show. We're on our feet ten hours a day. The only good thing is that it pays me twice what I made at Ad-Film. Oh, and one other good thing. Well, potentially a good thing, anyway. The producer of this show has a friend that is casting for a Gershwin revival of *Girl Crazy*. It's going to play up at a summer stock theater in Connecticut."

"Wasn't that a movie?"

"It was. The movie stared Judy Garland. It has great songs, like *Embraceable You, But Not for Me*." She began singing: "They're writing songs of love, but not for me."

"As far as I'm concerned, you've got the part."

"Thank you, Mr. Carraway. When I meet the director, I'll tell him you said so. Unfortunately, in order for him to let us audition for the show, I'm told we have to first attend his acting class—which I'd have to pay for."

"That doesn't sound right to me."

"It's not. But if it gets me a chance at an audition, it'll be worth it."

"When they hear you sing, they'll give you the lead. Count on it."

The conversation rattled on for several minutes before Joanna interrupted herself. "I forgot to ask: Did you get the job with that company ... what was the name?"

"Film Arts. Yeah, they hired me as a production manager. No more Mr. Go-fer. It's going to be a terrific learning experience. They owner plans to do a feature and if it happens, I'll get to work on it."

"Nice people to work with?"

"Yeah, they are. The owner, Elliott, is terrific. He's a really good director and has an unbelievable amount of energy." Jay went on to describe the early morning jog and how Elliott had all but run him into the ground.

"You said his name was Elliott?" she asked, her tone curiously guarded.

"Yeah."

"What's his last name?"

"Pierce. Ever hear of him?"

Jay waited for her answer. Joanna said nothing for such a long time, he thought they might have been disconnected. "Joanna? Are you there?"

"I'm here," she said. There was no mistaking that the bright color in her voice had changed to a dark brown.

"I thought we might have been cut off."

"No. I was just wondering if it's the same Elliott Pierce that ..." She fell silent and then said, "It's been eight or nine years since I've heard that name."

"Hard to imagine two people in this business named Elliott Pierce."

"I suppose not. It's probably him."

"What is it I hear you saying that you're not saying?"

"Well," she hesitated, "that he has," she paused again as if searching for the right word. Finally, she said, " ... a reputation."

"You mean as a director?"

"I'm talking about his personal reputation."

"Which is?"

"Let's just say that a whole lot of people back then didn't like him very much."

"Really? Why?"

"He was a user. The kind of person who would do just about anything to anybody to get what he wanted. And if, in the process, someone got fired or got hurt, too bad."

"I wonder why Baskham never said anything?"

"Maybe he doesn't know that side of Pierce. Or maybe John's being used and hasn't figured it out yet. Or maybe Pierce has changed ... which I doubt."

"So far he's ... well, he seems OK," Jay said, wondering if he had missed something in his assessment of Elliott. Yes, he was like a wind-up doll that never seemed to unwind. His relationship with his wife was … well, detached. But, a user? So far, he hadn't seen that.

"Just keep in mind that some people are not always what they initially appear to be."

Clearly, the three of them would not be having dinner together. "I appreciate the heads-up, Joanna. I really do," he added with emphasis to be sure she understood that he meant it. "Now, let's talk about something else." And they did, for the next half hour.

Finally, she said, "I've got to be up at six tomorrow. We're moving on to Atlanta, so I hope you won't think me a party pooper if I say I love you and go to bed."

"Just know that I envy the bed."

Joanna said nothing for a moment and Jay thought he detected a slight sigh. Finally, she said, "About Elliott Pierce. Just be careful, OK?"

"OK," he answered and began to wonder about all the things she hadn't said.

15
The Bid

"I think it's time we accelerated your education," Elliott announced as he arrived at the office just after nine. "This is a lesson I call, 'The Bid' or 'How to Get an Agency Asshole to Give You the Commercial.'"

"Agency Asshole?" Jay needed clarification.

"That's what most advertising agency account executives are. According to their job descriptions, they're supposed to manage an account, but most can't manage their way to the men's room. Agency assholes have virtually no talent and no ideas worth a damn. They don't create anything—in fact, there's very little they can do except go to lunch. That and they can kiss a client's behind and make it look like a performing art."

"Not exactly the kind of people you want for your best friends," Jay said.

"Ah, that's where you're wrong. When an Agency Asshole walks in our door with a storyboard that he's putting out for bid, he is magically transformed into one of the most intelligent, insightful and fascinating people in the world. Every word he speaks is a pearl of wisdom, a quotable quote. Especially when he says, 'You've got the job.'"

"And if he doesn't give us the job?"

"In that case, he immediately reverts into an Agency Asshole. And he stays that way until he comes around with the next board."

Jay could hardly contain himself. Elliott was really on a roll.

"Today, Stud, you're going to meet Sigmund Hillman, who went to bed last night a sorry sack of shit, but awoke this morning as a wonderful human being. What makes him wonderful is that he is coming to our office with a big fat package of commercials he needs produced for his client, Willys-Overland."

"They make Jeeps, right?"

"Right. The important thing is that he intends to award the contracts to some truly deserving company."

"And we are a deserving company," Jay added.

"Very deserving. That makes him our very best friend for as long as it takes to get his boards. Now, what you should understand is that most agency assholes are whores. They don't award bids; they sell them to the producer who gives them the best blowjob—figuratively speaking, of course."

"Figuratively," Jay echoed. As a student, Jay was having a hard time separating the metaphors from the realities. Elliott began to fill in some of the holes.

"The bid process usually works like this: Somebody at the car company or soap company—whatever—signs off on a storyboard. The agency guy gets the board and immediately calls … let's say, five production companies. He gives each company a day. Ace Films, you've got me Monday, Duce Films, you've got me Tuesday, Tri Films you've got me Wednesday and so on until they run out of names. What he's doing is setting himself up to play *Queen for a Day*, every day for five days in a row. Each producer gets to go through the same routine. The Agency Asshole comes to their office, they show him their sample reel, take him to lunch, tell him how wonderful he is and how they make great commercials. The agency guy loves it. He's Mr. Wonderful. If, at any time, he decides he wants to drop his pants and crap on the table, everyone has to smile and applaud his dump."

"I hope this Hillman guy will spare us that."

"The point, Stud, is that if the Hillman decides he wants something, all he has to do is ask and it's his. Or it will be, as soon as it can be found or purchased or cooked or poured or paid to get naked in a bed. And why is he the recipient of all this generosity?"

"Because he has *money* in his pocket," Jay volunteered.

"Right. And because he can mean the difference between handing out paychecks and handing out pink slips. Now you know why the minute Mr. Sig Hillman steps off the elevator in his Gucci loafers, we're going to do everything we can to make this the best day of his month."

As Jay listened, he sensed almost a delight in Elliott's voice. He was really looking forward to putting on a show for Sig Hillman. On the other hand, Jay got the impression that Elliott worked very hard at creating the impression that *he* was the manipulator, the pusher of buttons. But it seemed to Jay that Elliott was a little like the dutiful lackey who depends on his master to dole out money, but hates him for it at the same time.

"It sounds to me like today could end up being very expensive for Film Arts."

"Don't think of it as an expense," Elliott said. "This is an investment."

"I agree, so long as you end up with the commercials. But what if he gives them to someone else?"

"Hey, any producer who doesn't want to play can always go get a real job. But don't worry. This one is in the bank. His ass is mine."

"How can you be sure?"

"Because I've got something he wants."

"Which is?

"It turns out that Mr. Hillman has a bad habit of living beyond what they pay him for being an Agency Asshole. However, he knows he can count on me to *feed* his bad habit. But, that's beyond today's lesson. It's way up there, almost graduate school level."

Elliott excused himself, walked out of his office into the reception area and revealed another talent: he put two fingers to his mouth and let out a whistle that would have broken glass. "Now hear this," he called out to the staff. "We are in a 'bid mode.' Condition green as in *money*. Our best friend and spiritual guide Sig Hillman from Battle, Bateman and Smith will be here in exactly one hour and fifty-five minutes. Let's make it look like we're busy as hell."

Everyone knew what to do. Lucy, she of the black hair, pointed features and shrill voice, began to clean up the reception area and dust the display of the various awards Film Arts had won. The rest of the staff made a reasonable effort to look busy.

Just fifteen minutes before Sig was to appear, two extraordinary-looking women arrived, saying, "We're here to see Elliott Pierce."

Elliott came out of his office to meet them.

"Hi, sweethearts. Just drape yourselves on the couch and read Variety or something. You should be outta here by 12:30. Lucy will pay you then."

"What are they for?" Jay asked

"Windows dressing," Elliott said, his quick visual inspection of the two women revealing his appreciation for the finer qualities. "Tillie and Millie, or whatever their names are, will provide a little sideshow for Sig. When your surround Sig with great tits and show him some nice asses, his brain drops right into his shorts. And when it's there, he never thinks to ask any of the important questions, like 'why am I going to pay you more than anyone else to do these commercials?'" Elliott was clearly pleased with his ability to manage his client.

"This is some course you teach, Professor," Jay said, just a little overwhelmed. "I can hardly wait to meet this guy." As he returned to his desk to await Hillman, Jay thought about how Joanna had described Elliott. "He's a user." In this case, Jay wasn't sure who was the user and who was the used.

Sig was on time, to the minute. As Elliott had predicted, he was wearing Gucci loafers and looked like something out of a Brooks Brothers catalogue. Jay gave him credit: this man knew how to buy and wear clothes. Sig had a face that echoed of years past when he was probably one of the most sought-after young men on his college campus. He had begun to grey and he parted his hair just off center, giving him a slightly English look. His jowls had begun to fill out and the slight roundness at his belt line suggested that he'd enjoyed more than his share of lunches at others' expense. As Elliott predicted, his attention immediately went to the two models. They smiled up at him.

"Have I seen you two before?"

"Don't think so," said Tillie.

"Maybe," said Millie.

"Here," he said, digging into his pocket and producing two business cards. "Send me your head sheets. If you've got anything of yourself in swimsuits or lingerie … or a lot less," he raised his eyebrows suggestively and laughed. "We do a lot of lingerie stuff at the agency."

Sig lied with an earnestness that Jay found reasonably convincing. Elliott waited until he presumed Sig's brain had descended to its final destination and then took him by the shoulder like a lost brother and guided him into the screening room. "You like those two, Sig?"

"I like."

"Tell you what, I'll have them wrapped up and sent out to your house tonight. I'm sure Betty won't mind setting a couple of extra places at the dinner table."

"You're a real cocksucker, Elliott," Sig said, laughing. "You'd probably do that to me."

"If that's what it took to get the boards, you bet."

Jay had assumed that this give-and-take was just their normal sparring. Then he began to wonder if Elliott was actually sending Sig a message. Obviously, interpreting this client/supplier doublespeak was something he'd have to master.

"Oh," Elliott said, realizing he hadn't introduced Jay, "meet Jay Carraway."

"Hi," Sig said, extending his hand with little enthusiasm.

"I'm breaking him in as my personal assistant."

"You got a great teacher," Sig said. Then, after a calculated pause, he added, "When it comes to giving blow jobs. I can personally vouch for that." Sig broke into spasms of laughter.

"You're really the quintessential agency asshole, Sig," Elliott said, joining the laughter.

"That's why you love me so much," he said, much amused with himself. "Now show me your fucking reel so we can get out of here and go to lunch. I need a drink. By the way, I'm free all afternoon." The message had been sent: You'll get the boards, but I expect to be entertained.

They showed six of Elliott's latest commercials, including the two that had been awarded Cleos, the advertising industry's version of an Oscar for best commercial. They were followed by a slick, high-speed performance commercial in which the car did everything but fly.

"Nice shit, Elliott. Good stuff."

The last commercial was not a commercial at all, but a clip from a pornographic movie. The actor—if one could call him that—was naked except for his black socks and a Lone Ranger mask. He had a "member" that looked to be a foot long, which he proceeded to show to a woman, who grabbed it, winked at the camera and then started to say something. The screen cut to black and a title came up reading: "Eat your heart out, Sig."

Sig found it very funny. When he stopped laughing, he turned to Elliott and said, "OK, let's talk about the package of commercials I've got. Here's the deal. The storyboards that are going to make you rich will be delivered to you in a couple of days. Give me a budget of not a penny over four-hundred thousand, OK?"

"Sig, knowing how you budget commercials, I'd say you're about two hundred short. What if I come in at a six hundred?"

Sig's eyes narrowed and Jay wondered if Elliott had just blown it.

"Ok, not a penny over a half million."

"Deal. Not a penny more." Elliott shook Sig's hand.

"I'll need your bid."

"Bid? Didn't you mean budget?"

"Budget," Sig corrected. "I need it by next week so I can put it through the system. Give me a lot of detail so that no one will give me any shit about not getting other bids."

"Why does anyone have to know you didn't get other bids? Maybe you just tossed them out when you saw they were over your budget."

"Yeah. Maybe I did. Or will. Whatever. However, you gotta do something for me in return for tossin' out the competition."

"Like what?"

"I need some shots of the Jeep CJs. Willys wants 'em running over sand dunes like they were some fuckin' dune buggies or something. I can cover your costs, but not much more."

"Yuma, Arizona would be perfect for that. Perfect," Elliott said with emphasis. "Cost you a little more for the travel time, but the shots we can get out there will make your clients wet their pants."

"Ok, I'll buy diapers. You make it happen in Yuma. Send me a bill for the costs and don't fuckin' pad it too much."

"Ah, maybe just a little here and there," Elliott said clapping Hillman on the back as if he was a dear old friend.

"Now let's get down to some serious work. Where we going for lunch and can we take the two pair of tits with us?"

"They left," Elliott said. "We're going to the Brussels."

Jay had learned that this was truly one of the class restaurants in New York.

"You must have read my mind. A classy place for classy people like me," Sig said, standing up. "Oh, I almost forgot. Our agency handles the British Tourist Board account. They're sponsoring an opera with some Brit company at the Met later this summer. The account executive gave me a couple of tickets. Me!" He sounded incredulous that anyone would have considered him someone who would attend an opera. "I told him that only faggots go to operas."

He pulled the tickets from his coat pocket and held them out to Elliott. "Know any faggots who might want them?"

"I'll take them," Jay said eagerly.

"Kid, you don't look like a fag."

"That's because Elliott won't let me wear a dress to the office," Jay retorted.

Sig found that funny.

"Here," he said, handing Jay the small ticket envelop. "I don't know why anyone would want to go hear a lot of fat people sing, especially when they're not even singing in your own language."

Elliott came to Jay's defense. "Simple. You're a 'beer, broads and baseball' kind of guy and Jay's not." Elliott punctuated the comment with a wry smile and slapped Sig on the shoulder.

Sig hesitated, seemingly unsure if he was being insulted or kidded. He decided on the latter, snorted a short laugh and said, "Give me a minute while I take a crap." With that, the classy agency asshole headed for the men's room.

"I'll join you," Elliott said.

"Love a guy who's willing to come along and wipe my ass."

"I'll wipe your ass. I'll wipe the street with it," Elliott said, laughing, as they left the office for the men's room.

Elliott returned before Sig, checked the messages Lucy had left on his desk and then put a question to Jay. "What did you think of my benefactor?"

"He's a piece of work."

"Well, that piece of work just paid for the option on *Grand Prix Racer* and, not so incidentally, greatly improved his standard of living for the next several months. I *love* that guy," Elliott said, sounding as if he really meant it.

16
A Tree in the Forest

Every night, after Joanna returned from the Westinghouse road show, she left the apartment and walked the few blocks up to the acting lessons that she hoped would lead to a part in the revival of Gershwin's *Girl Crazy*.

"Well, it's not what I thought," she told Jay, "but if this is a ticket to three weeks at the Westport Playhouse, so be it. You want to sit in on a class? I warn you, it's … well, it's the 'method' school of acting."

"As in …?"

"As in there's method in their madness. At least I hope there is," she added laughing.

Jay arrived well after they had started. The Actor's Lyceum—a somewhat pretentious name, considering that they had to rent space by the hour—held forth in a small theater located on the second floor over a grocery store on West 18th Street in Chelsea. Jay managed to slip unnoticed into the back of the darkened theater. It was a long narrow room that could seat no more than one hundred people. The stage was bare, but well lit. About twenty of the acting class students were on stage listening to the admonitions of an effeminate, slightly built, middle-aged man whom Jay assumed to be the acting teacher. Joanna and one other woman were seated on the lip of the stage.

"You are a forest," the acting teacher said. His prissy voice was thin and pitched somewhere in an upper octave. "Show me that you know what it feels like to be a tree." Several of the students planted themselves at random on the stage, raised their arms and gazed up at the heavens, transforming themselves into a forest primeval. "Do you feel the wind in your branches? Let me see the wind. Make me feel your leaves. Make me understand what it's like to have sap running under your bark." His arms flailed about as he pirouetted and tiptoed around the stage.

And Joanna is paying for this? Jay was not impressed, but he vowed to keep his opinion to himself. An extremely heavyset young woman extracted her beach ball-like body out of one of the seats in the front row and approached the director, whispering in his ear. He guessed her to be his assistant. Whatever she'd said caused the instructor to glare at Joanna and the woman sitting next to her.

"What are the two of you supposed to be?" the acting teacher asked with pointed derision. "Rocks?" Embarrassed, they accepted his admonishment and joined the forest.

After several minutes of treeness, the teacher instructed the students to leave the stage and take seats in the theater. He called two names; a girl in a long black caftan and a young man wearing yellow pants and a blue T-shirt with a beer company logo on it took the stage.

"What scene were you assigned?" the instructor asked.

"The one where Medea discovers that Oedipus is her son."

The instructor raised his hands and paused in a manner that demanded silence and attention. "Remember the lessons of the forest," he commanded, sounding even more effeminate than before.

Jay was not sure who suffered more, Medea or those who had to watch the tortured performance. When they finished, the acting teacher leaped onto the stage to offer his critique.

"I didn't feel the sap. Where was the wind in the leaves?" The instructor's comments were so heavily laden with metaphors that Jay had no clue as to what he was talking about. The actors must have, because they left the stage with their heads down and bodies stooped, bearing the weight of their mentor's caviling.

Several other pairs of actors took their turns on stage, each performing the scenes that had been selected for them. Even those who gave strong performances were subjected to the instructor's obsession with trees and sap.

Jay began to dread what might happen to Joanna and he was relieved when class ended without her having gone on stage. The lights came up and Joanna smiled when she saw Jay waiting for her.

"Ahh, my very favorite tree," he said, taking her hand. "If your sap has stopped running, maybe you'd like some food."

"It's stopped running and yes, I'd like some food."

They walked down the street to Duex Gamin, a small bistro that was mostly empty at this hour. After they had ordered, she asked. "What did you think?"

"For what it's worth—and it's probably not worth much—I didn't see any potential James Deans or Julie Harris' in there. Of course, I didn't see you onstage, other than playing the part of a tree. Between you and me, that's not exactly typecasting. No offense, but your director is really a piece of work."

She nodded in agreement. "Peter Potter does take himself pretty seriously."

"Peter Potter? He sounds like a nursery rhyme. Plus, he seems to be light in his loafers."

Joanna laughed. "Just a little."

"What I want to know is what all this has got to do with casting a musical?"

"Not a lot, actually. But we don't get to audition if we don't take the class."

"That's crap, if you will forgive my French. Let me see if I understand this correctly. To be allowed to audition for *Girl Crazy*, you first take an acting class from Lightfoot? And he charges you for the acting class? This sounds like a scam to me."

"Well, I agree it's a bit unusual, but I would kill to get a part. If taking his class gets me to the audition, so be it."

By the way, who was the girl who gave Peter a big hug—or maybe it was the other way around."

"You mean Tina?"

"Yes, if that was her name."

"A friend, I guess."

"Is she up for the lead?"

"If she's in the class, she'll be at the audition."

"Could the fix be in?"

"Maybe, but she doesn't exactly look like Judy Garland and she dances like a cow. No, I think I have a legitimate chance. I mean, Peter's reputation is on the line. If he puts on a lousy show, who's going to hire him next time?"

"Who hired him this time? I think his sap has gone to his head. Peter Priss wouldn't know talent if he saw it. That guy is so hung up on trees, he should think about becoming a forest ranger. Are you going to be doing a scene for him?"

"He wants me to do Streetcar."

"A Streetcar Named Desire? What's that got to do with *Girl Crazy*?"

"Nothing. Remember, this is supposed to be an acting class."

"You going to read for Stella?"

"No, Peter wants me to read Blanche."

"Blanche?" he echoed incredulously. "Blanche Dubois is an aging southern bell. Why would anyone want you to read for Blanche? Talk about miscasting. Did Peter tell you why he chose that role?"

"He said it would be a good stretch for me."

Jay shook his head, indicating his acceptance of what seemed an outrageous rationalization. "I guess if that's what it takes to get an audition, then that's what it takes."

"And if they hate it, well ... I haven't had my ego bashed for almost ..." She waved her hand as through trying to recall the last time she'd subjected herself to rejection.

It was nearly ten when they started walking back to Sheraton Square. "Two invitations I want to talk with you about. One is ok, the other is terrific. Which do you want first?"

"Let's work up to the terrific."

"Ok. My brother has invited us to go sailing next Saturday. Just for the day. I told him I'd let him know. The not-so-good news is that he's bringing Tolova and I'm not sure I want to spend a day with my sister-in-law."

"Jay, what you're saying is that you're not sure if *I* want to spend the day with Tolova."

"Actually, I was speaking for both of us."

"I know you'd like to see your brother, so say 'yes.' One-on-one, I'm sure I can deal with her."

"Ok, we'll leave the city about nine."

"And the second thing?"

They waited for the light to change and then crossed over 14th Street. "This, you'll like a lot," Jay said giving her his arm. "There was an agency guy at Film Arts the other day by the name of Sig Hillman."

"Grey hair, slight build, about six feet, well-dressed?"

"Yeah, that's him? Do you know him?"

"He did some work at Ad-Film. He was only slightly less despised than Jackson Korman. All my women friends at Ad-Film agreed that he gave a whole new dimension to sleazy."

"Well, Mr. Sleazy gave me two tickets to La Bohème. The London Royal Opera company is going to be at the Met the first week in August and we have great seats —thanks to Hillman— in the orchestra. You said you wanted to see La Bohème, so now you can."

"That's great!" she responded, genuinely pleased. "What does one wear to the opera?"

"It's dressy. On Saturday night, a number of the men will be in tuxes. A suit will do it for me."

"Where did Hillman get the tickets? He doesn't seem the opera type to me."

"Somebody at his agency gave them to him. You're right, he's not the opera type. I'm not sure what type he is, actually. All I know is that the man's mind is constantly in his shorts."

Jay paused for a moment. "You know, I was thinking about what you said about Elliott being a user. When it comes to those two, I'm not sure who's using who."

"Has Elliott been treating you OK?" she asked tentatively.

"Yeah. However, it sort of depends on which Elliott you're dealing with. Sometimes he's like a rubber ball, bouncing all over the place, hard to catch and impossible to nail down. There's no end to his energy. Makes you believe he's your best friend and always will be, so long as you can keep up. Unless, of course, you're Sig Hillman. And then it's all an act. He doesn't necessarily hate Hillman, but he certainly has no respect for the man. The other Elliott ... well, I've only seen glimpses of that one. With the other one, there's no bounce. Just a moody, almost angry guy who has no compunction about saying things that cut people to the bone. I'm talking about his own employees. The people he depends on."

"How do they react? Do they say anything?"

"I guess they know Elliott well enough to just to ignore him and wait for the rubber ball to start bouncing again."

"I remember when I worked at Danner and Moore Advertising, it was the same sort of thing. No one ever knew which Elliott Pierce would walk in the door in the morning." There was unmistakable derision in her voice.

"You worked at the same agency?" Jay asked a little surprised. "When you said that you'd heard of him, I didn't realize that you actually *knew* him."

Joanna blanched slightly, slipped her arm out of his and stopped to look in the window of an appliance store as if she'd just seen something she had to have. With her back to Jay, she said, "Well, ahh ... well, it was a big agency. Hundreds of people worked there. So I guess you could say I knew who he was, but it was all the things I'd heard about him that I didn't like." She turned and started to walk down the street, forcing Jay to catch up.

"Like what things, for example?" Jay asked. "I'd really like to know what kind of guy I'm working for."

"Look, I don't want to talk about him," she said sharply. Her stern tone jolted Jay. "Let's just say that if it were my choice, you'd be working for someone else. But since it isn't my choice, I'll just hope that you get out of there and find something better before ..." she stopped, looked up at the black sky and nervously ran her hand through her hair, all the while avoiding eye contact. "Before ... before whatever." She turned away from him and started walking again, her pace a little faster. Again, Jay caught up. "It's getting late and I've got a temp job tomorrow."

There were so many questions Jay wanted to ask. What was it that Elliott had done or said that had had such a negative residual effect on Joanna, all these years later? How many people at the agency had he hurt or offended, or worse? The questions, he decided, would have to wait. It was time to talk about something else. "You know, this street sort of reminds me of the street scene in the second act of La Bohème—except that it takes place in Paris and it's full of people and nobody talks."

"Nobody talks?"

"No. They sing."

"In an opera? How unusual," she said facetiously, but her brightened expression told Jay that she was clearly glad he had chosen not to ask more questions about Elliott.

"Tell you what," Jay said. "I'm going to buy you a synopsis to read. Because unless your Italian is better than mine—which is non-existent ..."

"Ditto here."

"Then you really need to know the story before you see it."

"But if I read the synopsis, I'll know how it ends."

"In opera, especially La Bohème, everybody knows how its ends. There are no surprises in opera, unless the soprano falls into the orchestra pit."

"Has that every happened?

"Not that I know of. But it would certainly be a surprise."

As they turned the corner off Seventh Avenue onto Sheridan Square, Joanna took his arm once again. "I hope there are no surprises in our life," she said wistfully.

"Just good ones. Only good ones."

17
Yuma

On the following Sunday, Elliott and Jay were sitting in first class on a plane to Yuma via a connection through Phoenix. Behind them, in economy, sat Barney Lockerman, Sig's sycophant producer.

"What do agency producers do?" Jay asked, once they were airborne.

Elliott responded with a large grin. "Absolutely nothing. Sig might not have any talent, but at least he can hand out business. Barney not only has no talent, he doesn't control any business. All he's going to do is stand around watching us work. And every once in a while, he'll claim that he's seen some dirt on one of the fenders or that he doesn't like the catered lunch or that a certain shot doesn't look like the way it was drawn up on the storyboard. He's just excess baggage. That's why he's riding in the back and you and I are up front. The really good news, however, is that Barney loves golf and he's brought his clubs. We won't see much of him."

The best hotel in Yuma was called the Starlight. Some locals contended that it owed its name to the holes in the ceiling of the atrium, which, according to legend, had been put there by Billy the Kid. The lobby decor was grossly Western, almost as if a set decorator from a "B" movie had been commissioned to make it look like what Easterners thought a Western hotel should look like. A long, ornate, gold-painted mirror hung behind the bar, which was directly opposite the registration desk. The area in front of the bar was filled with wooden tables and chairs that, mostly empty now, looked like they were waiting for a casting director to bring in refugees from a John Wayne movie.

Jay saw a sandy-haired man seated at one of the tables look up from his paperback book and wave at them.

"Hey, Mike," Elliott said. "Any problem getting here?"

"No. Arrived about an hour ago."

"Mike, this is my production manager, Jay Carraway. Jay, meet the best car shooter in America, Mike Livesey."

"If I'm the best, then my fee just went up."

"Are you kidding? I'm letting you shoot this one for the experience." Elliott clapped him on the back and laughed. "What kind of crew have we got?"

"As you asked, we're going short. Assistant cameraman, two grips and a couple drivers. Since you said tomorrow would be a location scout day, I didn't figure we needed to bring them in today. Saved you a few bucks."

"You're my man."

"We doing diner together tonight?"

"Absolutely. Be down here at seven and we'll see what Yuma has to offer."

"Nice meeting you Jay. I'll see you guys later," Mike said and made his way to the elevator.

Fifteen minutes later, Barney Lockerman—who had taken his own taxi from the airport because his golf clubs wouldn't fit into the one that Elliott and Jay shared—plopped his luggage down in the middle of the hotel atrium and looked around, sizing up the place. He spotted Elliott at the bar and called out, "I hope the golf course isn't as beat up as this hotel. What a shithole."

Barney was forty-something and had the look of a man who was going nowhere but had yet to figure it out. His smallish head sat atop a rather substantial torso, which showed no signs of having been subjected to any exercise other than getting in and out of a golf cart. His bulbous nose and heavy lips seemed grossly out of proportion to his close-set eyes, which his full face made appear closer than they actually were. Jay instantly decided that this was a man who'd honed his inadequacies and deficits to a fine edge, making him instantly unlikable.

"This place looks like something I'd expect to find in one of those banana republics you read about. I mean, we still are in the United States of America, aren't we?"

Elliott grinned at Barney, but it was a deceiving, secretive sort of smile, suggesting that he was about to prove himself unpredictable. Then he spoke to Jay, never taking his eyes off the agency producer. "Jay, is this the best hotel in the City of Yuma, Arizona?"

"The best," Jay answered with conviction. "These are first-class Yuma accommodations."

"So there you are, Barney. First class all the way. Now, if staying in this hotel should prove to be too emotionally debilitating for a man of your discerning tastes and status, you can catch the next flight back to Phoenix. I understand the golf courses are much better up there. You just say the word and I'll have Jay run you back to the airport."

"Once I know you guys have got things under control, I just might," Barney said, looking at his watch. "It's only one o'clock.

I can still get a round in today. I wonder where the hell the golf course is?"

"I think we passed it on the way in from the airport," Jay offered.

Barney grunted and then directed his attention to Jay. "Why don't you see if you can get me a tee time at about two?"

"Tee time?" Jay was tempted to say something about that not being in his job description.

"Yeah. Tee time."

"You mean as in tea and scones?"

"Hey, I don't like wiseasses, ok?" Barney hissed. "Elliott, remind this little fucker who I am."

Elliott did not miss a beat. "I forgot. Who are you?"

***

Jay found Elliott and Mike Livesey waiting for him in the lobby just after 7AM.

"Ready, Stud?"

"Ready," Jay answered, looking around. "Where's Barney?"

"Still in bed. He told me last night he hated the golf course, so I convinced him that if he wanted to head back to Phoenix, it was OK with me. Told him I'd make sure Hillman would never find out. Of course, I lied. If that asshole gives us any problem, I'll be on the phone to Hillman faster than he can take a crap." Elliott seemed to salivate at the prospect of doing exactly that.

"Mike, the Jeeps are in the parking lot in the back. Why don't you get one of the CJs and bring it around front? I need to talk to Jay for a minute." Livesey disappeared through the back door and Elliott turned to Jay. "Change of plans. I'm going to stick with you guys today while we look at locations. Then tonight, I'm going to L.A. to see my friend George Gatley."

"Is he the guy you told me is going to raise the production money for the film?"

"He's the guy and that's the deal, anyway. I buy the option on the book and direct the film, he arranges for the production money. and we split fifty/fifty. That's what we've agreed. Unfortunately, we made our deal on just a handshake and lately he's beginning to sound a little iffy. Like maybe he thinks he could do the film without me."

"How can he? Gately doesn't have the rights to the book."

"I don't have 'em either. And he knows that. The option won't be mine until I write a check for fifty grand and I can't do that until Hillman gets the check for the first third of the budget through their payment system. Unfortunately, that may take a few weeks. The other option is to put a second mortgage on my house, which I'll do if I have to. What I need to make sure, like right now, is that Gatley isn't playing games with me. A lot of Hollywood assholes will cut your balls off if they think there's a better deal to be had with someone else. Once I've spent a couple days with him, I'll know if he's thinking about fuckin' me over."

"I'll keep my fingers crossed," Jay said.

"Me too," Elliott said with a forced laugh. "So, here's the deal: I'm going to leave you and Mike here to shoot the running shots. This is really a no-brainer. Lots of great locations out here. Sand dunes, off-road courses, the Colorado River—all kinds of great places to shoot Jeeps. Mike has done this a thousand times. He's a really good car shooter. You'll find him a great guy to work with. All you have to do is point and he'll shoot. In three days, you'll put more in the can than Hillman will ever need. You should be able to get back to New York on Friday."

"What if Hillman finds out that you've left?"

"He won't. Not with Barney playing golf in Phoenix."

***

West of Yuma, just over the California state line, there is a remarkable stretch of desert that is nothing but sand. The sand has been shaped by the wind into enormous hills that, in many cases, are ten stories high. In the early morning and late afternoon, the sun paints the area with light and shadows creating spectacularly dramatic backdrops.

Elliott led Jay and Mike to the top of one of the dunes. "Is this perfect for Jeeps or what?"

"Perfect," Livesey said. "I've shot here before and you can run a Jeep right up around the rim and leave tracks in the sand. Like a jet contrail. It looks great."

"At sunset, you could really get some spectacular shots," Jay added.

"You're right on. That's the best time," Elliott said. "What I'd like you to do is shoot most of stuff out here between sunrise and maybe nine and ten o'clock and then after four in the afternoon until sunset. Midday, shoot what we saw down by the river."

"We can get some nice shots of the Jeeps crossing those little streams."

"Shoot everything and anything you can think of."

"Count on it," Jay said, doing his best to contain his excitement.

***

Back at the hotel, Jay waited with Elliott for the taxi that was to take him to the airport. "Any questions?" Elliott asked.

"Can't think of any."

"You've got the number where I can be reached in L.A.?"

"I do."

"I'll check in with you tomorrow evening. You won't let me down, right?"

"Not a chance. I can handle it," Jay said confidently. Then, as Jay thought about the reason for Elliott's departure, he said, "Do you think Gatley will come through with the money for the film?"

"Hey, if he doesn't, I'll have to make him aware that we're cousins and that's something he doesn't want to hear about."

"Cousins? You're his cousin?"

"Pay attention, students," Elliott said, breaking into his role as instructor of the uninitiated. "There are two kinds of cousins in this world; those related by blood and those that have a relationship based on sex. Gatley and I are not blood cousins, we're sexual cousins."

Jay made no secret of the fact that he had no idea what Elliott was talking about. "Ok, I'm the student. Educate me."

"You're sexual cousins when two men—two guys that know each other—have both slept with the same woman."

"And you and Gatley have slept with the same woman," Jay surmised.

"Right. His wife. Of course, he doesn't know that. But if my cousin should try to screw me out of our deal, I'd have to tell him."

18
Bloodletting

"If you were to mount a couple of canons on the foredeck, you could loan it to the Navy. How long is this thing?" Jay and Joanna stood on the dock at the Greenwich Yacht Club alongside the 109-foot sailboat.

"Dad went a bit overboard, if you'll forgive the pun," Scott Carraway called back from the foredeck. "Needs a crew of four just to sail it."

"Don't forget the cook, that's five," Tolova Carraway added.

"Steps are over there," Scott said, pointing to the aft deck. "Permission to come on board, sailors," he said, offering a mock salute.

Jay and Joanna climbed over the side and made their way to the deck seating area where Scott and Tolova waited for them. Scott immediately gave Joanna the kind of approving head-to-toe assessment that most men avoid in the presence of their wives. Obviously, Scott had forgotten himself. "Now that you're on board," he said directly to Joanna, "we will be the envy of the harbor. Nothing like having a beautiful woman to improve the look of your deck."

Jay glanced at Tolova, who made no effort to hide her immediate resentment of Scott's effusive compliment. Had Tolova's eyes and been drills, there would have been two large holes in her husband's head. Jay attempted to come to his brother's aid. "The only thing better is having *two* beautiful women on the same deck," he said, directing his comment to Tolova. She was having none of it.

Scott glanced at his wife and knew instantly that he was in trouble. He did his best to cover his tracks. "Right, nothing like having two beautiful women aboard."

Joanna was clearly embarrassed and did her best to defuse the situation by turning her attention to Tolova. "It's good to see you again. Isn't this a beautiful day? Do you and Scott sail often?"

Tolova only grunted her response making it clear she did not intend to talk to anyone. "I'm going to look for my friends," she said making her way aft.

Scott rolled his eyes as an indication of his resignation to this wife's embarrassing performance as hostess. "Oh, let me introduce you to our captain," he said pointing to the middle-aged man in the blue blazer and white cap. "This is Captain Dave. He keeps me out of trouble and the boat off the shoals. Dave, this is my brother Jay and his friend, Joanna." Dave tipped his cap and Scott turned to Jay. "You know of course, that this is your boat, too. Dad bought it for the family."

"As the designated black sheep, I think there are some limitations on what our father might consider to be mine."

"Nonsense! He may be letting you bankroll yourself in the City, but it ends there. Believe me, anytime you'd like to use the boat, call Captain Dave and let him know when you want it and where you want to go. Hey, you and Joanna could sail to the Caribbean this winter if you like."

Jay glanced in the general direction of Tolova.

Scott picked it up. "By yourselves, I should add."

Jay shook hands with the Captain and exchanged some brief pleasantries. Then Dave excused himself and headed for the cockpit, calling out instructions to the other crew members.

It was but a short time later that Tolova reappeared to introduce two women friends that had been below deck. Jay wondered if Tolova had hidden them down there like stowaways, waiting to reveal them only after they'd left the dock. Had Tolova announced to her friends that Joanna was a refugee from a leper colony, her introduction could not have been more acrid. The two women understood the tacit message and found seats at a discreet distance on the deck. By the time the boat had cleared the harbor, the two women had followed Tolova below deck, not to be seen again for the better part of the day.

"I get the feeling that maybe I should have used more deodorant," Jay said to Joanna. "Honest to God, I don't know how my brother puts up with her. As my sister says, 'Tolova is burdened with an unfortunate personality.'"

"I knew there was a reason I liked Ceci."

***

"Tolova!" Scott shouted down the companionway stairs that led to the main salon. "How about being a good hostess and giving Joanna a tour of the boat while I teach my brother how to handle this thing?"

After several minutes, Tolova appeared, all smiles, exuding saccharine sweetness. In a voice that reeked of manufactured sincerity, she said, "Joanna, dear, I have been a terrible hostess. Why don't you come join me and my friends in the salon? We're having such an illuminating conversation."

Joanna glanced at Jay with the expression of a woman who had just been asked to walk the plank and was looking for a last-minute reprieve.

Jay shrugged, indicating he saw no way to tactfully refuse the invitation. Once Joanna had disappeared below deck, Jay joined his brother in the cockpit. Though Scott was twelve years his senior, Jay liked and admired his brother. Even in the face of the constant admonitions by his mother to be "more like your brother," Jay had always looked up to him. When Scott had gone to war, he'd shared his parents concern that his brother might never return. When they'd heard that Scott had been parachuted into France on D-Day, they prayed for his safety. For the next year, Scott fought his way with his unit across France, Belgium and into Germany. Then, one day, the war was over and he could come home.

Jay followed Scott's football career at Yale with pride, he was his best man at his wedding and he privately thanked his brother when he supported his decision to say 'no' to the family business and follow his dream.

"Take it," Scott said, indicating the wheel.

Jay took the helm. "Steady as she goes, right?"

"Until you get the feel of her."

"Feels just like the Sunfish I used to sail at camp. Except they had a tiller and this has a wheel."

"Well, it's a little different from a Sunfish," Scott chided.

"Yeah, a little different. This is maybe a football field longer."

Scott looked up to check the sails. "How are things working out for you in New York?"

"I'm making progress. At least, I think I am. It's going to be a long haul, but I'm learning a lot. Some of which has nothing to do with making films. This business has a lot of assholes," he said. Then he quickly added, "And a lot of nice people as well. It's a different world."

"Not exactly North Greenwich, I guess."

"Not exactly."

"Well, my advice, for what it's worth, is to pursue the dream. But, I should warn you, Dad is going to do whatever he can to talk you into moving back to Greenwich and joining the company. He figures this film thing of yours is just a short-term fascination and that you'll get tired of it. Of course, if you do, the door is always open at Carraway International. Dad would welcome you back in a second. Frankly, so would I. Having said that, let me say again that you should do what makes you happy, not what makes Mother and Dad happy."

"I appreciate you're saying that. I really do. I know how much Dad wants to maintain the company as one of the oldest family-owned businesses on the face of the earth."

"Or at least in the U.S.," Scott corrected, laughing.

"The point is, he's got you to carry on the name. What's more, he's got the smarter brother in line to take over."

"That's debatable."

"Are you getting much pressure from Mother?"

"About you?"

"Yes."

"Of course. But forget Mother," he said in a flippant tone. "I have. A long time ago." His voice was edged with a distinct bitterness.

Jay was about to ask for an explanation when suddenly Scott bent over, grimacing and shouting. "Damn! Sonavabitch!"

For an instant, Jay thought his brother might have been having a heart attack. "What's the matter? What is it?"

Scott, still bent over, rocked back and forth and then straightened up gritting his teeth, shaking his head as if trying to mitigate the pain. Finally, the pain began to subside. Scott took a deep breath and wiped tears from his eyes. "Goddamn it! Second time this week."

"Where does it hurt?" Jay asked, making no effort to hide his concern.

"Right here," Scott said, touching his mid-section.

"Have you seen a doctor?"

"I have an appointment next week," he said as the pain continued to subside. "I don't know, are there ligaments in your stomach? Really feels like I pulled something." Then dismissing any concern he might have had, he said confidently, "My doctor will figure it out."

The brothers fell silent, Scott composing himself and Jay staring blankly out to sea. The sound of the boat splashing through the water and the wind teasing and snapping the sails pervaded the deck.

After a time and with no prompting, Scott said, "Tell me about Joanna."

"What do want me to tell you?"

"Is this going anywhere?"

"I sure hope so."

"Can you imagine what it would be like to wake up every morning with that face on the pillow next to you?"

"To tell you the truth, I've thought about it. A lot," Jay added.

"Well, my advice is to go for it. I think she's terrific."

"I wish our mother felt the same. She disliked Joanna before she even met her."

"Our mother is still living in the 19th Century when parents arranged marriages. If she gets her way, she'll have you married to what's-her-name, that friend of Ceci's."

"Brooke Whitney."

"Yeah. My advice is to not let mother near Joanna." Scott looked around to see who might be within earshot. When he saw that the nearest crew member was well forward, he leaned close to Jay and said. "She talked me into marrying Tolova, you know."

"No, I didn't know. Do you regret it?" Jay asked.

"If I did, I'd never admit it to anybody. Not even to my little brother." Scott's thoughts drifted off to the windward and his eyes roamed the distant Long Island shore as though he were looking for something—maybe Gatsby's Green light. "Did I ever tell you about Emily?"

"Emily who?"

"Emily Potsworth."

Jay shook head, "Don't think so. Wait. Was this the girl you met in England?"

Scott nodded. "After we were told Germany had surrendered, they rotated my unit, what was left of us, out of the Ruhr Valley and back to England. We were told that we'd probably get shipped to the Pacific for the planned invasion on Japan. For a while, it seemed like they'd almost forgotten us. It was during that time I met Emily Potsworth. She was an RAF nurse and we met at one of those social evenings the Brits arranged for the troops."

"It might have been the war and everything I'd been though, but I fell madly in love with her. She was funny and she was bright. She was not knock-your-socks-off beautiful like Joanna, but pretty and there was something about her that ... well, there was something about her that was magnetic. When they dropped the bomb on Japan, we were told we were going home. Since her home had been destroyed by the blitz, she didn't have any address other than the hospital where she was assigned and they were going to release her. So I told her to write me in Greenwich and promised that once I was discharged, I'd come back. I was higher than a kite when I got home."

"I was only about ten or eleven, but I remember, all you could talk about was Emily," Jay said.

"What you probably don't remember is that Mother was appalled when she learned Emily was not British royalty. Her father was a pit musician in the London theater and her mother had run off with some soldier, years before. About two weeks after I got home, I received a letter from Emily with her new address. She said it was temporary and that she'd let me know when she had a more permanent flat. I wrote back and said, forget the flat; I'm coming to take you to the States. That was the last I ever heard from her."

"She never wrote back?" Jay asked.

"That's what I assumed. I figured maybe with the war being over, she'd had second thoughts. It must have been about five years later, Tolova was pregnant with Scott and I was looking through the attic for something. I think maybe some of my baby things. Guess what I found?"

"Her letters."

Scott nodded. "All nicely tied up in a bundle. When I confronted Mother, she admitted she had hidden them, in her words, 'to prevent me from making a grievous mistake.'"

"What did you do?"

"What could I do? What could I say, other than tell her how angry I was? I was married. We were expecting our first child. So I wasn't about to leave Tolova and start looking all over England for Emily. End of story."

"Why did Mother keep the letters? You'd think she would have burned them or something."

"I asked her that one time."

"What'd she say?"

"Just that 'I thought I should keep them.'"

"That's all she said? 'I thought I should keep them?' Why?"

"Said she didn't know why. And if she did, she wasn't about to tell me."

Jay weighed the next question before he decided to ask it. "Do you ever think of her? Of Emily?"

"I try not to," Scott said in a way that made it clear their talk about Emily had come to an end. "You want something to eat?" he asked as he stood up. "I'll bring something up from the galley."

"That would be nice."

As Scott climbed out of the cockpit he said, "Turkey OK?"

"Sounds good. See how Joanna is doing."

"If the wind changes, just holler for Captain Dave. He's back there on the aft deck."

Scott and Joanna appeared to change places in the companionway. She stepped onto the deck, looked up and down, spotted Jay and joined him in the cockpit.

"What's going on down there?" he asked, expecting to hear about her tour.

"A bloodletting."

Jay looked at her quizzically.

"Mine."

"What?"

"Tolova and her friends took out their little knives and cut me up pretty good. They made it very, very clear that the bimbo from Brooklyn is *persona non grata* and needs to recognize that she is not only socially handicapped, but intellectually inferior as well."

Jay made no effort to restrain his temper, "What the hell did they say to you?"

"Nothing as blatant as 'you're a dumb broad from Brooklyn.' It was far more subtle. They asked me questions like 'where did you prep?' and 'what sorority did you belong to in college?' Once they skewered me for my lack of formal education, they started on my travel experience. 'Do you prefer Claridges or the Ritz?'"

"You should have told them to ..." he stopped short of an expletive.

"When we got to clothes, it was 'Now, tell us, Joanna, which boutique on Fifth Avenue do you prefer, Channel or Dior or Yves St Laurent?' I told them I preferred the bargain basement at Macy's. That's when I left them to give myself a tour of the boat. You know, I thought I'd met some pretty cruel and cutting women during casting sessions, but not one of them could hold a candle to those three."

"Those Goddamn arrogant women. Who in the hell do they think they are?"

"I'm sure they'd be happy to tell you."

Jay was angry, really angry now. His jaw was tight and he was bent on retaliation. "I think I'll just go down there and have a come-to-Jesus session with those bitches." Jay made a move to signal Captain Dave to take over, but Joanna stopped him.

"Don't," she pleaded. "It will only make things worse."

"I think something needs to be said. And who better than me to say it? You're my guest and they've treated you like shit."

"Please Jay, I know you mean well, but there's nothing to be gained by going down there and making a scene. They'll just give you their most innocent, 'we don't know whatever you're talking about' look. I can hear them; 'If the poor little girl from the city can't manage to participate in a friendly conversation, what hope is there for her?'"

Jay felt a great wave of sadness wash over him. "OK, for your sake I won't say anything." Inwardly he was distraught that what should have been a nice day on Long Island Sound had turned into an emotional debacle for Joanna. His mother, he knew, would say it was because Joanna was "not one of our kind, a social inferior who could never be accepted by the society in which he'd grown up."

"Jay," Joanna said, putting her arm around his shoulder and putting her head close to his. "You can't go through life trying to protect me from the Jackson Kormans or the Tolovas, or her friends, or even your mother." There was no anger, no resentment in her voice, only an element of resignation. "I could never get used to your sister-in-law and her friends. With the exception of Ceci and Scott and maybe your father, I don't like these people up here. While this boat is … well … what can I say? It's spectacular. But to be honest, right now, I'd much rather be in a rowboat with you in Central Park, heading for the Isle of Innisfree."

"I'm really sorry, Joanna. I promise we won't do this again. Our life is not here, it's in New York."

Joanna said nothing. Her eyes seemed to scan the horizon like a sailor in a turbulent sea, looking for a safe harbor. "Remember what I said to you as we left your house after the polo picnic?"

"You said you felt like a foreign exchange student from a distant country that no one had ever heard of."

"Well, today I realized that this exchange student can't speak their language. And I don't know that I want to even try."

19
Paul Newman

Elliott burst into the office, surfing on a wave of excitement. "Newman's agent has got it and said she'd pass it on to him with her recommendation!" He was almost shouting. "The treatment is physically in his hands. He's got to love it, right, Lucy?" He hugged the receptionist. "He's got to love it! Jay, I'm telling you, this is his kind of film."

"You don't have to convince me." Jay did his best to show some enthusiasm,

but the Film Arts roller coaster ride was beginning to wear him down.

"Are we under control?" Elliott asked.

"Still no check from Hillman," Jay reported.

"It'll be here," Elliott said confidently, to no one in particular, but to everyone who might be within earshot. "Now, the previous question: Are we under control? If we aren't, I don't want to hear about it."

Jay realized that Elliott wasn't going to let anyone or anything ruin his mood with a cold dose of reality.

"We did get the Bromo spot," said one of his salesmen.

"Tell me it's a big budget?"

"I can tell you it will pay some rent, but that's about it. Shoots next week. I put it on your calendar."

"Ok, give Nathan the particulars so we can send 'em an invoice."

"Already have."

"You're a good man, Gunga Din. What time is it?"

"Just after six," Jay answered.

"Quittin' time! Come on, Jay, I'll buy you drink over at the Monkey Bar. It's got to be a quick one, because I have a meeting at eight."

They left the office and walked the six blocks to the Elysee Hotel on East 54th—which Elliott often referred to as the Easy Lay—that housed the Monkey Bar, a favorite after-work meeting place for many of the advertising people who inhabited Madison Avenue. Normally, Elliott settled in at the end of the bar. So Jay was a little surprised when he asked for a table near the door.

When the drinks they ordered arrived, Elliott took a large gulp of his martini and said, "I want to talk about *Gran Prix Racer*."

"Sure."

Elliott took another gulp of his drink and seemed to be looking for somewhere to start. "I've been thinking about the book and what it's going to look like on the screen. The one part that has to be absolutely right is the end. The audience has to understand why Eddy Merrill turns his racecar into the wall. The author does such a terrific job of making you understand that ending his life is his only option. The words jump off the page and you actually *feel* what Eddy feels in your gut."

"I agree. That's what makes *Death of a Gran Prix Racer* so powerful."

"The only problem is, so much of what happens in the book takes place in his mind. How do I get what's inside his head onto film?"

"I don't think you want him to deliver a ten-page soliloquy, running down the track at 200 miles per hour."

"You're right, I don't. But, the question remains: How do I make them see that Eddy's dream of winning—the chase, the *getting there*—is far more important to him than the *fact* of winning? Deep down, Eddy knows he doesn't have what it takes to be a champion. He's a guy who, all his life, in one way or another, has finished back with the pack. He's good, but not super-good."

"And, as the book makes clear, if he wins, they'll say it was a fluke. To him, that would be worse than never winning at all."

"Exactly. But more even more important, I have to make the audience see that his life is about to catch up with him. All that wreckage: the marriage that has gone south, the girl he's gotten pregnant, the car owner that he blackmailed to get the ride, the debts that are going to wipe out everything he has ever had, all the people who bought his act only to discover that they have been left holding the bag. It's all waiting for him at the finish line."

"That has to come through on the film."

"Right and that's the challenge. But how do I put that on the screen? How do I capture that moment when the finish line is less than an eighth of a mile ahead and he knows—just as everybody at the track knows—that he's going to win? Then suddenly, in the last sweeping turn, he steers into wall. That scene explodes in the book."

"Obviously, the same thing has to happen in the film."

Elliott looked at him remotely, like a man lost in the desert, desperate for someone to show him the way to the nearest oasis. "I'm not sure I know how to do that." And then, the painful admission, "Maybe it's not in me." Elliott stared blankly at his empty glass.

This was an Elliott that Jay had not seen before. What had happened to erode his bravado, his supreme confidence? Where had this rush of self-doubt come from? Maybe what Jay was seeing now had always been there, lurking just below the surface. Jay wanted to say something, but he knew whatever he said would be gratuitous at best and more likely inconsequential. As he looked at Elliott Piece, Jay realized that the martini had carried him off to some distant place where he was all by himself with his demons.

Then, as if this were a film, Elliott's mood cut from a dark night scene to one in bright daylight. From pensive to expectant, in less than the twenty-four frames that make up a second of film time.

"Look, this meeting I have tonight ... actually, it's not so much a meeting as it is a casting. A guy I know has this friend up in Scarsdale, a teacher who wants to get into commercials. So she's coming in tonight for a casting session and she's going to audition for a part that calls for her to play the entire scene on her back." A salacious grin slipped across Elliott's face as he reached into his pocket and pulled out a hotel key. "She will be performing on the king-sized bed in Room 765."

He's got to be kidding, Jay thought. *He's not kidding.* The truth of what he was planning was written all over his face. So, the casting couch lives. *How low do you have to be to take advantage of some unsuspecting girl's aspirations to get her to go to bed with you?*

Jay asked himself. That was beneath contempt and he began to wonder what kind of man he had chosen as his mentor. Jay decided that his only response was to ask the obvious question. "What happens if she decides she doesn't like the part?"

"She'll like the part," he said with a wicked, confident look on his face that implied he knew something Jay didn't.

But what about Sherry? Jay wanted to ask. Elliott was about to tell him.

"Do me a favor, Stud. Stay put here for a minute while I make a phone call. I forgot to tell Sherry that I'd be working late and might not get home tonight." He stood up and started toward the phone when he remembered something. "This woman I'm meeting—her name is Pat McDaniel—she's due here any minute and was told to ask for me. Buy her a drink and tell her I'll be right back."

"You want me to buy her a drink," Jay repeated, wondering when entertaining Elliott's sexual quests had become part of his job description.

Elliott stopped and turned back, looking down at Jay with a cheeky kind of smile. "Stud, don't get any ideas about holding your own casting session." With that, he turned and disappeared in the clot of people that had squeezed themselves into the limited space in front of the bar.

Jay imagined the little cheerleader and her children waiting for Elliott to come home. Then the phone call and the disappointment. Daddy won't be home again tonight. Jay wondered if Sherry knew, or at least suspected the truth about her husband.

"I'm here to meet Mr. Elliott Pierce," said a woman's voice. Jay looked up as the maitre d' pointed in his direction.

"Elliott?" she asked as she approached the table. Pat McDaniel looked to be in her mid-thirties. She was blond, about five six and just slightly on the pudgy side. She was nicely dressed in a black cocktail dress that had been scooped out at the neck to afford her ample breasts breathing room. If she thought Jay was Elliott, she showed no surprise at his clearly youthful appearance.

"No," Jay said quickly, "I'm Jay Carraway. I work for Elliott. He's on the phone. He'll be back in a minute." He stood up and held her chair as she sat down. "Would you like a drink?"

"Love one. Martini, very dry, with two olives." The waiter, who had floated up behind her, overheard the order and nodded.

Pat McDaniel was not at all what Jay had expected. This was not your typical aspiring actress who's decided to exchange her favors for a boost in her career. Pat was very relaxed, looking for all the world as if she had just stepped out with old friends for dinner.

"I like this place. Haven't been here in years." She glanced about the bar, giving it her considered approval.

"I understand you're a teacher," Jay said. He was intent on satisfying his curiosity.

"Yes. History and English." The martini arrived and she took a long sip and pronounced it good. "I'm sorry I'm late, but it took me longer than I expected to get the kids to bed."

"Kids?" Jay was confused. "Do you teach in a boarding school or something?"

"No, no. I'm talking about my kids. I have three of my own and my husband was late getting home."

There was a disconnect somewhere. Kids? Husband? Maybe Elliott's friend had screwed things up. Maybe this was some kind of practical joke on Elliott. He pressed on. "Are you looking to get into commercials?"

"Not really. I mean, if someone wanted me to ... you know, stand in the background or something, that might be fun."

Do you really understand why you're here tonight? Jay wanted to ask. *Do you know that you're expected to audition on your back in Room 765?*

"Actually, I'm more interested in meeting Elliott. My friend says he's really a terrific guy."

Substitute "stud" for "guy" and you've nailed him, Jay thought. He glanced toward the bar, hoping to see Elliott. It seemed that he'd been gone for a long time. As Jay watched Pat inhale a second martini, he wondered what he would do if Elliott had had a guilt attack and decided to go home to Sherry. He needn't have worried.

"You must be Pat," Elliott said, presenting himself for inspection.

It did not take her long to give him a passing grade.

"I see you've taken good care of her, Jay. I know you've got stuff to do, so I'll take over here."

Jay welcomed the invitation to leave.

"Nice to have met you," he said to Pat as he pushed his chair back and stood up. "See you tomorrow, Elliott."

Jay stared at the two of them, thinking that what he should be feeling was contempt. Instead, he just wanted to laugh. He thought he'd seen—or at least heard of—everything. Who would believe that a thirty-plus-year-old woman with three kids and a husband baby-sitting at home had gotten all dressed up to come down to the Elysee Hotel to let Elliott—whom she'd never met before—cast her for a commercial she wasn't interested in doing? *I've lived a very sheltered life,* Jay decided.

"Jay?" Elliott said when it appeared that someone had nailed his shoes to the floor. "You forget something?"

"I guess I forgot to go," he said clumsily and beat a direct path to the door.

***

Jay walked slowly back to the office. The urge to laugh had been replaced with images of Sherry, the sad little cheerleader, waiting at home for a husband who was bouncing off another woman in Room 765. Maybe Sherry should call Mr. McDaniel. They could keep each other company and they'd certainly have something in common. The bizarre thought made him laugh out loud.

He returned to the office and found Nathan Best in the conference room, surrounded by stacks of folders and account books. He was surprised to see John Baskham sitting in the corner smoking his pipe.

"John, what are you doing here?"

"Hi Jay. I'm waiting for my friend here to finish so he can buy me dinner," he said, nodding toward Nathan.

"I didn't know you two knew each other."

"Too well," Nathan volunteered. "By the way, Teddy screened the running footage you shot in Yuma. Terrific stuff."

"Thanks mostly to Mike Livesey."

"Not necessarily. Teddy said that Mike gives you a lot of the credit. Says you've got a good eye and that you set up a lot of really great shots."

"Coming from Livesey, that means something."

"Have you seen our leader?" Nathan asked.

"I just left him."

"Is he coming back to the office?"

"Ah … I don't think so."

"We had a meeting scheduled. He promised he'd be here. Did he go home?" Nathan asked. He made no effort to hide his frustration.

"He's having a meeting?"

"With who?"

Jay decided there was nothing to be gained in covering for Elliott. "It's not a meeting; it's a kind of casting session."

"Anybody we know?" Nathan asked.

"No, she's a schoolteacher from Westchester."

"A schoolteacher?" Nathan was incredulous.

Jay told them about babysitting Pat McDaniel while Elliott made his phone call. "What really confuses me is that I don't think she cares if she gets into commercials or not. Is there something I'm missing here?"

"What? You think it's strange for a husband to stay at home with the kids while his wife spends the night screwing someone she'd never met before?" Nathan's voice was heavy with sarcasm.

"He hasn't changed, has he?" John asked, knocking his pipe into an ash tray.

"The company is going in the shitter and he's out getting laid." Nathan made no effort to hide his disgust. "Hell, if he doesn't care about this financial mess, why should I? It's gotten so that I hate to open the mail because I know I'm going to have to deal with another disaster. We're being dunned by several suppliers and we've got two very official looking letters announcing that henceforth Cinemagnetics and MovieLab will accept Film Arts orders on a C.O.D. basis only."

"Have you talked to him about this?" Baskham asked.

"I've tried," Nathan said, shaking his head. "We set up meetings and he doesn't show up. Take tonight. He promised he'd be here. Maybe I misunderstood. Maybe I was supposed to take the books to the hotel and go over them while he plays Teacher, May I?"

"Elliott never has been a numbers man."

"Unless you're talking numbers of women." Nathan's frustration had turned to disgust.

Jay could feel his stomach sinking and he tossed out what he hoped would be a life preserver. "That package of commercials that Sig Hillman has promised him ought to help clear up some of this," he said as he gestured toward the stacks of file folders in front of Nathan.

"Yeah, assuming two things: one, that he actually delivers the business and, two, that Elliott doesn't blow the budget."

"Funny," Baskham said. "Elliott has more raw cinematic talent than any guy in this business. His stuff is magic. When it comes to selling, he can convince you to buy the shirt off your own back and make you feel like you got a great deal. But he's reckless. He's reckless with his marriage, he's reckless with the people who care about him, he's reckless with his company. And worst of all, he's reckless with himself."

Nathan threw up his hands. "Well, there's not much more I can do here without Elliott." He began to stack the folders.

"Good, I was beginning to think you were going to welsh on dinner," Baskham said.

"One piece of good news," Jay said in an attempt to lift some of the pall that had settled in the room. "Elliott learned that Newman's agent has given the film treatment on to him."

"Jay, let's do a little reality check," Nathan said with heavy skepticism. "Do you know how long he's been talking about doing that feature? Two years and nothing's happened. But, let's say for the sake of argument that the treatment actually gets inside Newman's house. Keep in mind that Paul Newman gets dozens of treatments and scripts a week and that he probably never looks at more than one or two."

"You don't think the fact that the treatment was given to him by his agent will make a difference?"

"Who knows? Elliott's an eternal optimist and that's one of the things that drives him. Me, on the other hand, I'm the kind of guy who likes to see the check in the bank before I get excited about anything. For all our sakes, I hope it happens. However, if I were you, I wouldn't spend a whole lot of time planning how you want your credit to read on the end titles." Nathan scooped up the folders. "John, I'll be ready as soon as I put these away."

John had turned his attention to his pipe. "Before you go, let me mention one thing. Please don't consider what I'm about to say as an offer. Consider it more an option, just in case."

"Just in case what?" Nathan asked.

"Just in case things go south here and you find yourselves looking for work. Let me make it clear that I'm not looking to steal any of Elliott's people. I wouldn't do that. But I do have an option for you, if Film Arts should go belly up."

"You're finally starting your own shop," Nathan said.

Baskham smiled and nodded. "I think I'm getting close. Not there yet. It looks like—thanks mostly to you, Jay—I can count on Tasti-Feast and I have a tentative commitment from three other agency producers I know I can trust. Plus, I'm in line to get a couple corporate image films. And a guy I know who handles Renault here in the U.S. is ready to give me a couple dealer films. Again, this is not an offer, but if it happens—and there's still a big 'if'—I know that I could always find a place for a couple good people like the two of you."

"Well, good luck. I hope it happens for you," Nathan said.

"Thanks, John. I appreciate the offer," Jay added.

"You want to join us for dinner?" John asked

"No thanks, I've got a couple things to clean up here."

After John and Nathan left, Jay wandered into Elliott's office and found himself asking, *What is it about this guy?* There was the Elliott who had the remarkable ability to create one-minute visions of a fabricated reality on 35mm film at 24 frames a second—the man who dreamed of making great feature films. Then there was this other Elliott Pierce, an intentionally reckless man who mortgaged his days and lived his life by rules that he alone understood. Two personalities, living side-by-side in unresolved conflict.

Jay looked around the room at the production stills, which Elliott had hung on his office walls with the same disregard that he showed most aspects of his life. Was it Jay's imagination, or did the walls seem to be developing cracks?

20
La Bohème

"**W**here's Joanna?" Ceci asked as her brother opened the door to his apartment.

"She's on her way up. What's that?" Jay asked pointing to the large, rectangular box under Ceci's arm.

"A surprise for Joanna," she said putting it on the table.

"I love this place, Jay," Ceci said, flitting about the room like a butterfly looking for a place to light. "It's like out of a movie."

"I think I recognize that voice," Joanna said as she entered the apartment.

"Joanna!" Ceci said excitedly and gave her a hug. "Thank you, thank you, thank you, for inviting me in today. I've never been to Greenwich Village. It's sort of like Paris but with American cars."

"Parts of Paris, maybe," Jay corrected.

"This is what you'd imagine an artist's garret to look like," she said, indicating the large window overlooking the Square. "And you even have an easel." She inspected Jay's attempt at art. "Did you paint this?"

"A work in progress."

"It's terrible. Stick with making films," she said, laughing.

"No argument, there."

"Oh, Joanna, I've brought you a surprise," Ceci said, indicating the box. "Jay told me that he's taking you to the opera tonight."

"Yes, he is."

"Well, everyone dresses at the opera and I decided that you should wear the dress you wore at the picnic. It was a little formal for Mother's picnic, but it will be perfect for a summer evening at the opera." She opened the box and pulled out the dress, holding it up. "Consider this a gift for showing me Greenwich Village today."

"Ceci, I can't …"

"Yes you can," she interrupted. "As I told you, you looked so beautiful in this dress that no one else would ever be able to wear it." Ceci folded the dress and laid it casually on top of the box.

"This is so nice of you. I don't know how to thank you."

"All I want is for Jay to take your picture in it and send it to me."

"Consider it done," Jay said. "Thanks, Ceci. Now I remember why you're my favorite sister."

"I'm your only sister."

"Then by elimination, that makes you my favorite."

Ceci ignored Jay's attempt at humor. "OK, I'm ready for the tour. You know, Mother would kill me if she knew I was here." She turned to Joanna. "She's afraid Jay's going to corrupt me and that I'll escape like he did."

"Where does Mother think you are?"

"I told her that I was meeting a college friend from Vassar and that we'd be making the rounds of Saks, Bonwits and Bergdorf. Think how proud of me she'll be when I tell her that I shopped all day and didn't see a thing I wanted to buy."

"She'll probably call a doctor to see if you're sick."

"Oh, Jay, I don't shop *that* much."

"I've seen your closet. I rest my case."

Ceci ignored him and turned to Joanna, "Is this your first opera?"

"It is. I'm looking forward to it."

"Daddy's had a box for years and years at the Met. He started taking me to the opera when I was eight. I hated it at first, but then I got so I liked it. But only Puccini and Verdi. Wagner was like torture. What are you seeing?"

"La Bohème."

"That's my all-time, very, very favorite. I cry every time I see it"

"Jay gave me the synopsis to read."

"I love the way Rodolfo meets her in the first act. She knocks on his door because her candle has gone out. He relights it. She's about to leave when she discovers she's dropped her key. A draft blows out her candle again and then he blows out his and pretends he can't find her key."

"Sneaky fellow, that Rodolfo," Jay volunteered.

"Then there's the scene in the third act when we discover that she's sick and he's too poor to help her. Rodolfo tells his friend that she'll only get worse in the poverty they share. At first, they think it would be best if they were to part. But then they realize how much they love each other. So they decide to stay together until spring. The snow continues to fall as the lovers start for home in each other's arms. It's so beautiful."

"But the last act ... it's so sad when she comes back to Rodolfo's garret to be with him when she dies," Joanna said.

"That's what makes it a timeless love story," Jay said. "You have two people who fall in love and then fate, bad timing, circumstances beyond their control, egos, misunderstandings—you name it—all conspire to determine their fate. Unfortunately, *stuff* happens in life. We all want a happy ending for Mimi and Rodolfo, just like we want one for ourselves. But, because we realize what happens to them could happen—in one way or another—to us, we see ourselves in the story."

"He doesn't look it, Joanna," Ceci said, "but my brother's really a romantic ... like Rodolfo."

"I know," Joanna said, smiling at Jay. "Believe me, I know."

Jay decided it was time to change the subject and move on to something else. "Are we going to talk opera, or are we going to show you the Village?"

"I'm ready," Ceci said. "I hope we see some Bohemians."

"You mean, in addition to the two of us?"

"You guys aren't Bohemians. Bohemians have long hair and scraggly beards."

"Oh, so that's what those people are," Jay said, laughing. "I thought they were just vagrants. Come on, let's go find some."

It was a soft summer afternoon in the Village. They began with a walk though Washington Square Park and paused to watch the serious old men hunched over their checker and chessboards. They strolled past children playing on the swings and then left the park, heading for NYU, where Jay pointed out the buildings where he'd learned to make films. At just after one o'clock, they stopped for a long lunch at a small bistro. Jay pointed to two reasonably scruffy, unshaven people in the far corner and said, "Ceci, take a look. Real bohemians. Or just two guys who don't get along with their barbers."

After lunch, they browsed through some of the of colorful and funky Village shops. Ceci bought some trinkets that she vowed to hide from her mother. At six, they returned to Sheridan Square and found the Carraway Cadillac waiting for Ceci.

"This has been about the best day of my life," Ceci said with her usual expansive exuberance. "Really, I mean it," she said to her brother, as he appeared to cast some doubt on her claim. "Do you think Mother would hate me if I told her I wanted to move to Greenwich Village and become an artist?"

"No, she'd hate me," Jay said. "'How dare you corrupt your little sister,'" he said, mimicking his mother.

"I think I'd like to be corrupted," she said as the chauffeur held the door. "I just love you guys."

"Ceci, I don't know how to thank you for the dress. It's just wonderful."

"All I ask is that you don't forget to take a picture."

***

The seats at the Met were excellent: Row M on the right center aisle. Physically, the tenor didn't look like a starving writer who had missed very many meals. And the soprano did not appear to be about to die of consumption. None of that mattered when they began their duet; everyone in the opera house seemed to sense that they were witnessing something extraordinary. Several times, Jay glanced over at Joanna. The music and the story had swept her total attention onto the stage and into the garret with Mimi and Rodolfo. Their story became her story. La Bohème had won another convert.

As the lights came up at the end of the first act, Joanna said, "I can't believe the voices. And I thought I could sing."

"But you can."

"Not compared to them."

"But there's other music besides opera. And I'll take your Cole Porter anytime."

"I think you're prejudiced."

"Very."

***

As they left the opera house, Jay asked her if she'd like to stop for coffee.

"If you don't mind, I think I'd just like to go home," she said quietly.

"Is something wrong?"

"No," she answered unconvincingly. It wasn't until they were in the taxi heading down Seventh Avenue toward the Village that she said, "I'm afraid, I don't handle sad stories very well. They were so in love at the end of Act Three. I sort of wish it had ended there. That way, you could imagine that not only would they stay together until April, but forever. As you said this morning, happiness is what we want for them and it's what we want for ourselves."

"Unfortunately, life is sometimes more like Act Four. Things don't always end up the way you'd like them to."

"I know and maybe that's why I'd just as soon skip the last act."

"Do you want to come up for awhile?" Jay asked as they entered the building.

"Let me change out of Ceci's dress."

"Correction. *Your* dress." Then he remembered his sister's request. "We promised Ceci a picture."

***

Joanna stood in front of his garret window. The lights from Sheridan Square provided a backdrop that wrapped her in an opalescent glow. She draped her hair over one shoulder and was waiting for his approval. He could feel his heart rate double. "If that dress could talk, it would be saying thank you, thank you, thank you," he said.

"You are so good for a girl's ego," she said, only half accepting the compliment.

"Don't move. Let me take some pictures." Jay got his camera, loaded it and repositioned her in front of the garret window. Using his lamp and a little ingenuity, he managed to direct just enough light onto her to balance the back light from the window. "Give me a fashion magazine look."

She turned toward him, looking directly into the camera. Her face was aglow with a smile that he knew reflected the love she felt for him. "These are going to be terrific," he said. "I'll send one to Ceci, but I'm keeping the best one for myself."

"Let me change," Joanna said, heading for the door." I'll be right back."

About twenty minutes later, Jay heard her tapping on his door. When he opened it, he found Joanna standing there in her nightgown holding a candle. He made a feeble attempt at a joke. "Don't tell me, it's Mimi."

"Just me," she said, her face full of sadness and tears in her eyes.

"What's the matter?" he asked gently.

"I don't want to be Mimi. I don't want to end up like that."

Jay had never seen her like this before. There was fear in her face, like a little girl waking from a bad dream, looking for someone to make her feel safe. "You won't end up like Mimi. Not a chance," he said in a confident voice, hoping that it would reassure her. Then, in an attempt to lighten the moment he said, "Tomorrow I'll write a new Act Four for Mr. Puccini and I guarantee it will have a happy ending."

There was no change in her sullen expression. It was going to take more than words to lift whatever cloud had settled over her.

"I want to stay with you tonight, Jay," she whispered. "I don't want to be alone."

"You're going to stay with me for the rest of your life. I promise you that."

"Maybe you shouldn't make a promise that might be hard to keep."

"What do you mean?"

"There's so much about me you don't know. I may not be what you think I am. There are so many things in my past that I'm ashamed of. If I thought that something I'd done might hurt you ... I couldn't take that. I think I'd just disappear." She started to cry again.

"Joanna," he said, taking her in his arms. "Joanna, the important part of my life began on May 2nd, the morning I first saw you at Ad-Film. Anything before that time, in my life or yours, does not matter. All that matters is what has happened between us since that day. There is no past for us, only now, today and tomorrow and every tomorrow. That's all that can ever matter."

"I want that to be true. I really do."

"It will be, I promise." He blew out her candle and led her to his bed. He lay down next to her and she pressed herself into his arms. She continued to sob. "Hey," he said, raising up slightly and kissing her on her tear-streaked cheek. "It's all right, I'm here. I'll always be here."

She snuggled close to him. "I love you, Jay. I love you so much. You're all I have." She closed her eyes and nestled her head near his chest.

At some other time, maybe with some other woman, Jay would have assumed that the happy ending script would have called for them to make love. But he understood that physical love was not what she had come for. After a while, her breathing became slow and regular. Mimi had fallen asleep in his arms and he dared not move for fear of waking her. His last conscious thought was how much he wanted to write their own Act Four.

21

CJ

"This is your big break, Stud," Elliott said mater-of-factly when Jay walked into the office. "I'm going to let you direct a film."

"You're kidding!"

"Based on what I saw from your Yuma footage, you can handle this easy."

"You've screened the Yuma footage?"

"Last night. I guess I should have called you. Sig and I looked at it about eight. He really loved what we shot."

We? Who's we? Jay asked himself. *You were in LA with your 'cousin' and the wife you shared.*

"But then, I really couldn't have had you here. You understand, of course, that there was no way I could tell him that I left you there with Livesey while I went to L.A. He'd have shit. What Hillman doesn't understand is that anybody can shoot running footage, especially if you've got Livesey behind the camera."

"Thanks for the compliment," Jay said sarcastically.

"What do you want me to tell you? That you did a nice job?" Elliott did not wait for an answer. "Ok, Stud, you did a nice job," he said, patting him on the head in a demeaning sort of way. "Feel better now?"

Jay decided not to tell him how he really felt. Instead, he asked, "So what's my big break?"

"Here's the deal. Hillman wants me to do him another favor while the check for the package makes its way through their system."

"More running footage?"

"Basically. Willys-Overland is holding a series of meetings for their dealers and they want a film to open the meeting, featuring the new CJ5 Jeep. It doesn't have to be fancy. Just two to three minutes of running shots and some hot, upbeat music. Maybe you can find some way to have a little fun with it—maybe create a little story line or something. As long as the stuff is in focus, they'll love it. However, there are some problems. Problem number one: Sig has next to nothing in the budget for this, but I'm going to let him squeeze my balls until I get my hands on the check. Problem number two: I haven't got time to do the film, which is why this is going to be your baby."

"What's the budget?"

"Peanuts. Five grand ... maybe six, if we really make him happy."

"Can I hire Livesey to shoot it?"

"Hire whoever you like, so long as you don't go over budget. Shoot it in 16. No need to spend money on 35."

"When do I start?"

"Now," Elliott said, looking at his calendar. "One last problem: there's no time. Sig and the VP of Marketing from Willys are going to be walking into our screening room a week from Friday and they're going to want to see something."

"Can I hire a couple of helpers? Like someone to drive the Jeep?"

"Sure, as long as they'll work cheap. Can you do it?"

"Absolutely." Jay made no effort to hide his excitement.

"Attaboy, Stud!"

***

"I want this Jeep film to be more than just a bunch of running shots," he said to Joanna as they shared a pizza that evening in an Italian Restaurant on Grove Street. "I'd like to blow them away. Really do something that they'd never expect."

"Have you got any ideas?"

"Tell me what you think of this: This guy comes out of his house like he's going to work. He climbs into his Jeep, pulls out onto the highway and finds himself in a traffic jam. The Merritt Parkway in Connecticut would be perfect for this. Anyway, he's getting impatient. He looks at the traffic and then he looks off to the side into the woods and says, 'Hey, I've got a Jeep. I don't need a road.' So he turns off the highway, cuts into the woods and for the next two minutes he drives the Jeep over every kind of terrain you can think of—sand, streams, mud, hay fields, whatever we can find. Eventually he ends up at his office."

"I've got a great tag line for you." Joanna said.

"Which is?"

"As he gets out of the Jeep and goes into his office, the camera centers on the Jeep and the narrator says, 'Jeep. Who needs roads?' Or something like that."

"I love it! It's simple and clean and really says it all. You missed your calling, Joanna. You should be a copywriter."

"If it will pay the rent, I'm your girl."

22
The Visit

The intercom buzzer woke Jay. *Who is ringing me at this hour?* He wondered as he got out of bed and went to the door, where the intercom was located.

"Yes?"

"Jay, is that you? It's your father."

"Dad?"

"Can I come up?"

"Wait a minute," Jay said. He opened the door, went out on the landing and leaned over the railing to look down the stairway shaft to the first floor. "I'm up here. It's five flights."

"You don't have an elevator?"

"Sorry. Wait a minute, I'll come down."

"No. I'd like to come up. However, if you don't see me in ten minutes, call for an ambulance."

Jay went back into his room, slipped on his pants and shirt and straightened up his bed.

As Wilfred Carraway walked into Jay's apartment, he said, "There's a lot to be said for buildings with elevators, son."

"But then how would I get any exercise?"

"There are other ways, I'm sure."

"Welcome to my humble hovel."

"I wasn't sure I'd find you in."

"I had an all-nighter. Didn't get home until 6 AM."

"An all-nighter?"

"I was working with our editor on a film that has to be ready for a client screening on Friday. I'll be going back in around one to finish up. Want something to drink? Water? Milk? Coffee?"

"Water and oxygen."

"We're a little short of oxygen up here, but I can handle the water."

"That'll be fine," his father said, settling into the one comfortable-looking chair. Unfortunately, looks were deceiving. The springs had long since decided to give up their primary function, so that Wilfred Carraway found himself, sinking, sinking, until his bottom, he was sure, was on the floor. "Is it me or is it this chair? I feel as though I'm being held captive."

Jay laughed. "Newest thing in furniture design. Great for trapping women."

"Would you mind helping me to get up from here?" He held up his hand to Jay. "First time I've ever needed to be rescued from a chair."

"There always a first for everything," Jay said, pulling him up.

His father looked around for another place to sit and opted for one of the wooden chairs at the table near the kitchen. Jay delivered the water and sat down across the table from him.

"I suppose you're wondering what's brought me here?"

"Yes, as a matter of fact. Anything wrong?"

"I'm due at a meeting on Wall Street at noon and your mother insisted that I stop buy and check out your ..." he paused and looked around the room, "your living conditions."

"First class, don't you agree?"

"This is worse than your room at the fraternity house."

"Ah … but it didn't have this view," he said, indicating the large window.

"Your sister was very impressed with that."

"She told you about coming here?"

"Just me. We conveniently kept it from your mother who … well, you know your mother. Ceci certainly is impressed with that friend of yours."

"Joanna."

"I understand you took her to see La Bohème. Did she enjoy it?"

"She did. She really did."

As often happened when talking with his father, the conversation fell into a hole. His father looked out the garret window over the rooftops as though he'd found something of profound interest. Finally, he turned to Jay and said, "Well, how's this career of yours going? Are you happy?"

Jay nodded, "Yeah. I am. I just completed my first film. We're working on the final cut. The editor thinks it's good. Really good."

There was a soft knock at the door.

"It's open," Jay called.

The door swung open and Joanna stepped into the room.

"Jay, I … " she said, stopping short as she caught sight of Wilfred Carraway. "Oh, I'm sorry. I didn't know you had company."

"Joanna, you remember my father?"

"Of course. How are you, Mr. Carraway?" she asked and held out her hand.

They shook briefly. "Nice to see you again. Well, Jay, I now understand the attraction of this apartment building." He looked up at Joanna. "Just your being here totally improves the complexion of this apartment."

"No argument there," Jay said.

"I want to thank you for giving my daughter the grand tour of Greenwich Village."

"She's a very sweet girl. We had a really good time."

"I must say, she is very fond of you."

"That goes both ways."

"And I understand you enjoyed the opera?"

"I had a wonderful tutor," she said, nodding toward Jay. "Those voices were out of this world. The power when the soprano, Renata Tabaldi, hit those high notes ... it made me embarrassed to think that I thought I could sing."

"You were lucky. You saw one of the great divas. They're not all like that."

"Jay's promised to take me to Madame Butterfly next."

"I'm glad that all those years I dragged him and his sister to the opera are paying off." He turned to his son, "Jay, you and Joanna will have to use my box this winter." Then he turned back to Joanna. "Mrs. Carraway and I don't seem to get to the Met as often as we used to. Half the time, our box just sits empty."

"I'll take you up on that, Dad."

"Well, let me not interrupt any longer," Joanna said to Mr. Carraway. Then to Jay, "I just stopped in to tell you that I'll be working late tonight."

"Me too, I think. I'll give you a call when I see where we are with the edit."

"Maybe we'll grab a bite if it's not too late."

"Sounds good."

"Oh, something else. The audition is set for next Thursday."

"Audition?" Wilfred Carraway asked with interest.

"Yes," Jay said, "Joanna is up for the lead in the Westport Country Playhouse production of *Girl Crazy*."

"Really," he said, seeming genuinely impressed. "My mother was a performer. Amateur theater. Did Jay ever tell you that?"

"No, he didn't."

"Well, he'll have to fill you in. Anyway, good luck."

"Thank you. It was nice seeing you again."

"The pleasure was mine. By the way, if you have any influence over my son, you might see what you can do about getting him to shape up this apartment."

"The truth is, I plan to make some improvements, like real furniture, but I just haven't had time to shop."

"I'll be sure he finds time."

"Good. You may be the only person who can control him." His father's tone and the look on his face told Jay that he liked Joanna. *One more family member in her corner,* he thought.

"G'bye," she said and left.

"She seems like a very nice girl."

"Fantastic is a better word."

Jay watched as his father made a quick visual inspection of his apartment. "You know, if you'd like to move out of here and maybe find something a little better, I'd be happy to help you out … financially."

"Thanks, but our deal was that I would do this on my own or not do it all. What time is your meeting?"

"Noon. This is going to be interesting. I'm meeting with the CEO of a little company up in Rochester to talk about investing in a machine that they're developing. It makes plain paper copies direct from the original document. It even copies three-dimensional objects. And then there's computers. My friend Tom Watson talked me into investing a significant amount of money in his International Business Machines Company. He's convinced the world is going to explode with this computer thing. And Scott is looking into expanding into television."

"Television?"

"Yes. He's been approached by some folks who produce those situation comedies—you know, the *I Love Lucy, Jack Benny* kind of thing. Scott thinks maybe we should consider buying a controlling interest in one of the production companies. He believes and so do I, that TV production is going to be a big business. With your experience here in New York, that might be something you'd be interested in getting involved in."

He's baited the hook and dropped it in the water, Jay thought.

"I tell you Jay, we're on the edge of a revolution. Computers, office equipment, television … the horizon is expanding every day and I want the company to take advantage of it. Of course, I'm still hoping that you'll decide to be part of the company's future."

"Dad, you don't need me in the business. You've got Scott and …" He cut himself off. "Speaking of Scott, did he see the doctor about the pain he was having?"

"Yes."

"And?"

"They're doing more tests. They're not sure what the problem is. The good news is that I've got him with the best doctors in New York. They'll figure it out and get him right." Again, the conversation fell into an uncomfortable hole.

"More water?"

"No, I'm fine. I probably should get going." Wilfred Carraway pushed back from the table, stood up and looked around one more time. "Do promise me you'll do something about the furniture."

Jay nodded. "Will do."

Jay followed his father down the five flights of stairs and out onto the Square. Wilfred Carraway paused to look around. "Interesting neighborhood. If I recall my literary history correctly, the author O. Henry lived somewhere near here, around the turn of the century."

"So I've heard. I'll have to do a little research on that," Jay said.

The chauffeur opened the door to the Cadillac and Wilfred Carraway got into the back seat and rolled down the window.

"Not to beat the same drum, but if we do buy a production company, I would sure like you to give some thought to coming home and getting involved."

"I appreciate the offer, Dad. But, right now, I like what I'm doing here in New York. And then there's Joanna. For her, Greenwich is just ..." He stopped. Not the right time or place for that discussion, he decided. "Say hello to Ceci," he said and then, almost as an afterthought, "and to Mother."

"I'll tell her you asked to be remembered," he said rather formally.

Jay read the disappointment on his father's face. The fishing expedition had not been successful. Jay had not even given him a nibble.

"I'd better be off," his father said and rolled up the window as the limousine left Sheridan Square.

23
Sig in Love

"I have some good news, I think," Teddy O'Keefe said as Jay sat down in the editing room. "Got a message from Hillman that the Willys-Overland guys won't be in on Friday. I think they're looking at late next week."

Jay thought for a moment and then said, "Let's take advantage of that. There're some changes I'd like to make and this will give us time to make 'em. Instead of having our guy ending up at work, what if he drives up to a really elegant house? Honks his horn and this gorgeous woman in a pretty summer dress comes out. She gets in the Jeep and they take off across an open field and end up at polo match. The last shot would have them standing in front of the Jeep with the polo players on their horses in the background."

"Sounds great, but have you got time to find a house and I don't think the budget can afford having you stage a polo game."

"Not a problem. I know a house I can use and there's a polo match every Sunday in Greenwich at Conyers Farm."

"Can you get permission to shoot during the game?"

Jay smiled knowingly. "I know somebody who can arrange it for me."

"How you doing on budget?"

"Elliott said we had between five and six thousand and we've spent less than three."

"If you can get Livesey and the actor driving the Jeep back for a day, go for it. I'm sure you can call the agency and get a good-looking woman for no more than scale."

"I think I know where to find one."

For the next hour, Jay made phone calls. The last one was to Joanna. "We'll shoot it at my Dad's house on Sunday and then do a couple of quick shots during the polo match. I've got three hundred dollars in the budget that has to be paid to somebody and I can't think of anyone I'd rather give it to than you."

"Am I going to have to face your mother and Tolova?"

"No. Fortunately, the whole group will be sailing up to Nantucket on Friday. They won't be back until the middle of the week, so only the housekeeper will be there. The house will be ours."

"What do you want me to wear?"

"The dress Ceci gave you. I want a really elegant look."

"You're sure you want me to do this?"

"I'm sure."

***

Elliott was among the missing on Monday. Jay and Teddy were in the editing room, screening the footage Jay had shot on Sunday.

"This is terrific stuff. Looks like we paid a fortune for these set-ups. I love the way you had all the polo players ride up and surround the Jeep to take a closer look."

"I think they were taking a close look at Joanna."

"The actress?"

"Yeah."

"Very nice-looking lady," Teddy said approvingly. "Where'd you find her?"

"She's a friend of mine."

"Good friend?"

"Very good."

"Lucky guy."

"Nathan, Jay! "Elliott's shouts came from the reception area. "I need to see you guys in my office, like now!"

"Sounds like a crisis," Jay said.

"You'd better see what our leader wants."

Jay followed Nathan into Elliott's office.

"We've got a bit of a problem."

"What kind of problem?" Nathan asked.

"I learned that on Friday, my benefactor, Mr. Sig Hillman, was promoted to an even higher level of incompetence. They made him a V.P. and he's in charge of all production."

"So that's good, right?" Jay asked.

"Normally, you'd think so. But it seems the anointment has gone to Mr. Hillman's head. He announced yesterday that he's made an *executive decision* to pull our invoice. He's *decided* to put the package of Willys commercials out for bids and I quote, 'just to make sure I'm getting full value for my client's money.'"

"Bull!" Nathan observed.

"Exactly."

"So what are you going to do?" Jay asked.

A slow, oblique grin spread across Elliott's face. "I've decided the best thing I can do for Mr. Hillman is to show him the misguided nature of his *executive* decision."

"How?"

"Stud, welcome to your graduate course in the commercial film business. I will let you learn by observing when you and

I take Mr. Hillman to dinner tonight. By the way, don't say anything about directing the CJ film. He thinks I'm doing it."

"Aren't you going to tell him Jay did it?" Nathan asked.

He answered Nathan while looking directly at Jay. "At the right time. Tonight, however, is not the right time."

"I suppose it wouldn't do any good for me to ask for an explanation," Jay said.

"No, it wouldn't do any good," Elliott said with a sharpness that took Jay by surprise.

"Are we going to sit down with the books today?" Nathan asked.

"Right now is good for me," he said and then looked back at Jay. "My mentor and spiritual guide here has just served to emphasize the importance of my dinner with Mr. Hillman. Not only do we need that package of commercials to pay the rent, but I've got to write a check for $50,000 for the option on *Grand Prix Racer* or I'm going to lose it."

Nathan frowned. "Elliott, forgive me if I ask the obvious. Based on the budget you gave Hillman, there's very little profit beyond our overhead. If you write a check for $50,000, we're going to be razor thin. I mean, we might as well be doing social work for Willys. Need I remind you, we've got some serious bills to pay? Somehow we need to find an extra thirty grand to get the creditors off our backs. Any suggestions?"

"We'll just have to cut it out of the production budget."

"Cut it out where?"

Elliott ignored Nathan's question. "Best-case scenario: If I get Newman to indicate an interest in *Death of a Gran Prix Racer*, our money problems will be history."

"Elliott," Nathan was pleading. "I think it's time for us to quit playing *let's pretend*. This company can't survive on ifs and maybes."

"Have you heard anything from Paul Newman?" Jay asked.

Elliott shook his head. "No. He's on location and won't be back for a couple more weeks. But if we don't pick up the book option, it won't make any difference." Elliott stared blankly at his desk. Then, like the circus performer who's been shot from a cannon, he bounced out of his chair and began to pace, stabbing the air for emphasis. Any sign of concern for his financial plight had disappeared. "Not to worry guys, I'm going to make this happen. Jay, you're out of here. Nathan, I'm all yours, but please be gentle, will you?"

"Yeah, I'll be gentle like a sledgehammer."

***

Chanticleer restaurant on 49th Street was a bright, French restaurant that featured a long, inviting bar in the front and a cluster of elegantly set tables in the rear. Sig was feeling very good. There was an element of self-assured arrogance in his demeanor. His attitude toward Jay was deprecatory and he was clearly annoyed that Elliott had deigned to burden their dinner with so insignificant a functionary. Almost immediately he began to lace his conversation with barbs and implied threats relating to the award of the commercial package. There was no mistaking that Sig was on a mission. He aimed to make it abundantly clear to Elliott that he deserved a higher level of homage, especially from those whose business and personal survival he held in his hands.

The maitre d' seated them at a table not far from the end of the bar. The first round of drinks arrived. Jay followed Elliott's lead and paid rapt attention to Sig as he explained the import of his new role and how he planned to change the tone and direction of the agency's advertising. He talked at length about bringing a new image and a new look to their commercials. It was obvious to Jay that Sig was fully intent on torturing Elliott with the possibility that 'the Film Arts approach to filmmaking,' as Sig called it, might not meet the clients' expectations—and, not so incidentally, *his* needs. Jay thought if ever a man was working hard to earn points for the "Asshole of the Year" award, Sig was it. He was way out in front of whoever might be in second place.

By the time the waiter brought the second round of drinks, Jay had become aware that they were being watched by a rather stunning young woman sitting at the bar. She was wearing a tight, very low-cut dress that dramatically presented her essential charms. Had not Sig been sitting with his back to her, Jay was certain that she would have instantly become the focus of his attention. He wondered if Elliott had seen her. Almost as if on cue, Elliott interrupted Sig and nodded his head toward the bar with a look that said he'd found something far more interesting than his conversation. Sig turned around to see what had attracted Elliott's attention and nearly spilled his drink. The woman looked directly at Elliott, who smiled and gestured for her to come join them. As she left the bar and walked to their table, each of her body parts seemed intent on upstaging one another in a sensuous way. Her dress, which Jay would have initially described as tight, looked more like skin. She wore her blond hair long and slinky and she had a face that, except for a slightly off-center nose, almost qualified her as beautiful. Whatever anyone might say about her components, any survey conducted among the male diners who watched the traverse from the bar to their table would have confirmed that she was definitely imposing.

Elliott stood up to greet her, "Lisa, long time, no see!" He gave her a peck on the cheek. "Are you in from Chicago?"

"Just arrived."

"How long are you here for?"

"Just a few days."

"You still see much of Hef?"

"Of course. I spend a lot of time at the Mansion."

"I bet some of that time you're even wearing clothes."

Sig was doing his best not to drool on his tie. Jay expected that, at any minute, he'd raise his hand like a student at a lecture asking Elliott to call on him so that he might meet the provocative Lisa.

"Where are you staying?"

"Thinking about paying me a visit are you?"

"Hey, you know me. I always like to make visitors to New York feel welcome."

"Still a one-man welcoming committee, right?

"That's me."

"I'm staying where I always stay. At The Plaza. Playboy always puts me there."

Elliott abruptly turned to Sig, acting as if he had inadvertently forgotten his obligation to introduce his friends. Jay found his seeming embarrassment totally out of character.

"Lisa, I apologize. Here I am jawing away with you and I haven't introduced my guests. This is Mr. Sig Hillman. Sig, this is, Lisa Jones. Lisa works for Playboy in Chicago." Then to Lisa, "Sig here is one of New York's major advertising executives. That's Jay Carraway, who works for me," he said and barely nodded toward Jay.

As far as Lisa was concerned Jay was on another planet.

Sig stood up and took her proffered hand. "It's a pleasure," he said, clearly meaning it. Immediately his eyes dropped to her breasts. From the look on his face, it appeared Sig had just discovered he could see all the way down the front of her dress to her toes.

"What brings you to Chanticleer?" Elliott asked.

"I was supposed to meet a friend here, but I just got a message saying she can't make it."

"Then join us. Do you mind, Sig?"

Sig most certainly did not mind.

The conversation bounced back and forth between Lisa and Elliott and Jay found the content curiously banal and uncertain, like two actors thrown into a part at the last minute who'd had no time to learn their lines.

"So you're in advertising," Lisa said, turning her complete attention to Sig.

"Yes," Sig replied, helping himself to another look at her breasts. "I think you are, too." He laughed.

Lisa laughed as well and turned to Elliott. "Your friend has a sense of humor. I like people who make me laugh." Again, she turned her attention back to Sig. "So tell me," she said, inviting him to impress her, "what does a major New York advertising executive do?"

Sig accepted the invitation and for the next several minutes he described someone that neither Jay nor Elliott had ever met. It was all Jay could do to hold back a smile as Sig painted a picture of himself as a man whose steady hand at the helm of the agency was the difference between the company's financial health and ruin. No matter what he said or how outrageously he stretched reality, Lisa bought every word. Her appreciation for his importance was growing exponentially by the minute.

Sig paused in his self-aggrandizement long enough to complain to Elliott that neither he nor Lisa had been offered another drink. Lisa took the opportunity to say to Elliott, "I knew you had important friends, Elliott, but I didn't know they could be important and so ... " she seemed to be searching for a word and turned back to look at Sig, "attractive and magnetic all at the same time."

I'm going to be sick! Jay thought. *What a line of crap.* Sig was eating it up like a kid turned loose on a bowl of jellybeans. His ego had gained at least ten pounds.

Elliott called for the menus and Lisa insisted that Sig, who had pronounced himself one of New York's unsung gourmets, ordered for her. He did and she responded to each of his recommendations with "Ummmm" and "Yum" and other assorted pleasure-related sounds. *What in the hell is going on here?* Jay wondered. He managed several sideways glimpses of Elliott who gave not the slightest hint as to what he was thinking.

During dinner the conversation stayed focused on Sig, but it was interrupted with an occasional comment from Lisa delivered directly into Sig's ear. Each time, Sig's face would light up like a man who knew that tonight he was going to get lucky.

As they drained the last of the '49 Pommard, a woman wearing a red tutu, a black bustier and fishnet stockings appeared with a camera and said, "What a wonderful looking group!" When she pointed the camera, it was immediately obvious to Jay that she had only Lisa and Sig in her lens. Without prompting Lisa put her arm around Sig and planted a kiss on his cheek as the flash went off. Quickly, the fishnet lady took a second, then a third and fourth. With each picture, Lisa adopted increasingly suggestive poses. For the last one she stood up behind Sig, bending over to provide both the camera and the right side of the restaurant with a full view of her breasts. Lisa was working very hard to create the impression that she was a good deal more to Sig than just arm candy. Finally, the woman turned and took a picture of Elliott and Jay. "Thank you," she said. "Prints are $3.00 and you can order on your way out." With that she disappeared through a door in the back of the restaurant.

Sig's forehead crinkled and he lowered his brow as he leaned over to Elliott. "I think I'd like those pictures *and* the negatives. Can you take care of that?"

"Done." Elliott excused himself from the table. He wasn't gone more than a minute before he returned. "Mission accomplished." Sig's comfort level returned and he resumed his conquest of Miss Lisa Jones.

They all passed on dessert and Elliott announced that he and Jay had to go back to the office to rework their budget on the commercials that Sig was holding hostage. Elliott made a point of asking Sig to be sure that his friend Lisa got home. "I don't think she should be walking around the streets at this hour looking like that."

"Rest assured," Sig replied. "I have full intention of getting Lisa safety back to the Plaza."

With that, Elliott stood up, leaned over, gave Lisa a kiss on the cheek and said, "See you next time."

"See ya," she said, totally ignoring Jay and re-devoting herself to the man of the hour, Mr. Sig Hillman.

As they left the restaurant, Jay could not help but notice a change in Elliott's demeanor. He was clearly buoyed and the familiar bounce and pace of his walk had returned in full. "Well, Stud, what do you think?"

"I think Sig is going to get lucky tonight."

"Wrong. *We* are the ones getting lucky tonight. Although, it's not luck, but the sure and certain knowledge that Sig goes though life dick first. That was probably one of the best $650 investments I've ever made."

"Six-hundred fifty? Jay repeated. "The bill was only $200."

"Plus $150 for the Plaza and $300 for Lisa."

"She was a hooker," Jay said, beginning to realize what had just transpired.

"A very good-looking one, I think you'll agree. About an hour from now, Sig will be having a night to remember. What he won't remember, because he won't have seen it happen, is that his driver's license is going to fall out of his wallet and Lisa will find it after he's gone. Then, at about ten o'clock Monday, pictures of Sig and Lisa enjoying each other's company at Chanticleer will be delivered to our office."

"The lady with the camera in the restaurant—you arranged that too?"

Elliott's smile acknowledged that he had. "About eleven, I will call Sig and tell him I have this wonderful collection of photos, which I'm sure he'd like for his scrapbook. I will also inform him that Lisa found his driver's license, but not to worry, she plans to drop it by his house this afternoon. Of course, if he'd prefer, I can always have her drop it by our office. Just before I hang up, I'll remember to ask him if there's some way we can clear up all the confusion about bidding out that package of commercials."

Jay was speechless and his dismay showed plainly.

Elliott responded to the look on Jay's face and smiled. "So now you know how it's done. If they try to screw you, ya' put their balls in a vise and squeeze until they cough up the business. This is hardball and I can play hardball with the best," he said, his tone exuding victory. "Sig's always been an agency asshole. Only now, with his new responsibility, he's become something even worse: a vindictive agency asshole. After tonight he's going to be the same old compliant Sig who will make every effort to keep his best friend's company solvent."

"But won't he start screaming blackmail?"

"Jay, my boy, give me some credit. I will say nothing that in any way could be misconstrued as coercion. It's what I will leave *unsaid* that will make Sig see the error of his ways."

"Won't he try to get even?"

Elliott laughed. "No, because he thinks of me as a loose cannon. He knows that if I'm pushed, I'm not above lettin' loose with a barrel load of grapeshot. Deep down where it counts—in his pocketbook—Sig's a wimp. Sure, he'll be pissed and he'll call me a lot of names. But he's not going to risk that six-figure salary getting sliced up by some divorce lawyer. Once we have that contract signed sealed and the first payment in the bank, I'll let him off the hook ... maybe," he said, leaving his options open.

"Maybe?"

"I might decide I like having that fish on my line. I gotta admit, I'm going to love making that fucker squirm. Serves the bastard right. Fuck with me, will ya?" he shouted in the direction of the Plaza.

Elliott led the way back to the office. As they stepped into the elevator, he said, "Sig doesn't know it, but after tonight he and I are going to become cousins."

"Cousins? You've slept with Lisa?"

"I always insist on a test drive," he said, laughing. For a brief moment, he almost seemed pensive. "You know, I'm not so sure that I want to be cousins with that slimy bastard. Poor Lisa's going to earn her money tonight."

24
Taxi Talk

"I'm looking at a Mercedes Gullwing, or maybe a Ferrari," Tony Watkins announced to Jay.

Vivian Abato had been given four tickets to *My Fair Lady* and invited Joanna and Jay to accompany her and her new boyfriend, a rich stockbroker from Long Island. After a quick dinner on Christopher Street, they hailed a Checker cab for the ride up town. Jay, Joana and Vivian sat on the back seat and Tony squatted on the small, round chair that folded down from the back of the front seat. As he had during dinner, Tony continued to dominate the conversation.

"Of course, whichever one I buy, it would just be a second car. Wouldn't drive it around the city, of course."

"Those are pretty pricey automobiles," Jay said.

"Of course they are, but in my business you've got to look like you're successful. You know what I mean? And what makes you look more successful than a really upscale car?"

"Do you like being a stockbroker?" Joanna asked.

"Sweetheart, it's a license to steal. You charge your clients if they buy or if they sell. Even if they die, you can make money helping to settle their estates. You make money no matter which way the market is going. My boss gets up after every morning meeting and says, 'Ok, guys, the word for the day is ...?' And everybody shouts, 'Churn!'"

"Churn?" Joanna asked

"Which means convince our customers to … " he searched for a word and then gave up. "We churn their accounts."

"They encourage them to buy or sell—doesn't matter which," Jay explained to Joanna. "In either case, the brokers earn a commission."

"Yeah, exactly," Tony concurred.

"Do you churn your own portfolio?" Jay asked.

"Hell no! I'm holdin' my stocks for the long haul."

"Might that be good advice for your customers?"

"Maybe," he said, laughing, "but it's not good advice for me. I don't make money when clients sit on their stocks. Gotta churn 'em," he said punching the air and laughing.

Vivian clearly sensed the need to change the conversation. "Some news from Ad-Film," Vivian, said turning to Jay and Joanna. "John Baskham has left. He's starting his own production company."

"John told me he was getting close. I guess the accounts he needed came through."

"I'm sure it will be no surprise when I tell you that Marty is mad as hell. He's threatened to sue him if he tries to steal any of his clients."

"From what I heard," Jay said, "that's the way Marty got his start. When he left Fairchild-Reese, he took half the business and the people with him."

The conversation drifted to other news from Ad-Film, leaving Tony unable to contribute. Finally, having been ignored long enough, he broke in with a question to Joanna. "Vivian tells me you're an actress."

"Off and on," Joanna responded

"Off and on what? The casting couch?" His laugh turned the head of the cab driver and Tony only stopped when he realized he was laughing alone.

"Tony, please," Vivian pleaded, then said to Jay and Joanna, "You have to get used to Tony's humor, it's ... "

"Obtuse," Jay volunteered and everyone but Tony laughed.

Tony made an attempt to regain control of the conversation. "And what do you do? I take it you're not on Wall Street?"

"No, 48th Street."

"Yeah? What do you do on 48th Street, panhandle?" He laughed again.

"In a way. I guess you could call it panhandling. We ask people for money anyway."

"You ask people for money?"

"We call it making TV commercials. Actually, it's the commercials that ask for money. Or more accurately, they ask for people to spend money."

"No offense, but I hate commercials."

"A lot of people do," Jay said, "but they pay the rent. And I bet a lot of your clients would not be in a position to have their accounts churned if they weren't making money off those commercials."

"Excuse me, what was your last name again? Cartway?

"Carraway."

"Carraway. You aren't by chance related to the people who own Carraway International are you?"

Jay had no intention of confirming his family relationship to the master churner and was about to say 'no' when Tony answered for him.

"Of course you aren't. If you were, we'd have eaten at Lutece tonight and right now we'd be in your personal limo instead of this beat-up cab."

"Probably," Jay said. "Except there'd only be room for three in my limo, which means one of us," he looked squarely at Tony, "would be walking to the theater."

Once again Vivian sensed the conversation wasn't going well and abruptly changed the subject. "I have a joke. It's a theater joke, which I figure is appropriate for where we're going tonight. Shall I tell it?"

"Vivian really knows how to tell jokes," Joanna said. "Go ahead, Viv."

"Ok. This guy, he wants to be a Shakespearean actor. He's dying to play Hamlet. But he's terrible. Every time he goes to an audition, they all but throw him out because he's so bad. Frustrated, the guy decides that the only way he's ever going to get on stage doing Shakespeare is if he rents a theater and stages the play himself. But that, he knows is going to cost a lot of money. Money he doesn't have. The only way to get the money he needs is to marry a rich woman, which eventually he does. Using her money he rents a Broadway theater and casts himself as Hamlet. Opening night the theater is full and he is just as awful as ever. His speech is affected. His gestures are overdone. Terrible. So he comes to the big speech. 'To beeeeee or not to beeeee,' he shouts, waving his arms. 'That ... is the question.' Well, the audience starts to boo, hiss and throw programs at him. Suddenly, he breaks out of character, turns to the audience, his arms up in protest and says, 'Waaaait a minute! Waaaaaait a minute, I didn't write this shit!'"

Joanna and Jay broke up. "Very good, Vivian," Jay said through a choking laugh.

"I told you she was good," Joanna said, applauding.

They all looked at Tony, who had not joined in but was smiling weakly.

"Tony?" Vivian asked, "You didn't like it?"

"I don't get it. That guy didn't write it. Shakespeare wrote it, didn't he?"

There was stunned silence and then Jay said, "I think maybe you should stick with churning accounts."

***

Later, after a quick post-theater desert at Sardi's, the four said good night. As they left the restaurant, Joanna took Jay's arm and they walked toward Broadway in search of a cab.

"Jay, when Tony asked if you were related to the Carraways, why didn't you tell him?"

"Because if I had, he would have decided to become my new best friend. I learned a long time ago that our family name and bank account can attract all kinds of new best friends, real quick."

"I found Tony really obnoxious."

"Makes you wonder what a nice woman like Vivian sees in that creep?"

"What's to wonder? You know what she sees in him," Joanna said.

"I do?"

"A checkbook. A reasonably good-sized one, I'm told. Money does have a way of helping you overlook a lot of character flaws."

"Is that why you love me?"

"My secret is out. Now please call for your Mercedes or your Ferrari and let's go home."

"How about this yellow limo?" Jay said as he waved down a taxi.

"My kind of guy," she said, grabbing his arm and giving him a quick kiss.

"Sheridan Square," Jay said to the cab driver.

"Jay, what did you think of what Vivian told us about John Baskham?"

"You mean that he's starting his own production company?"

"Yes."

"I think it's great. He's a good guy and I think he'll do well."

"Would you ever consider working for him?"

"Sure. In fact, when I saw him a month or so ago, he talked about leaving Marty Oppenheimer. At the time he said that if things didn't work out at Film Arts he had a job for me."

"Maybe you should take him up on the offer."

"You think so?"

"Why not?"

Jay had actually given the idea of leaving Elliott some thought after watching him set up Sig Hillman with Lisa. He didn't consider himself a prude and he certainly had no love for Hillman, but the whole affair had been like watching the prologue to a pornographic movie. If Elliott was not above blackmail—and that's certainly what it was—what else might he not be above doing? "It's a thought," he said.

"It would make me very happy if you did," she said.

Jay sensed that there was much she was saying that she was not putting into words. Those unspoken words, he believed, began with "Elliott Pierce." He decided to bring him into the conversation. "You'd really like me to walk out on Elliott, wouldn't you?"

"Yes, I would," she said and then changed the subject.

25
'Go, team! Go!'

"Well, the good news," Nathan announced to Jay, "is that we got Hillman's payment for the first third of the production costs. The bad news is that Elliott wrote a fifty-thousand dollar check for the option on the book."

"That really shoots a pretty big hole in the budget."

"More like dynamites it."

Jay spent the afternoon with Nathan going over the budget for the commercials that Hillman had awarded them. Several times they worked through the projected expenses and redid their figures. The bottom line always came out the same: there was no way they could break even, particularly now that Elliott had paid for the option on *Gran Prix Racer.*

Nathan tossed his pencil onto the pile of budget forms and leaned back in his chair. He was strangely sedate, like a man who had finally accepted his trip to the firing squad. "Hillman has really sandbagged Elliott on this budget. Even if Elliott hadn't written that check, there would not be enough money to deliver what's in this contract."

"What do we do now?" Jay asked, realizing that the company was teetering on the edge of financial disaster.

"We lay this in the lap of our leader."

Jay shuffled through the budget pages again, shaking his head. "I don't understand it. Why did Elliott agree to this budget? There's no way anybody could produce these commercials for this kind of money. Even I can see that."

"This is what happens when you pull numbers out of your ass. Which is exactly what he did. Sig tossed him a number, Elliott upped it, Sig agreed to half and the deal was made. Elliott never took the time to look carefully at the storyboards, price out all the production elements and put a real budget together. All he saw was all those zeros and the money he needed for the book."

"He's got no choice, does he? He's going to have to let the option go."

"Are you going to tell him that?"

"I don't think I'll have to. All he has to do is look at these figures. We're talking survival here?"

At six, Elliott returned to the office. He was in a hurry.

"We need to go over these budgets," Jay said as Elliott stopped by Lucy's desk to check for messages.

"We'll do it first thing tomorrow, Stud," he said, then went into his office and closed the door. Minutes later he bolted out into the reception area and hurried toward the front door. He was clearly excited about something. "Folks, what you're about to see is me leaving," he said as he slapped Jay on the back and faked a playful punch at Nathan. "Just found out that I've got a client who needs some serious servicing tonight. Don't wait up!" He laughed and disappeared out the door, leaving Jay and Nathan looking at one another and shaking their heads.

"Someday that guy's pecker is going to drop off," Nathan said. His tolerant disgust had metastasized into a kind of morbid bemusement. It was if he'd decided to hang around on the deck and enjoy the music as the Titanic went down.

***

It was about seven when Jay heard the last of the staff call a "good night." Jay looked at his watch and promised himself he'd only spend another hour before going home. He sat down at Teddy's moviola to look at the final cut of his Jeep film one more time. He was halfway through when he thought he heard the door from the elevator lobby open and close. The voice was tentative: "Elliott?"

It sounded like Sherry Pierce.

Louder this time. "Elliott?"

Jay left the editing room and went into the reception area.

"Oh, hi, Jay," Sherry said. She appeared to have just come from a party. Jay could see she that she was having a bit of problem remaining steady on her feet.

"Is Elliott here?" Her speech was slightly slurred.

"Ahh ... " Jay said and hesitated.

Sherry continued. "We were supposed to meet at seven in the Palm Court at the Plaza. It's my birthday and he's taking me to Cote Basque."

Jay felt flushed and was sure his face had turned red. He had no idea why he was taking it upon himself to feel embarrassed for Elliott.

"Have you seen him?"

"He was here earlier," Jay said, "but he went out."

"Did he say where he was going?"

"I think he said something about seeing a client."

Sherry's expression evolved from expectation to disappointment to resignation. "He gets so busy sometimes, he forgets things. I guess he forgot I was coming in."

"Well," Jay said fumbling, "maybe he'll be back. I'm sure he wouldn't forget your birthday. If you'd like to sit down and wait, I'll make some calls and see if I can find him." Already Jay was thinking about calling the Elysee Hotel, which was where he stayed on those nights when he chose to stay in town and "service his accounts."

Sherry sank heavily into a chair and stared blankly at the wall that displayed Elliott's production pictures.

Jay put in a call to the Elysee and found that he was not registered. "I'm sure he'll be back soon," Jay said, trying to comfort her with what he knew to be an out-and-out lie. *What a rotten bastard! He's out porking some broad on his wife's birthday,* Jay said to himself in utter disgust.

"Can I get you some coffee or a soda?" he asked, more out of desperation to break the silence than because he thought she'd want something to drink.

"No, no I'm fine. Thank you for asking."

This is awful, he thought. *What am I going to do?*

More silence. Lots of it. And then from deep within the haze left by too many martinis, she said, "Things aren't like they used to be between us. I think it's the pressure he's under."

Listen to her, he thought. *She's making excuses for him.*

"He works so hard and to have to deal with people like that Hillman person every day. It wears on a man." Then from nowhere, "Do you have a girlfriend, Jay?"

"Yes, I do."

"That's nice. It's fun to be in love."

"Ahh, yeah," he responded wondering where this was going.

"Did you ever play football, Jay?"

"No, it wasn't my sport."

"Elliott did. He was a halfback. Set all the records at our high school. That's where we met and began dating. Even then being in love with him was exhausting. He was a whirlwind. Flowers, presents, surprises, we couldn't get enough of each other. We were married our senior year in college and were so in love those first few years. Then somewhere along the way, I don't know when, everything changed. I sometimes wonder if he loves me anymore."

Jay was growing increasingly uncomfortable as she began to talk more openly and frankly about her marriage. He really didn't want to hear all this.

"We used to touch a lot. Not just sex. We touched in a way that always made me feel that there was a special connection between us. But that doesn't happen anymore. We used to talk about us, our lives and his dreams. Sometimes we'd talk all night. Now, it's just bills and kids and ... well, it's never about us. His life has just become too complicated." She tried to hide her embarrassment behind a thin, disconsolate smile. "Listen to me go on. I sound like I'm talking to a therapist. It must be too many ... " Her voice drifted off. Clearly, the alcohol was taking control.

Sherry slipped back into her soliloquy, but it was like the futility of struggling against the certainty of drowning. Her account of the slow dissolution of the love in their marriage served only to hasten the submergence of her spirit. Jay found himself wondering what he could do or say to comfort the little cheerleader who, as she sat listlessly in front of him, looked to be a long, long way from her last "Go, team! Go!"

"Jay?" Her voice was faint, almost a whisper, making its way past the welling tears. "Would you mind holding me, just for a little?" She stood up and walked toward him.

"I ... ah ... Mrs. Pierce. I don't know what to say," Jay said as he stood up. Was there any way he could gracefully to extricate himself from the room without appearing to reject her? She was on an emotional edge and he did not want to do anything that might topple her.

Without looking at him, she laid her head on his chest and put her arms around him. "Hold me just for a little while," she said. Jay felt helpless as she pressed herself into him, his arms suspended in space. Reluctantly, he put them around her while hoping that Elliott wouldn't suddenly bounce into the office. That was all he'd need to make this a night to remember. After what seemed like several minutes, though in retrospect he decided it was more a matter of seconds, she pulled away. She looked up and him and said, "If you can, try to always love that girl of yours. It hurts so much when it stops."

Sherry turned her back on Jay, paused to pick up her handbag and then doing her best to balance herself like a tightrope walker, made her way slowly to the office door. She opened it looking around the office as if undecided as to what she should do next. "Thank you, Jay," she said, in the same tone she might have used with someone who had just delivered groceries. Then she left.

Jay slumped into a chair. When he was sure that he heard the elevator doors open and close, he began to ponder which was greater: the acrid disgust he felt toward Elliott, or the pity he felt for Sherry Pierce.

26
The Audition

"My name is George Kukoris." The man in the sweater and black pants was speaking to nearly fifty people seated in the small theater on West 18th Street. "I have been asked by the producers to take over the direction of *Girl Crazy* from Peter Potter for a variety of reasons, which I don't think I need to discuss at this time. We'll be auditioning the singing parts first and we'll simply go in the order of the signup sheet."

"OK, Number One, Gail Thorpe."

Kukoris found a seat next to several people whom Jay later identified as the producers of the show.

"What number are you?" Jay whispered to Joanna.

"Eighteen."

After Jay had listened to several of the women, he turned to Joanna and said, "When they hear you sing, this isn't going to be a contest."

"I appreciate the vote of confidence."

"I mean it. You're going to knock their socks off."

Jay watched as several more women came out onstage and sang a few bars of *Embraceable You*. By the time it was Joanna's turn, only three of the actresses had been asked by Kukoris to stay. Most never got past the first chorus before a voice said, "Thank you Miss," and cut them off.

"I'm Joanna Olenska," Joanna announced to the shadowy forms seated in the seats in front of her in the darkened theater.

"Is that your stage name?"

"I usually go by Joanna Olen," she said.

"Ok, anytime you're ready."

Joanna turned her back to the audience for a moment and then nodded to the piano player, indicating she was ready. As the piano player began, Joanna turned and began to sing: "Embrace me, my sweet embraceable you ..."

Jay assumed that, as with the other singers, Kukoris would interrupt, indicating he'd heard enough to give him a good idea of her voice. He was both surprised and pleased that no one said a word until she had completed the entire song.

"Mr. Gershwin would have been very happy to hear that," Kukoris said. "Very nice. Please have a seat; we'll want you to show us a few dance steps."

When she returned from the stage and slid in next to Jay, he said, "What did I tell you? You not only knocked their socks off, but their shorts as well."

"I couldn't believe it when he didn't stop me. I almost forgot the words."

"I gotta tell ya, you do look absolutely fantastic up there. I don't see how they can cast anyone else."

It was almost an hour before they called up the six women they'd asked to stay.

"Ok, ladies," Billy Burson, the choreographer, said. "We're not going to do anything fancy. All we need is to see how you move. Ok, hit it," he said to the piano player. Burson showed the women the steps and then had them follow him as he moved back and forth across the stage. They all showed they knew how to dance, but in Jay's eyes, only Joanna seemed to flow with the music.

"Jimmy," Kukoris said to the piano player, "I'd like to hear them do *But Not For Me.*"

The remaining women were called out, one at a time, to sing the second song. Joanna was last. Once again, the director let her complete the song.

"Wonderful, Joanna. Mary Martin couldn't have done it better. Could you wait a minute?" he asked. Then he appeared to go into a huddle with his assistants and the producers.

Jay could not make out their faces, but from their gestures and the low, earnest tone of their voices, he felt sure that they were seriously considering Joanna for the part. *She's going to get it,* he thought. *No way they won't give it to her.* Jay felt confident in his assessment. *Nobody on that stage is anywhere near as good. A couple are OK, but they look like kids. Finally, she's going to have something good happen for her in this business.*

Kukoris' conversation with his associates and producers became more animated and it appeared that the group could not come to an agreement. Finally, he broke away from the meeting and turned to the stage. "Joanna, speaking for myself, I have to tell you that you have a terrific voice. Best we've heard today. I really like the way you handle those songs. And when it comes to your dancing – great. No one looked better."

Jay's stomach felt like he swallowed a bowling ball. He could feel a *'but'* coming. And not a good one. He didn't have to wait long.

"But, in talking with my producers we've decided that you're not quite right for the part. We'd like a younger look. Sort of a twenty-year-old Judy Garland type. So, thank you for coming in. Maybe another time. We'll certainly keep your name on file."

"I can play younger," she protested. "I can do my hair differently to give you a Judy Garland look."

"We discussed that. But you just don't look twenty. Which is not a bad thing, mind you. Except when it comes to this part. I'm sorry."

Jay could see Joanna absorb the rejection like a fighter taking a sucker punch. Her head dropped and her body slumped as she turned and walked off the stage.

***

Jay waited for her at the entrance to the theater, knowing that she would need help to repair the ravages inflicted by the audition. As Joanna approached, he noticed she had pasted a thin smile on her face as if to mask the pain. "Well, that's a new one to add to my list of rejections." She shrugged under the weight of her disappointment." Nothing like being told you sing great, dance great, but are too old. At thirty I'm over the hill. I can't tell you how much this hurts. I don't know, maybe it's time for me to get real. It's never going to happen for me."

"Don't say that," Jay said. "It was obvious that the Kukoris was really impressed."

"Then why didn't I get the part?"

"Because you just don't look like a teenager or whatever Judy Garland looked like when she made the movie. And for what it's worth, on her best day, Judy Garland never looked half as good as you do."

"So what good does that do me? I would probably have had a better chance if I looked like Mickey Rooney."

Jay could not help but laugh. "No, somehow I don't think that would have helped."

As they walked across 9th Avenue, she suddenly realized they were going the wrong direction. "Where are we going?"

"This will just take a minute. There's a studio in the next block where Elliott's shooting a Bromo Seltzer commercial. I've got to drop off the pay vouchers for the crew. I'll be in and out real quick. Promise."

"You won't mind if I don't' go in," Joanna said. It was not a question, but a statement. "Seeing that S.O.B. would just about do it for me today."

The front of the building that housed the soundstage took up half the block. The entrance was at the far end of the building, well to the left of a loading dock. "I'll wait here," she said, stopping by the loading area. "Who knows? Maybe someone will offer me a job as a truck driver."

"If someone does, promise me you'll say 'no,'" Jay said running off toward the main entrance to the stage.

Jay walked into the studio and saw Nathan parked at a table, working on the time sheets. "How'd it go?" he asked, handing him the pay vouchers.

"Fine, I guess. We just wrapped. Simple shoot. No big deal. No big money either, but it should pay the rent this month. Or some of it, anyway," Nathan said gloomily.

"Where's Elliott?" Jay asked, looking around the studio.

"He just left," Nathan said. "You must have passed him on the way in."

"No, didn't see him."

"Then he must have gone out through the loading dock."

Past Joanna? Not good, he thought. Jay hurried toward the loading dock exit and stepped onto the sidewalk. Up the street a short way, he saw Elliott talking to Joanna. It was obviously a one-sided conversation. He talked while she did her best to ignore him. Each time she turned her back or tried to move away, Elliott quickly moved to block her, like a jungle animal teasing its prey.

"Joanna!" Jay called as he ran toward her.

Elliott turned sharply when he heard Jay's voice and his expression showed that he was clearly surprised to see Jay running toward him. "Hey, Stud." Elliott said. "What's up?"

"They need you inside," was all Jay could think to say.

"Let's go, Jay," Joanna said, hooking her arm in his.

"Don't tell me you know this guy?" Elliott's tone was both amused and dismissive at the same time.

"Yes, I know him," she answered, her voice full of animus. "I'm only sorry he knows you." She turned away and began pulling on Jay's arm. "Come on. Let's get out of here."

Elliott grinned, seeming to take a perverse pleasure in the unpleasant encounter. "Joanna, don't be a stranger. Give me a call so we can catch up," he said cheerily as they hurried away.

"There's a taxi," she said, flagging it down.

Jay opened the door and she slid in.

"I hate that son-of-a-bitch!" she said.

"Sheridan Square," Jay said to the cab driver. He turned to Joanna and said, in a tone that promised understanding, "OK, I think it's time you told me what's the deal between you and Elliott. I know you don't like him. A lot of people don't like him. But I have the feeling that it's more than just his reputation that's bothering you. I'd like to know what it is."

She turned away, staring out the window. She was obviously upset and when it seemed that she was not ready to tell him, he decided not to press her. He didn't have to.

"Back when we worked at the same agency, there was this girl, Julie. We were very close. We both got jobs in the steno and typing pool. Whenever some manager or producer needed to dictate a letter or a report, one of girls in the pool—there were about twenty of us—was sent up to the man's office. That's how Elliott met Julie. She'd been called up to take dictation, but he hardly got past 'Dear So and So' before he started coming on to her. He was very smooth. Pushed all the right buttons. Like me, she'd never had anybody like Elliott pay attention to her."

"They started to date. He took her on trips and found ways to write it all off on the company. He convinced her not to say anything about their relationship to anyone because the agency, he claimed, didn't permit employees to be married, or even to date. It was a lie, of course, but she was too dumb to check it out. I was the only one who knew what was going on."

"It went on for six or seven months. She was absolutely convinced they were going to get married. He talked about it all the time. When she tried to press him for a date, he always had some excuse for putting it off. She was gullible and naive enough to believe him. When some of the girls in the typing pool found out about their relationship, they tried to warn her. They tried to tell her that she was just one in a long line of girls he'd led on. But she wouldn't listen. Then one day, she discovered a small problem. He'd somehow forgotten to tell her that he was married and that his wife was six months pregnant."

"I had a feeling that was coming," Jay said

"Well, she didn't. She was too blind, too stupid, too ... too trusting. Maybe sucker is a better word. Aside from being a bastard, he was a very convincing liar."

"I'm afraid he still is."

For the first time since she'd begun to tell the story, she turned and looked at him. It seemed to him that her eyes pleaded for understanding—he was not sure why. Knowing Elliott as he did, there was no need to ask for understanding. "To think, he was talking marriage to my friend while his wife was pregnant. Could any scum be lower than that?"

"Well, from what I've seen of him, he's found a way to get lower."

"That doesn't surprise me."

"What happened to Julie?"

Joanna took a deep breath. "She thought long and hard about committing suicide. I like to think I talked her out of it. Jay, Elliott Pierce nearly destroyed that girl. If she'd gone through with it, he would have been responsible for her death, as much as if he'd killed her himself. It took a long time for Julie to get over what had happened. People tried to help her, but she didn't want help. She quit the job. There was no way could she face all those women who'd tried to warn mer. Within a week, she had moved out of her apartment. Then, the Julie I knew just disappeared."

"Disappeared?"

"Vanished."

"What do you mean, vanished?"

"I mean the girl that I knew was no more. And that's why I hate Elliott Pierce. End of story."

"Two fifty," the cab driver said.

Joanna was out of the cab and walking toward their apartment while Jay was still fishing in his pocket for the fare. He gave the driver three dollars. "Keep the change." Jay caught up with Joanna as she was opening the front door of the building. "It's almost six. You want to have an early dinner?"

"I'm not hungry," she said. "This has not been a great day for me."

"I know, I understand," he said, "but ... "

She cut him off sharply, "No you don't! You don't understand anything. You don't know what it's like to want something so badly ... so badly that you believe, really believe, you can reach out and touch it. Then, just as you're about to grab it, it's snatched away, like someone teasing a hungry dog with a bone they won't let go of."

"Well, maybe I don't know what it feels like to go through what you did today, but I'm not so insensitive that I can't appreciate how you feel. There are lumps in my business as well."

Joanna pushed open the door and started up the stairs. "Jay, you don't know from lumps," she said bitterly. "For you, it's just ... just pretend. You think you're living the life of a struggling artist, but you're only kidding yourself. It's just a charade. If you really want to play the part, try living on a box of Cheerios for a couple of days while you're waiting for a check to arrive from some producer who's holding onto your money for a couple extra days of interest. Sit in a temp office praying they'll call your name and give you an assignment that pays by the day so you can get the electricity turned back on. Come home some night and meet the landlord at your door saying you've got five days to pay or you'll have to go. I don't know, Jay. We're from two different worlds. You're a rich romantic playing at being a bohemian, like those actors in La Bohème. I'm not playing." She started to cry. "I wanted that part so much. I was right for it. I know I was."

Nothing was said as they climbed to the third floor. In his desperation to try to give her some ray of hope, Jay realized that he had a solution. It was a wild idea, but one that he knew he could make happen. "I have an idea," he said as she made the turn toward the stairs leading to the fourth floor.

"I'm not in the market for ideas right now," she said sharply.

"Please, Joanna, hear me out." She stopped, appearing ready to listen, if not to look at him. "First, let's agree that you're a very good singer and you belong in a show—a good show. Second, I'm convinced, as I know you must be, that if you could get a show—an off-Broadway show, even—and if the right people saw it, that could change everything for you."

"Great," she said sarcastically as she turned to look at him on the steps below. "Know anyone who wants to put me in their show?"

"How about me?"

"What? What are you talking about?"

"What's it take to produce a musical off -Broadway? Twenty thousand dollars, thirty?"

"What are you suggesting?"

"You pick a musical. A revival. Maybe one of Cole Porter's. Then we'll find a producer and a director you like and I'll put up the money."

"Where would you get all that money? From Daddy?"

"Essentially, yes. My brother would do it for me. I know he would. Look, you're good. Really good. All you need is a break, an opportunity for people to see you. That's all it would take."

247

Her laugh was not one of joy, but of derision. "Then people could think of me like the guy in Vivian's story who wanted to play Hamlet. Can you imagine what everyone would say: 'She was not good enough to get a part the normal way, so she conned Mr. Carraway into putting up a fortune so she could star in a musical.' What would that say about me?" She shook her head and started for her door. "Maybe this—whatever it is that we think we have—is all wrong. Maybe we should just call it quits before one of us really gets hurt."

Jay felt like a man who had just been swept over a waterfall into a deep gorge and was fighting to come up for air. What should he say? What could he say that wouldn't sound defensive or pandering? He had no choice but to tell her how he felt. "Joanna, I never thought of myself as playing at this. Sure, I know if everything were to go to hell in hand basket, I could go home, I could work for my father. What you don't understand is that no one in my family ... no one has ever expected very much of me. Up to this point in my life, I haven't disappointed them. I'm doing what I'm doing because it's the only way I'll ever prove to myself that I can do something without having to depend on my father's bank account. A lot of people would say I'm crazy. Why not take the easy way? Have your Dad buy you an entire Hollywood movie studio. He's ready to do that for me. But what would I have to be proud of? What could I point to that I did on my own?"

"Now you know why I don't want you to produce a musical for me. I want to be proud of something I've done, too. I don't know, Jay. I don't know about anything anymore."

"I know one thing. Maybe you don't feel it's much. But I know that I love you and that I want to spend the rest of my life with you. Beyond that, nothing else really matters to me."

For a moment, she said nothing. "I need to be alone," she said, opening her door. "Just alone."

She closed the door, leaving Jay in the silent hallway.

***

Around midnight, he heard a rapping at his door. As he slid out of bed, he noticed that it was very dark. Extremely dark. He looked out the window. All the lights of the city were out. Power outage. Again the rapping, He opened the door. Joanna was standing there holding a candle. She blew it out. My candle has gone out."

"Let me light it for you," he said, taking her in his arms.

"I love you, Jay. I was terrible tonight, a royal bitch. Forgive me. I didn't mean any of what I said. I was so hurt by the audition and then meeting Elliott ... I took it out on you."

"The offer to produce a musical for you still stands."

"No, no. You're sweet to offer, but I don't want you to do that. If it never happens for me, then ... well, then it doesn't."

"Stay with me tonight."

"Every night, if you want."

"Forever." He took her hand and led her to his bed. He removed her nightgown. As he laid her down gently on the bed, it seemed to him that the moon had become a brush, painting her body in an opalescent azure light. He lay down next to her and drew himself close. Their mouths met, their bodies came together slowly, deliberately, as the softness of the night carried them off to Elysian Fields.

27
Dodging Bullets

"George Kukoris has recommended me and another singer for a job in Boston, at a convention!" Joanna was almost giddy. "We're to be the entertainment. We have one day rehearsing with the band, then we perform the next night and come back home the following day. It pays $400 plus expenses."

"Joanna, I think this is great," Jay said. "The fact that Kukoris liked you and that he's recommended you for this job … well, who knows where it could lead?"

"And something else—he said he'd set me up with an audition in September for a new musical that he thought had a part that I'd be perfect for."

"The audition is not until September?"

"The 15th."

"Well, let's mark it down. You know, not getting a part in *Girl Crazy* might turn out to be a break in disguise. At least now you've got the attention of a legitimate director, one who knows what you can do and is obviously impressed."

The phone rang and Jay picked it up. "Hello, this is Jay."

"It's Scott and it's not good news. Not good news at all," his father said. His voice was heavy and dark.

"Where is he?"

"In Greenwich Hospital."

***

"I feel like an angel just walked in," Scott said as Jay and Joanna entered his hospital room. "Not you Jay, her," he said, nodding toward Joanna and smiling. "I'd get up," he said, clearly in jest, "but they have me pretty well strapped down with these tubes. I feel I've been attacked by a porcupine with all these needles they've got stuck in me."

"I understand they have you on chemotherapy," Jay said.

"That's new, isn't it?" Joanna asked

"Suppose to kill the cancer, but it's making me sicker than a dog."

"If it works, then it will be worth it."

"Yeah, I guess, if it works. However, I'm not sure the cancer knows it's supposed to die before I do. But hey, I'm ready to go as many rounds with this thing as it takes to knock it out."

"Well, you've got the right attitude, anyway," Jay said.

"One of the fringe benefits of the airborne is, you learn that if you don't laugh at the prospect of dying, you can go nuts. After they dropped me into France on D-Day, I made it across France, Belgium—with an extended stay at the Battle of the Bulge—and then fought all the way in to the Ruhr Valley in Germany. There were only two other buddies of mine from Charlie Company that made it all the way. I should have died a hundred times, but I didn't. What that says to me is that, if I can dodge a million Kraut bullets, I can dodge this one."

"Just don't forget to duck," Jay said. "I know you're not the kind of guy to let something like this beat you."

Scott smiled weakly. "Not without a fight, anyway. But I'm not going to fight it here in this hospital. I've made arrangements for them to take me home tomorrow."

"What about all this stuff? These tubes and things?"

"Takin' everything with me, plus a couple nurses. I told Dad that if the hospital gave him any guff, to buy the place and move it all into my bedroom. Hey, can you guys stay a bit? The nurse won't be in to throw you out for at least another ten minutes."

"Sure, as long as you want us," Jay said.

"Sorry, there's only one chair," Scott said, pointing to the lone chair on the other side of the room. "Jay, you can sit on the end of my bed as long as you're careful and don't detach me from all this spaghetti."

Joanna retreated to the other side of the room and Jay eased himself onto the foot of the bed.

"I want to get serious for a few minutes, OK?"

"Sure," Jay answered.

"If all this nonsense doesn't work—and I'm not saying that it won't, because I believe it will—I'm going to need your help with Dad. He's not taking this well and if I should 'buy the farm,' it's going to hit him pretty hard. I know he'd feel the same way if it was you in this bed. He doesn't always show a lot of fatherly love, but he really loves the three of us. And then there's the company. You know, of course, that you'll get a lot of pressure to take over for me."

"I know. In some respects, it's already started. Can't break that chain of all those generations of Carraways running the company," Jay said, echoing a family refrain.

"Mother's going to be on Dad like rain to try and force him to make you come home. If she was the only consideration and I thought I wasn't going to make it, I'd sell everything we own tomorrow, send her to Palm Beach and say to hell with being one of the oldest family-owned companies in America. After we're all dead, who the hell is going to care who owns the company? With the proceeds, there'd be enough money to take care of the next five generations. They could all become worthless playboys—or go into the film business." Scott started to laugh. "Oooo. Can't do that. Hurts like hell when I laugh."

"You make with the humor and I'll do the laughing," Jay said, grinning.

"Seriously, what I want you to understand is this: We aren't royalty. This is not England. We're not handing a crown from one generation to the next. You do what you believe is best for Jay Carraway. All I really want you to do for me ... and for you and Ceci ... is to protect Dad from Mother. You don't see it as much as I do, because you've flown the coop, but she's really been tough on him. And you know Dad; when it comes to Mother, he won't fight back."

"What's her problem? What's she getting on him about?"

"Who knows? Little things, big things, anything. Nothing is ever right with her. I swear, I think she suffers from terminal menopause."

"At her age?"

"With her it's not the physical kind, it's mental menopause. Bottom line, what I'm asking is that you do whatever you can to help him. Help him get over me and give him all the reasons you can think of to let him spend time away from our mother."

"I think maybe it's best that you get well. I really don't want to have to deal with Mother."

"What is it the Bible says? 'For everything there is a season.' This may be your season with Mama."

"Get better, big brother. That's an order."

"Time's up," the voice of the nurse preceded her through the door. "We have to make Mr. Carraway comfy now."

"What she means is, she has to give me the bed pan and change the thing sticking in my you-know-what. Believe me, that catheter is worse than the cancer."

"I'll be back tomorrow," Jay said as he stood up.

"Joanna, I'm sorry I didn't talk more to you. I'd really prefer to look at you than this mug. Please come back. If you have to bring Jay ... well, I guess you have to bring him."

"Whatever you say. Please get better, OK? I'll say a prayer," she said.

"Can't hurt. Take care, kids," he said and then gave himself over to the nurse.

As they walked toward the elevator, Joanna took out a handkerchief and dabbed at her eyes. "He will make it, won't he?"

"He's a fighter. If anybody can, he can."

"After all he went through in the war, it doesn't seem fair that he might go this way."

"A lot's not fair."

28
Cousins

"I'm not going to be embarrassed by this, am I?" Elliott asked as they waited for Hillman and his clients from Willys-Overland.

"Embarrassed? Elliott, you're going to be knocked over!" Teddy O'Keefe, the editor, said. "Jay's little film is one of the best things I've ever seen come out of here. It really works. I haven't had as much fun editing anything in a long time."

Elliott recoiled slightly, as though Teddy had just slapped him in the face. His expression went cold and flat. Jay was sure Teddy had no intention of demeaning Elliott's talent—he loved the guy—but that was the way it had sounded. Had there not been a client to please, Elliott might have felt compelled to defend himself. Instead, he just asked for reassurance. "I've got your word that Sig and the guys from Willys are going to love it?"

"Hey, if Sig doesn't kiss your behind when he sees this, he's a bigger jerk than I thought he was," Teddy said.

Jay had begun to feel uncomfortable in the shower of Teddy's enthusiastic endorsement. The student, he knew, is not supposed to upstage the teacher.

Elliott turned to Jay. "What did this epic of yours cost us?"

"We actually made money. Not much, but we came in under budget."

"You could be starting a bad precedent," Elliott said with a strained smile.

The intercom buzzed and Jay picked it up.

"They're here," Lucy said.

Elliott got up and led the way to the screening room, where he greeted Sig and three executives from Willys-Overland with his normal, infectious enthusiasm. Sig introduced Wally Stubbs as the new V.P. of advertising for Willys. It was clear from the way the other two functionaries deferred to Wally that his weight was carried in more ways than just around his middle.

"Have we got a great film, Elliott?" Sig asked, looking for Elliott to make some commitment that he could use to hang him, should it turn out to be a disaster.

"You're going to love it," Elliott said with conviction.

The film began with the man in the suit coming out of his house and getting into the CJ5. The music was pretty, but without any excitement. The film cut to the Jeep in a traffic jam and the look on the man's face indicated that he'd decided to leave the highway. The sound track exploded and the screen became a blur of images. The shots were quick, dramatic and fast paced. The CJ was tearing through a woods. Then it crossed a deserted sandy beach and screamed along the water's edge, sending up a fishtail of spray. Then a hard cut to the Jeep screaming down a hill, like a skier on green snow, leaping off a small bank, landing on all fours in a stream and sending a wave of water—in slow motion—high in the air, momentarily obliterating the Jeep.

Slam cut to the Jeep pulling up and braking in front of the Carraway house. The front door to the house opened and the camera cut to Joanna. A full shot at first that zoomed into a close-up of her face as she looked at the Jeep like a woman about to seduce her lover. Smash cut to the man and Joanna in the Jeep, taking off across an open field. Then suddenly, the Jeep was on the sidelines at the polo match. No sooner had Joanna stepped out of the CJ than she and the Jeep were surrounded by the polo players on their horses. It was not clear which they were more enamored of, the Jeep or Joanna. Just before the scene faded to black. The deep, resonant voice of Alexander Scorby was heard to say: "Jeep. Who needs roads?" The Willys logo appeared, accompanied by a musical sting.

The screen went dark and there was silence. All eyes went to the Wally Stubbs. Sig Hillman's head seemed loosely attached to his neck as he waited for the results. He reminded Jay of a bobble-head doll.

Finally, Stubbs said enthusiastically, "That was great! Just great! The dealers are going to come out of their seats when they see this."

Now the others felt comfortable adding their comments. "Elliott, that was goddamn brilliant," the second Willys functionary said.

"Who the hell was that model?" Sig asked. "Never seen her before."

"Jay, was that Joanna Olenska?" Elliott whispered the question in Jay's ear.

"Yes," he said, wondering now why he'd exposed her to Elliott. *Dumb move*, he silently admonished himself.

Elliott decided to answer Hillman's question. "She's just a model we use from time to time."

"Use? Knowing you, I'm sure that you *use* her from time to time." He laughed. "Bring her in for a casting session. I might want to *use* her for something."

"*Something* is right," said one of Sig's assistants, laughing.

It was all Jay could do to restrain himself.

"Elliott," Wally Stubbs said, "I love this film. I hate to say it, Sig, but it's better than any of the commercials you guys have done for us in the past. I know this film is too long for a sixty-second spot, but maybe we can cut it down."

As they discussed how they might edit the film for a commercial, the kudos for the concept continued to punctuate the conversation.

Jay waited for Elliott to acknowledge him as the director. It was clear that everyone assumed Elliott had made the film and he said nothing to disabuse them of that impression.

"It's not easy to come up with something like that in the little time you gave us," Elliott said. "But creating film miracles is what we're all about. However, I have to warn you: Don't get the idea that you can always get this kind of work for the miserable little budget you gave us. We did this as a favor, because I know you're going to continue to give us your commercials."

"Let's put it this way," Sig said. "We're going to continue to keep you as one of the top three companies on our list of selected production companies."

"That's great," Elliott said with barely disguised sarcasm. "And I'll keep you as one of the top three studs on Lisa's list."

"Who's Lisa?" Stubbs asked.

"Private joke." Sig gave Elliott a hard look. It was obvious he was not going to say anything to Elliott—at least not here and now.

"Could we run the film again?" Wally Stubbs asked.

"Racked and ready to go," Elliott said.

The film was shown again and the three men from Willys-Overland continued to express how pleased they were. When it was over, Wally turned to Elliott and said, "I love the tag line, *Jeep—Who needs roads?*" Wally turned to Hillman, "Sig, we ought to use that line in some of our print ads."

"Be our guest." Elliott said. "Of course, we'd like to be compensated if you do use it."

Sig was not pleased with Wally's suggestion or Elliott's response. "Well, we'll have to look at it in the context of the ads we're working on. I'm not sure that it fits with our strategy."

"The hell with context. Just make it fit," Wally said, showing he did not intend to mince words with Sig. "I like it and I want to use it."

Sig immediately did a one-eighty and said, "I like it too, I was just saying we'll have to rework our ads to make it fit. I'm sure we can do that. No problem."

"Knew you'd see it my way," Wally said.

Jay's attention during the back-and-forth between Stubbs and Hillman was riveted on Elliott. It looked to him as if Elliott had morphed into a predatory animal and was getting ready to spring. He was right.

"Oh, one minor bit of business, Sig. Because of the time frame and because of all the extra production value we put into the film —the rental of that house, paying off the polo people to cooperate —we went over budget.

"How much?" Sig asked warily.

"Not much, eight grand or so."

Sig was about to protest when Wally Stubbs said, "Hell, it was worth that and more. A lot more."

Elliott laughed and clapped Wally on the back. "Hey, if that's the case, then I'll bill Sig for ten."

"Whatever," Wally said. Then turning to Sig, "You'll take care of my man, here, won't you?" Wally put his arm around Elliott. "You guys can take it out of all the money I give your agency. Too much, if you ask me." He laughed a deep, throaty laugh interspersed with coughs, typical of a heavy smoker. Elliott immediately joined in, knowing full well that it's never a good idea to let the client laugh alone

"I think maybe we'd better get out of here," Sig said, nudging Wally toward the door, "before our friend here starts asking for our wallets."

Wally Stubbs laughed again, harder, until a wracking cough replaced the laugh. "Got to do something about that cough," he said, leaving the room.

"We'll talk about the budget," Sig said.

Jay could see that Sig didn't like being squeezed and he was doing his best to deliver that fact to Elliott via the tone of his voice.

"Yeah, let's talk," Elliott said as he followed him out of the projection room. "Over dinner tonight. Maybe Lisa can join us."

So Elliott was not going to let him off the hook. Jay wasn't surprised.

***

Jay stood in the reception area, totally deflated. Elliott had not given him credit for the film in front of the clients, nor had he even thanked him.

"Elllllyet!" Lucy bellowed from the reception area. "Call on two!"

Elliott immediately went into his office and Jay went into the editing room to report to Teddy.

"Verdict?" Teddy asked.

"They loved it," he said without enthusiasm

"You don't sound very enthusiastic."

"I'm sorry. Write it off to my ego," he said, struggling to climb out of the disappointing trench Elliott had left him in. "I was hoping Elliott would tell them that I'd directed the film and that you'd done your usual magic on the moviola. Not a word."

"Well, at least you know that it was your baby. As you heard me say to Elliott, this is one of best pieces of work that's come out of here in a long, long time. He's an idiot if he doesn't give you credit for it. Hell, he should be able to sell you all over town for jobs like this."

"I appreciate the compliment, "Jay said, clapping the editor on the back. "We'll see what happens."

***

It wasn't until four in the afternoon that Elliott called Jay into his office. "About this morning," he said. "I'm not happy, Stud."

"About what?"

"About the film.

"What are you talking about? They loved it."

"Yeah, but sometimes when you give a client more than they paid for, they get the idea that they can squeeze you on every budget and still get great work. I'm going to have to disabuse them of that idea."

"Can I ask you a question?" Jay did not wait for a response. "What would have been wrong with telling them I made the film?"

Elliott leaned back in his chair and swiveled around so that he could look out the window at the building on the other side of 48th Street. "Look, Stud, keep in mind that every foot of film that comes out of this shop is by Elliott Pierce. Comprende? My name is on the door. I'm the guy they pay for."

"Would my film have been an Elliott Piece production if it had been a disaster?"

"It would never have been a disaster. I know Livesey, I know how he shoots and I know he would never let you make him shoot crap. Plus, I know that Teddy can save just about anything—even crappy footage."

Jay was not about to let it drop. "But for argument's sake, what if it has been a disaster? What if Livesey's stuff wasn't all that good and what if Teddy couldn't save it?"

"Haven't you got something you should be doing to earn your paycheck?"

Jay was angry and not about to be dismissed. "Answer my question: What if it has been a total mess?"

Elliott spun his chair around and looked up at him with an expression that seemed to drop the temperature thirty degrees. "Then right about now, Stud, you'd be looking up from a shit hole at Hillman's ass as he dumped all over you."

"So this is the thanks I get for making a film the client loves and bringing it in for almost two grand under budget."

"Two grand? That's a fart in a windstorm."

"Well at least it's a profit. I didn't blow the budget. That package of commercials you've got from Hillman—you haven't shot a foot of film and on paper, you're already in the hole. As Nathan and I have been trying to tell you for the last couple of days, the budget is terminal. Unless you either get more money or convince Sig to make some major changes in their storyboards, we're going to take a bath on the production."

"Well, you're the production manager—so manage!"

"How can I when I've got a guy who spends more money getting laid than he does shooting film?"

"Fuck you!"

Elliott's continued perniciousness had pushed Jay over the edge. He closed Elliott's door, not wanting to make the confrontation an office spectacle. "What the hell is your problem, Elliott?"

"*You're* my problem!" He shot back with unbridled hostility. "You seem to have forgotten who owns this company. That's *my* name on the door. Elliott Pierce. You're nothing more than a fucking ingrate that I overpay who doesn't know enough to keep his nose out of my personal life."

How'd we get from the film to his personal life? Jay wondered. *Sherry must have said something to him. But what? What the hell had she told him?* Had she made up some story about what had gone on in the office to punish Elliott for having stood her up? Had she turned the hug into more than it was? Who knows what she might have said? Whatever, it was clear to Jay that Elliott wanted to see blood.

"You've got two options Stud. A; if you want to continue to work here, you're going to kiss my butt whenever I bend over; or B; you can haul your sorry ass out of here and work for somebody else. Lots of go-fer jobs around," he said with contemptuous ridicule.

Jay was doing his best to resist pulling Elliott out of his chair and giving him some of the same treatment he'd given Jackson Korman. Holding himself in check, he just stared holes in Elliott. The bastard wasn't even looking at him. He was thumbing through mail from his inbox, mail that he'd been ignoring for weeks. "OK," Jay said, once he was sure he had a full measure of self-control. "I choose option B. My sorry ass is out of here. After what happened here last week, I couldn't work for you any longer, anyway."

Elliott raised his head slowly, looking like a man who has just trapped his prey into an admission. "And just what did happen last week, Stud? You want to tell me your side of it?"

"Nothing. Nothing at all, except that a woman came in looking for her husband who had promised to take her to La Cote Basque for her birthday. And I had to act stupid and pretend that he was out taking care of the company business when, in fact, he was porking some bimbo. I don't think lying to your wife was in my job description. I'm outta here."

Elliott looked up at him, staring, saying not a word. Then, in an effort to inflict a parting shot guaranteed to seriously wound his now ex-employee, he said, "Ok, cousin, have a nice life."

"What did you call me?"

"Cousin," he said, punctuating the word with an abortive laugh. "You know what cousins are. I assume you're fuckin' Joanna, right? If she's anything like she was when I knew her, she's still one great fuck. That makes us cousins, Stud. Now get your ass out of here."

***

The heat of the afternoon assaulted Jay as he stepped out of the building. He barely noticed. As he made his way toward Fifth Avenue, one word kept echoing in his head: "Cousin! Cousin!" The implications of the word and the images it conjured up of Elliott and Joanna together conspired to tie his stomach in a Gordian knot of hatred and resentment. There never was a Julie. He should have guessed. His step quickened like a man who had no place to go but was in a hurry to get there. What was he going to say to Joanna? What should he say? How would she react once she discovered that he knew the truth about her relationship with Elliott? Even if he told her that it made no difference, that he didn't care what had happened nine years ago, that he regarded it as ancient history—it would, in the end, make a difference. No, he realized, no good could come of confronting Joanna with what he knew. It might destroy everything and place an elephant in the room that would never, ever leave. There was only one thing he could do and that was to say nothing. Not ever. The Joanna that had been led on by Elliott all those years ago had vanished, like the Julie in her story.

The sound of the traffic on the Avenue disappeared and in its place, he heard, beating in his ears, the words he had said to her the night she had knocked on his door after the opera: *Joanna, the important part of my life began on May 2nd, the morning I first saw you at Ad-Film. Anything before that time—in my life or yours—does not matter. All that matters is what has happened between us since that day. There is no past for us, only now— today, tomorrow and every tomorrow. That's all that can ever matter.*

As he waited for the light to change at 57th Street and Fifth Avenue, he turned around and looked at the building behind him. Suddenly he knew what he had to do and say. He pulled his wallet from his hip pocket and looked behind a flap in the bill compartment. The blank check he had put there almost six months ago for emergencies was still there. He would use it now.

***

Jay tacked a hand written note on Joanna's door for her to see when she returned from Boston.

If the woman who lives in apartment 4B would consider spending the rest of her life with the man who lives upstairs in 5A, he would very much like to have a word with her.

Joanna didn't bother to knock. "Are you the man who lives upstairs that left this note on my door?" she teased.

"I am that same man," he said. "Please sit down." Joanna sank into the chair without the springs.

"I think this chair is holding me hostage."

"I planned it that way. Now, I want to do this right," he said and bent down on one knee. "I would consider it a great honor if the very beautiful, talented singer who lives in apartment 4B would consent to lower her standards and marry me." He handed her a small black jewelry box.

She turned the box in her hand and read the name inscribed on it. "Tiffany?" she said, her eyes widening and a look of surprise lighting up her face.

"Only the best."

"Oh, Jay," she said opening the box and staring at the diamond. "It's beautiful. Are you sure you really want to do this?"

"I'm sure. But you haven't answered my question."

"Haven't I?" she asked, holding out her arms to him. "Come join me in this sinking chair and let me give you my answer."

29
Two Goodbyes

Joanna did not press Jay for details on his decision to leave Film Arts. All he said to her was that he and Elliott had gotten into it over the Jeep film and that he had decided the time had come to crawl out of the sewer. Elliott and the job were history as far as he was concerned. He left it at that, although it was enough of an explanation for Jay to see the relief cascade over Joanna's face. They would never talk of Film Arts or Elliott Pierce again. Two days later, John Baskham and his wife took Jay and Joanna to dinner to celebrate both their engagement and Jay's joining Baskham's new film company.

"I feel real good about the way things are shaping up. You and I are going to make some money with this company. For example, thanks to your film, I think we have a real shot at a Renault project."

"John showed me your Jeep film, Jay and I really liked it," Betty Baskham said. "However, I must confess there was something I liked even more than the way you shot it." Betty looked over at Joanna. "You've missed your calling, Joanna. You really should be in front of the camera."

Before Joanna could acknowledge the compliment, Baskham broke in. "She's right. TV is where it's at, as far as advertising is concerned. Agencies are sucking up talent like you wouldn't believe. With the addition of color to TV—which will eventually take off, once they start shooting shows in color—TV advertising is going to get bigger. To be perfectly blunt, men pay attention when a pretty face sells them something. And women don't mind looking at pretty women because they want to believe that, if they use this or that product, they'll look like ... well, like you."

"When they invent that product," Betty Baskham injected, "order me a truck load."

"You really think anyone is going to buy something from someone with a Brooklyn accent?" Joanna asked.

"From you, they'd buy anything, even if you spoke in Swahili"

"You're an actress," Betty said. "If you work with a speech coach, you can sound like you come from the Midwest in no time."

"Anyway," John said, "if you're up for a screen test, I'd like to show you off to a couple of clients. I'm sure I know a guy who would be willing to direct it.'

"Absolutely," Jay said.

A week later, Baskham let Jay direct another Tasti-Feast commercial. They used two cats this time, in a variation of the maze concept. It all went off without a hitch. Then Baskham gave him his first automotive assignment.

"Are you ready for this?" Jay asked excitedly, as he opened the door to Joanna's apartment. "John has picked up the Renault account and they want to do a film—in Paris—to promote the Renault Dauphine to the U.S. market."

"Thanks to your film, right?"

"It helped, but give John the credit for the sale. They like him because he's different. No bullshit. They can trust him. As far as the Renault job, I don't know why anyone in the U.S.

would want to buy that excuse for a car, but if they want a film, we'll give them a film. Now, guess who John asked to direct it?"

"Someone I know?"

"Correct. And guess whose fiancée is going to Paris with him?"

"You're kidding? We're going to Paris? When?"

"September 7."

"But wait, how is it I get to go? I'm sure I'm not in the budget."

"You're not. I bought you a ticket. The only downside is that we'll be sitting in the cheap seats out on the wing. But once we're there—hey, two can see Paris as cheaply as one, as long as the two people don't mind sharing a room."

"This person certainly doesn't mind. Just think," she said, assuming a pompous air, "I'll be able to compare notes with Tolova on how much I just love the Ritz."

"Ahh," Jay said, shaking his head, "chances are we're going to be staying someplace that's a couple of Michelin Stars below the Ritz. Maybe the whole galaxy of Michelin Stars below."

"What?" she said, feigning shock and indignation. "You'd take me to Paris and expect me to live like a peasant?"

"Not only that, but you're going to have to ride around in a Renault Dauphine."

"Are you saying that the Dauphine is not like a Cadillac?"

"Not exactly."

"I don't think I've ever seen one of those."

"It's ... it's truly ugly. Looks like a bloated bug with a case of psoriasis. One reviewer called it ... let me see if I can find it." He searched through his briefcase. "Here," he said, pulling out the newspaper clipping. "'The Renault Dauphine is the most ineffective bit of French engineering since the Maginot Line. It's a rickety, paper-thin, scandal of a car that if you stand beside it, you can actually hear it rusting.'"

"Is it fast?"

"Maybe going downhill. According to the specs, it would probably come in second in a drag race with a farm tractor. It takes 32 seconds to go from zero to 60 miles per hour."

Joanna laughed. "I can hardly wait to see it."

"I can hardly wait to see you in it. This car is so small, you don't just get in, you have to put it on." They both laughed. "Now, I've bought some travel books on Paris and ... "

The phone interrupted him.

"Hello?" Jay's face dropped. "When?" Again he listened. "I'll be up in a couple of hours."

"Scott?" Joanna asked somberly.

"I guess he couldn't dodge that last bullet," he said as the impact of the news took hold. "He died in the ambulance that was taking him home."

***

The service was held at Christ Church in Greenwich. Hundreds of people had come to pay their respects. As Jay and Joanna left the church, friends of the family came up to express their condolences.

"It's so sad. He was such a nice man," the voice behind them said.

Jay turned around.

"Brooke, how are you?"

"I'm fine. It's a very sad day."

"Oh, Brooke, this is Joanna Olenska. Joanna, this is Brooke Whitney, a neighbor and a friend of Ceci's."

"Nice to meet you." Joanna said.

"Ceci has told me a lot about you." Brooke caught sight of the diamond on Joanna's left hand. "Oh, it looks like congratulations are in order. You know, of course, you're a very lucky girl. All my friends consider Jay the catch of the century."

"If I'm the catch of century," Jay said in protest, "the fishing must be pretty sparse up here."

"No, there just aren't many guys like you," she said with a look that suggested she'd had more than just a casual interest in Ceci's brother.

"Did you take the job with your father, Brooke?"

"I start next week."

"Good for you."

"Jay, our condolences." An elderly couple pushed their way in front of Brooke. They were followed by another and Brooke took it as a cue to melt into the crowd.

Joanna turned to him as they approached the car Jay had rented to take them to the cemetery. "I think it's safe to say that Miss Brooke Whitney has a crush on you."

"Who? Brooke? No, no way."

Joanna nodded. "Oh, yes. I know that look."

"Well, I'm taken," he said, squeezing her hand.

***

The burial had been announced by the priest of Christ Church as "family only." The other mourners were to proceed to the reception, to be joined by the family after the interment. The military escort that Wilfred Carraway had arranged for his son followed the family to the cemetery. A canopy had been set up to cover the gravesite and folding chairs placed alongside. Eleanor and Wilfred Carraway, flanked by Tolova and her two children, sat next to the grave. Ceci, Jay and Joanna stood behind them. Other members of the family, uncles, aunts and cousins, found seats or standing places where they could.

The military escort arrived with the flag-draped coffin and carefully placed it on the straps that were to lower it into the ground. The priest led the final prayers and then the captain of the escort signaled for the twenty-one gun salute. Two soldiers positioned themselves at either end of the coffin and carefully, meticulously, with ceremonial precision, picked up the flag and proceeded to fold it in the time-honored tradition. Once it was in a tight triangle, the captain of the detail presented it to Tolova. Taps echoed in the distance and handkerchiefs were sought to dab at wet eyes and cheeks.

When the honor guard retreated, Eleanor Carraway stood up and steadied herself on Tolova's arm. She leaned over and placed a rose on the coffin, then turned around and glared cruelly at Joanna, forcing her to avert her eyes. Eleanor turned to Jay and virtually hissed, "I thought I made it clear that the interment was for family only."

"Mother!"

"Eleanor!" Wilfred Carraway said at the same time. "That was uncalled for!" Eleanor Carraway responded by showing them her back and walking away.

Wilfred Carraway turned to Joanna. He was clearly embarrassed, even humiliated by his wife's behavior. "I must apologize for my wife. She's been under a great deal of strain, as you can imagine. She's not herself. Please forgive her."

Joanna nodded her acceptance. Jay asked Ceci to walk Joanna to the car and hurried after his mother. "Mother, I won't even ask you to apologize to Joanna and me. Because if you did, I would not accept it. For the record, you should know that Joanna soon *will be* family."

"Not if I can help it," she responded with a clipped determination.

"Well, guess what? You *cannot* help it," he said, making no effort to hide his utter contempt.

"We'll see!" she shot back with steely resoluteness. Again, she showed him her back and started to walk away.

Jay grabbed her arm and turned her around so that they were face-to-face. "Mother, today you buried one son and just now you said 'goodbye' to your other son—forever!"

Jay realized the impact that his words had on his mother when she blanched, fully recognizing the enormity of what he'd said. Somehow, from somewhere deep in her sense of social propriety, she found the strength to suppress her desire to lash back at her son. She reverted to tears, instead. Whether they were for Scott or Jay or for herself, Jay found it impossible to tell. She had always been incurably dishonest when it came to shedding tears. As Jay turned and hurried away, she said, "Jay, my only concern is for your …"

Whatever else she might have said, Jay was not there to hear it. He found Joanna seated in his rental car. She was crying. "I don't know, Jay. How do we have a life together with her resentment or hatred or whatever it is hanging over us?"

"Easy," he said. "We cut her out of our lives. Permanently."

"Jay, you can't do that. There's your father and Ceci to consider."

"We can see them."

"Jay, I don't want you to one day believe that I was the reason you and your mother..."

Jay cut her off. "Joanna, understand that I have no respect for my mother. I feel no obligation of any sort. And this is not as of just five minutes ago. Our problems go way back. She is now, as she always has been, a self-centered, arrogant person, who knows no way but her way. There is nothing on this green earth that says I have to accept her behavior. Not now or ever." Jay glanced back at the gravesite where the cemetery workers were lowering the casket. In little more than a whisper, he said, "Good-bye, Scott. I don't apologize for what I said to Mother, only for any disrespect it might have shown to you. Hurry on now, your buddies from Charlie Company will be waiting." Then to Joanna, "Let's go home. I want to escape from all this."

"But can you?"

"Just watch me."

30
Generations of Carraways

"I need you, son," Wilfred Carraway said. "Now that Scott's gone, I need you to come home."

When Jay accepted his father's invitation to lunch at the Knickerbocker Club, he was sure he knew what his father wanted to talk about.

"Dad, I'm not Scott and I could never replace him. He had a sixth sense about business. That's not my thing."

"You're bright. You could learn."

"Maybe. But there are dozens of men who work for you who could step in for Scott and do a hell of a job."

"Maybe, but they're not Carraways. You are."

"I've got a feeling there are people who might argue that my last name does not necessarily qualify me for a top job in the company."

"I'd bring you in at a lower level and work you up, like I did Scott."

"Look Dad, I'm sorry to disappoint you. I really am. But, I don't want to be an incarnation of my brother. I don't want to come to work every day in the shadow of someone I can never emulate. My life is here in New York. I'm doing what I want to be doing. Besides, I think I have some talent and I want to see how far I can go with it. And then, there's Joanna to consider."

"What has she got to do with it?"

"I fully intend to marry her, Dad."

"Fine. She seems like a nice girl. I don't understand what's she got to do with your working for me."

"It has nothing to do with working for you. It's that I don't want to bring Joanna to Greenwich."

"I don't understand. Why not?"

"Because she would never be accepted there."

"Says who?"

"Ask Mother. Ask Tolova how they feel about Joanna. Do you think they're ready to parade her around Greenwich as one of the *family*? To introduce her to their very exclusive society? Maybe put her up for membership in the DAR? Mother and Tolova treat Joanna like some kind of social derelict. She would never fit in with the society out there. And frankly, the fact that she's nothing like them is one of the many reasons I love her. No pretense. No snobbish bullshit."

"I think you're wrong. With the Carraway name, she would be accepted—by everybody."

"The name would only be a temporary shield. You know as well as I do, Mother and her friends judge other women based on family wealth, social importance and which schools they graduated from. Those are the measures they use to decide who's acceptable and who needs to be turned away at the gate. God forbid they should allow anyone into their circle that had to work for a living. Or had to live in a fourth floor walk up or whose mother had never taken her on the Grand Tour of Europe. Mother and Tolova's friends are social piranhas. Put someone like Joanna in their pond and they'd eat her alive."

His father stared at his plate and move the asparagus from one side to the other, then looked up at Jay. "May I ask you a hypothetical question?"

"Sure."

"If you'd never met Joanna, would you still feel the same way about coming home and eventually taking over Carraway International?"

"I don't think one has anything to do with the other. So I don't understand the point of the question."

"I guess what I'm wondering is, which bothers you more: the prospect of subjecting Joanna to the kind of ugly social scrutiny that you describe, or the idea of taking over the responsibly of assuring that the Carraway name stays on the company letterhead?"

Jay thought for a while, trying to weigh his answer well before responding. "Look, if I all I ever wanted was to take my place in line with all the previous generations of Carraways, I'd have no problem letting you train me to take over the business. But since I was old enough to know what being a Carraway son was all about, I've never really wanted to limit my life to just being the next heir in line. What matters to me at this point in my life comes down to two things."

"Which are?"

"First, to be with Joanna and to live with her someplace where she can be happy and not intimidated by the Carraway aura. Second, I want to see if the man sitting across from you can do something on his own, without depending on the family money to do it for me. Who knows? Maybe one day I'll come crawling back home. If that happens, I hope Joanna will have had the good sense to leave me and not be there to see it. Bottom line, Dad, my life is here now. I'm sorry if I'm letting you down, but that's the way it is."

His father let out a long, resigned sigh. "Well, I can see that we're at an impasse on the subject. I don't want this matter to become contentious. You're my only son now and I'd like us to remain friends, whatever you eventually decide." He paused to gather his thoughts. "I will not lie to you; I do hope that at some time in the future, time and events will help change your mind and that you'll come home to ... to carry on. As far as your situation with Joanna ... well, I can only say ... " Whatever he was about to say, he thought better of and, after a moment, diverted the conversation. "Are you interested in looking at the dessert tray?"

"No, I've got to get back. I'm going to Paris next week to shoot a film for Renault and I've got a lot to do to get ready.""

"When are you due back?"

"I have plane reservations on the 12th."

"Are you taking Joanna?"

"Yes. Sort of a pre-honeymoon, you might say."

"You're not planning to get married over there, are you?" There was a note of concern in his voice.

"Actually, I looked into that, but French law makes it very difficult for foreigners to be married there. It's OK to cohabit, but not get married," he laughed.

"So, at least you'll wait until you get back."

Jay nodded. "We'll wait."

His father's gaze drifted off to some distant place. The look on his face was intent, unmoving, as though he'd been commanded to listen to the voices of prior generations of Carraways reminding him of his responsibility to pass the firm on to a Carraway son.

He would need more than ghosts to help him make that happen.

31
I Love Paris

J ay found Joanna seated outside at Les Deux Magots café on the Boulevard San Gemain, having a coffee and nibbling at a very tempting pastry.

"Mon cher, je voudrais que vous fassiez l'amour."

"I don't know what you said, but it sounded good."

"It's my best French pick-up line."

"You're the fourth guy who's tried that in the last fifteen minutes."

"Only three guys have tried to pick you up? What's wrong with these Frenchies? Are they all blind?" He sat down next to her.

"Forget them, I love it here. I'm not ever going to leave," she said, leaning over and giving him a kiss.

"Ah, but you are."

"I am?"

"We're on a 9AM flight to Nice tomorrow."

"What? Why?"

"Because I want you to see the south of France."

"What about the film? Aren't you supposed to start shooting tomorrow?"

"Well, I was. But when I met with the Renault people today to look at the car, they told me it wasn't ready."

"Wasn't ready? What's to make ready about a car?"

"They've made a few changes and said they'd need a week before they could release it for the shoot. So, I had them call Baskham—it took a couple hours for the overseas operator to get the call through—and he said there was nothing I could do but wait and why didn't I just take a little holiday and bill the expense to Renault? I told him I thought that was a great idea. So instead of spending the next four days with a rusting bucket of bolts, I'm going to spend them with a beautiful woman on the Cote d'Azur."

"But then we probably won't be back in New York by the 15th, which means I'll miss the audition George Kukoris set up for me." She made a snap decision. "Forget the audition. I'd rather be here with you. I probably wouldn't get the part anyway."

"Why don't you go back on the 12th as we planned? Then I'll come home as soon as we finish shooting. I'm sure I'll be home by the 18th or 19th. I really don't want you to miss the audition, especially since Kukoris has gone to the trouble to set this up for you."

"You won't mind?"

"Of course not. Chances are, you'd get bored sitting around watching the shoot."

"I could just spend my time here, trying to snag good-looking Frenchmen."

"Another good reason to put you on a plane."

"Look," Joanna said, pointing to the troupe of jugglers that appeared on the street in front of them.

"Paris street theater," Jay said.

They watched for a while as the mimes with their white faces, black bowler hats and black leotards performed various stunts and tricks. After several minutes, Joanna took his hand and turned her face toward his, her eyes roaming his face like an artist surveying an inviting landscape.

"What?" he asked, anticipating a question.

"If a few minutes ago you said what I think you said, maybe we should go back to the hotel for a little while."

"Ah, mais oui, mon amour!"

***

"You're going to love this guy. His name is Vladimir and he says he's a White Russian as opposed to a Red Russian. He's got a 1949 Cadillac and he's going to take us to St. Paul de Vance."

"Where did you find him?"

"The concierge here at the Negresso found him. They know everything and everybody here in Nice and along the entire Cote d'Azur.

They loaded their luggage in the back of Vladimir's Cadillac and he drove them out of the city and into the countryside. "There," he said as they approached the walled city. "That's St. Paul and just off to the left you see one of my favorite hotels in all the world, La Colombe d'Or."

"All I see is a stone wall," Jay said as Vladimir pulled up and stopped just outside the entrance to the village.

"*Mais, oui.* That's its charm. You see that small door in the wall? That little sign over the door is the only evidence that there is a life inside."

Once through the door, they saw that La Colombe d'or had the look of an old, stone, French farmhouse surrounded by lush gardens dotted with fig and olive trees and tall cypress pointing their narrow forms toward the azure sky. The reception area had a warm antique ambience echoing back to the sixteenth century. Through the doors and windows, they could see the terrace and the stone passages that led to the pool. "Let me give you a brief tour first and then I'll bring in your luggage." Vladimir pointed to the walls. "What do you see?" he asked.

"What I see, at least what I think I see, are some incredible works of art," Jay said.

"Yes, there's a Chagall, a Picasso," Vladimir said. "Over there a Matisse and here's Renoir."

"How did they get here? Looks like someone robbed a museum," Joanna said.

"Not quite. When these artists—like Miro who's over there—were young and unknown, they paid for their room and board here with their art."

"Can you imagine what these must be worth?" Jay mused.

When they had completed their brief tour of the art, Vladimir led them to the reception desk. "I have requested that you have Room 25. It has the best view of the village. After one night here, you will not want to leave. However, since I understand you, Monsieur, have business in Paris next week, I will return on Saturday to take you both to the airport."

***

Jay stood on the balcony outside their room, looking out at the village, the fields and vineyards below the walls surrounding St. Paul. The trees were just hinting at producing the first collage of autumn colors. "Can you imagine what it must have been like for artists who came here around the turn of the century? The light here is so incredible."

"You know Jay," Joanna said, taking his arm and pressing her body into his, "I am, at this minute, completely and deliriously happy. Yet for some reason I feel so ... so fragile. I'm afraid that if you were to drop me, I'd break into a million pieces like a China doll.

For the first time, Jay realized that the shell that had been so slow to crack and open to him, the protective armor she had strapped on to defend herself —all of it was totally gone. She stood in his arms, emotionally unprotected, completely vulnerable to the slightest provocation, trusting that he would protect her. He happily accepted that responsibility. He would be her armor. He would see to it that nothing would ever get close enough to diminish her happiness.

"Know this, my China doll," he said. "First, I will never drop you. However, if you should ever suffer even the smallest break, I will be there with the world's strongest glue to put you back together."

She smiled. "Good thing I didn't compare myself to Humpty Dumpty. All the king's men could do nothing for him."

Jay laughed. "That's because they were amateurs when it comes to gluing things back together."

"Look, Jay, doves." Joanna pointed to a flock of white doves as they rose up from the other side of the garden wall, riding on unseen currents, gliding effortlessly toward destinations known only to them. The late afternoon sun seemed to be painting their wings. "They almost look gold."

"They are and thus the English translation of La Colombe d'Or: The Golden Dove."

"I'd wondered about the name."

"Ah, but those aren't just ordinary doves, you know. They're magic doves."

"Are you sure?" Joanna said, willing to play along.

"Absolutely. Do you see how they're flying off in different directions?"

"Yes."

"That's because they've been given a mission to bring somebody home. They're fulfilling the promise of the legend."

"What legend is that?"

"It's an old Greek legend. The story goes that Aphrodite, the Greek goddess of love, lived in the land of perfect happiness with her lover, Jason. Everything was terrific until one day Ulysses comes along and says, 'Hey, Jason, I need every man I can find to sail with me on this little voyage I have planned.' Well, years passed and only Ulysses comes back. Naturally, Aphrodite wants to know where Jason is. Ulysses informs her that, unfortunately, he'd lost him along the way and that he is probably wandering aimlessly somewhere in the world. So she does what any mythological Greek living in Elysium would have done: she calls on the magic doves. She tells them to find Jason and bring him home. Instantly, the doves obey her command and take off to the four winds. And guess what?"

"They found him and brought him back to her?"

"Exactly and that's why Elysian Field doves are very special."

"So if, for some reason, you get stuck over here, all I have to do to bring you home is to call on my magic doves?"

"Believe me, this Jason won't need magic doves to bring him back to you. Pan Am will do the job nicely."

For a long time, they just stared out at the fields and patches of forests that seem to stretch all the way to the blue mountains of the Luberon which rose like stationary waves of stone on the distant horizon.

"Have I ever told you why I love you?" She did not wait for him to answer. "I love you because you don't hide your emotions, because you're not ashamed to be a hopeless romantic and because I know that you love me for me. I don't know if there are such things as soul mates—but if there are, then that's what we're all about."

"I believe there are. And I believe we are." Jay took her in his arms, their mouths coming together slowly, irrevocably. It was a kiss from across time that made myth and reality one. "I'm going to work very hard to give you a good life Joanna. I'm going to do everything in my power to make you happy."

"Just be you, Jay. Just always be what you are today and I'll never ask for more."

"Well, you might want to ask for a *little* more. I mean, I don't think rent money and food are unreasonable requests."

"When I want you to be funny, I'll ask," she admonished him with a smile. "When I want you to be romantic ..."

"You won't have to ask," he said, covering her mouth with his.

***

Their plane landed at Orly around noon. After checking into the Windsor-Reynolds Hotel, they took a taxi to Montmartre. "This is the highest point in Paris, almost 500 feet," Jay said. They got out of the taxi and began to stroll around the square with its open-air café and dozens of artists, standing at their easels, creating art-on-demand for the tourists. Just beyond the square, at the highest point on the hill, the white travertine marble Sacre Coeur Basilica stood watch over all of Paris.

"There's something magical about this square," Joanna said. "Do you think we might see Mimi and Rodolfo at the café over there?"

"Never know."

"What are all these artists doing here?"

"Painting Paris for the tourists," he said. "Since we're tourists, I think we should find one that we like and buy it."

"A perfect souvenir of this week."

They found that most of the artists were working on Paris street scenes, buildings and the Basilica itself. "I have a feeling that many of these guys have probably been painting the same scene for years."

"What do you think of this one?" She motioned for Jay to take a look. The artist had painted the café in the square with its colorful umbrellas shading the tables. Horse-chestnut trees hovering over the square created a leafy backdrop. To the left on the canvas, towering over the scene, was the majestic white dome of the Sacre Coeur. The artist appeared to be adding the last couple of touches.

"I like it," she said.

"I have an idea," Jay said, tapping the artist on the shoulder. "Pardon, Monsieur, je voudrais acheter votre peinture."

"Très bon. Merci."

"Je voudrais vous faire mettre mon fiancé et moi dans l'image se reposant à cette table."

"No problème. Pourquoi vous ne vous asseyez pas là-bas," the artist replied.

"What was all that about?" Joanna asked.

"I've asked him to paint the two of us into his picture. We'll sit over there at the table."

Jay held a chair for her and then seated himself. A waiter appeared almost immediately and they ordered two glasses of Chardonnay.

When the artist finished, he brought the painting to them for their approval.

"I love it," Jay said

"It's perfect. This will be the first painting we'll hang when we get an apartment. It will always have a special place, wherever we live."

***

It was about four in the morning when Jay was awakened by the nasal, rasping whine of the motor scooter passing under their window. He raised himself up on is elbow, listening as the crescendo of the motor rose and then fell away as it continued down the street. *Maybe a baker on his way to produce the morning's croissants*, he thought. He looked over at the face on the pillow next to him with unfathomable delight and savored the thought of a lifetime of such moments.

Her eyes fluttered open and she looked up at him. "I was having a dream. I don't remember what it was, except that it was nice and it was about us."

"The best kind."

"Has this been a dream Jay? Am I going to wake and find that all of this—that you and me—that it's all been a dream?"

"Would you like me to pinch you?"

"I'd rather you kiss me."

He moved toward her and brought his face to hers. Then, as he felt her legs part, he lifted his body over hers. Slowly, he found her and they began to move in unison—slowly, inevitably toward Elysian Fields.

"It's not a dream," she whispered.

***

The next morning, they took a taxi to Orly and checked her in for the New York flight.

"I miss you already."

"This has been so wonderful, Jay. I'm so sorry it has to end."

"End? This is just the beginning. We have a whole lifetime of this ahead of us."

"I hope so," she said.

"You have doubts?"

"No doubts, just fears that somehow this is all we'll ever have."

"Joanna, trust me. There's a lot more to come. When we get back to New York, if you still agree, we'll put the second ring on your finger."

"You're sure you want to do that?"

"Positive! As in, I can't wait."

"But what about your parents? Your mother may never forgive you for marrying me."

"That's her problem, not mine. And it's not ours."

"I'm so afraid that somehow I'll disappoint you. If I thought that I might one day hurt you—in any way—well, I'd just want to vanish."

"Hey," he said, taking her in his arms. "No more of that. The only thing that would ever disappoint me, that would ever hurt me, is not marrying you. That would haunt me all my life."

The voice on the public address system cut in. "Le vol d'Air France le numro quatre pour New York City embarque maintenant au nombre 5B de porte." Then in English, "Air France flight Number Four for New York City is now boarding at gate Number 5B."

"This is goodbye," she said, the tears welling in her eyes.

"No, you should say, *Voyez-vous bientô*—see you soon, like in about four or five days."

"See you soon," she said, her eyes no longer able to contain the tears.

"Knock 'em dead at the audition, OK?"

"I'll do my best."

"I'm going up on the observation deck to watch you take off. Look for me. I'll be waving madly."

I love you," she said, her voice heavy with melancholy as she took her place in the line leading to the door.

He stood there watching her, acknowledging each of her glances as the line of passengers slowly advanced, past the agent taking tickets, toward the door. *Why am I letting her go?* He asked himself. *I'll ask her to stay. There will be other auditions.* Why should they let this unique moment in time when Paris—when all of France seemed to be in love with them—why let it end so soon? He hesitated, wondering if he was letting the emotional strain of their parting cloud his better judgment. *She deserved the audition*, he thought. *It might be the break she's been looking for.* Could his need to have her with him justify denying her that opportunity? *There will be other opportunities.* He labored to convince himself of that fact. *I'll make sure there are.* Decision made. He would not let her go. "Joanna! Wait! Joanna!"

"Appel final pour le numéro de vol d'Air France le numro quatre pour New York City embarque maintenant au nombre 5B de porte." His words were drowned out, erased by the piercing female voice that blasted out of the public address system. By the time the announcement was over, Joanna had disappeared through the door that led down the stairs to the tarmac and the waiting plane.

Jay hurried to the observation deck and caught sight of her as she climbed the stairway to the plane. "Joanna!" he shouted, waving frantically. "No. Wait! Come back! I want you to stay with me!" The wind in his face blew his pleas back at him like leaves tossed into the face of a maelstrom. He saw her pause on the top of the stairway, turn around shading her eyes against the sun, searching for him. His arms waved frantically, beckoning her back, wishing her back. He continued to shout, but to no avail. He could see that she was looking for him at the other end of the observation deck. Unable to find him and pressed by other passengers waiting to board, she turned away and stepped inside the plane. There was no calling her back now.

He stood, frozen, unable to move as he watched the door close and the ramp workers roll away the stairs. The engines fired and the plane began to taxi. Minutes later, it was rolling down the runway and lifting off. Jay stood on the deck, waving one last goodbye in the futile hope that she might see him. His eyes welled with tears as the plane became little more than a speck in the azure blue sky and vanished into the high clouds.

A torrent of depression swept over him. He'd never felt more empty or alone. When he turned around and looked back toward the city, Paris was empty.

32
Everyone You Ever Knew

The Renault Dauphine, to no one's surprise other than Jay's, was not ready and the shoot was delayed several more days. It was not until the twenty-first of September that he was able to schedule a flight back to New York. He had sent several telegrams to Joanna alerting her to his delay. Twice on the night of the nineteenth, he'd waited in his hotel room for the overseas operator to complete a telephone call to her. He was informed both times that there was no answer. The next morning, with nothing to do and almost twenty-four hours before his plane was to leave, he decided to take a walk and make mental notes of all the places he and Joanna would visit the next time they were in Paris.

The late morning was bright and pleasantly warm. He walked over the bridge to the Ille St. Louis, then crossed over to the Ille de la Citè and stopped for a quick visit to Notre Dame. From there he made his way to the Louvre and strolled into the Jardin Tuileries where he sat for a while and watched young boys sail their boats in the large circular pond. By mid-afternoon, he was on the Rue de l'Opera and decided to stop for a coffee at the Café de la Paix. He found a chair at one of the outdoor tables that seemed to have seized the lion's share of the sidewalk in front of the restaurant. He opened the Paris edition of the Herald

Tribune, which he'd purchased earlier and noted that, for the most part, the world was still intact. As he sipped his coffee, he could not help but overhear an American at the next table. He was telling his companions that Parisians contend that, if you sit at the Café De La Paix long enough, everyone you know will eventually pass by. In Jay's case, only one person he knew passed by: Mike Livesey.

"Hey, Mike!" he shouted. "You must be lost."

After sharing their surprise at running into one another, Livesey told Jay that he had just arrived in Paris and that he was to meet up with his crew the next day and begin shooting a travelogue.

"Have you got time for a coffee or a drink?" Jay asked.

"Always have time for a libation."

After Jay briefly told him about what he'd been doing for Renault, he said, "So catch me up on what you've been doing since our Jeep film."

"Of course, you heard about Elliott."

"Has he got the feature off the ground?" Jay asked, expecting confirmation.

"Then, I guess you haven't heard. Elliott was killed in a car accident two weeks ago."

"What? When? How did it happen?"

"It happened about 2AM on the Merritt Parkway. Don't know what he was doing up in Connecticut in the middle of the night, but I have an idea," he said with a look that assumed Jay needed no further explanation. "Police said he had to be doing over one hundred when he hit a bridge abutment."

"Was he drunk?"

"You know Elliott, he could drink five martinis and still not be drunk. I never knew a man who could drink as much as he did and still function like he was cold sober. My opinion—and I'm not alone in this—is that he committed suicide."

"Suicide? Why?"

"His business had just rolled over and died. Everything seemed to fall apart at once. First, his buddy—if you could call him that—Sig Hillman got canned for God knows what. You gotta believe, knowing that son-of-a-bitch, it was a pretty good reason. Then Barney Lockerman took over. You remember Barney. He was a golf player we had with us out in Yuma."

"Mr. Congeniality."

"Right. Well, it was no secret that Lockerman hated Elliott. Apparently, he found some loophole in the contract Hillman had given Film Arts. The agency lawyers had it declared null and void in a New York minute. Nathan tried to talk him into going Chapter 11, but Elliott said he wasn't interested. So we all ended up on the street with paychecks that nobody could cash."

"Left everyone holding the bag."

"Afraid so. But I think what really turned him inside out was when the agent turned around the next day and sold the rights to that movie he wanted to produce, to guess who?"

"The guy from L.A?"

"Right. George Gatley. Between you and me, I gotta believe that Gatley had a deal for the book sitting out there all the time and was just looking for a chance to dump Elliott."

"I thought Elliott had the author's agent in his back pocket."

"I guess not."

"Losing that book really would have sent him over the edge."

"Absolutely. From what I was told, he hung around the office for a couple of days until the landlord locked him out. After that, nobody heard from him for almost a week. I'm not even sure Sherry knew where he was. Then one morning, his name comes up on the police blotter."

"Were there many people at the funeral?"

"Not many. Most everyone from Film Arts, of course. Hillman and Lockerman didn't show up. John Baskham was there, Sherry's folks and some of their neighbors."

"How is Sherry taking it?"

"I guess she's coping. At the funeral, she said something about going to live with her family. They're up around Boston someplace, I think. I understand her father has money, so she'll be OK financially."

Jay stared out across the Place de l'Opera, but his mind was filled with images of the past several months. All the scenes seemed to lack any sense of reality. It was as though he was watching an unrelated series of outtakes running through Teddy's moviola.

"What happened between you and Elliott?" Mike's question was tentative and a little cautious.

"What did *he* say?"

"Nothing. When people would ask about you, he'd just tell them that you were no longer with the company. No more explanation than that."

"Well, it's no secret that we didn't part on good terms. In fact, in the end, we didn't like each other a whole lot." Jay again decided to avoid the specifics. "I guess the root of my problem was that Elliott was like working for two people. One

I respected, because he was good at what he did. The other," he paused, "well, let's just say that we were very different people." A thought occurred to Jay. "You say he hit a bridge abutment?"

"Right. From what I heard at the funeral, it seems the police think the only way the car could have hit the bridge at that angle was if he actually drove into it. That's why I think he did it on purpose."

Jay thought for a moment and then asked, "Did you ever read *Death of a Gran Prix Racer*?"

"No, but I meant to."

"Read it some time. It may just be coincidence, but the way Elliott died was not all that different from the way the main character, Eddie Merrill, dies."

"How was that?"

"In the book, Eddie Merrill is leading the Formula One race at Dijon and it looks like, after years of trying, he's finally going to win one of the big ones. He's on the last lap and the finish line is not much more than a half mile ahead. What no one knows is that Eddy's life is a shambles. Everything that could go wrong has gone wrong and it's all come home to roost. No matter what the outcome of the race, win or lose, he's not going to be able to turn things around. Then, when the one thing he's wanted all his life is only a few seconds away, he deliberately steers his racecar into the wall. That's how the book ends and that's how Elliott wanted his film to end."

"Maybe that's how he wanted his life to end, too," Mike said.

Jay wondered if he was working too hard to find a parallel between the death of the fictional Eddie Merrill and the real Elliott Pierce. He laid both scenarios side-by-side in his head and decided there was enough similarity to make it a possibility. "Maybe you're right. Maybe Elliott did choose the wall."

33
The Note

As soon as he cleared customs at Idlewild Airport, he called Joanna. No answer. He joined the cue for taxis and, within fifteen minutes, was on the Van Wyck heading toward the midtown tunnel. The cab dropped him in front of the brownstone on Sheridan Square and he literally bounded up the stairs two, sometimes three at a time.

"Joanna?" he called as he knocked on her door. To his surprise, it swung open under the force of his knock. Instantly he realized something was wrong. It was a furnished apartment, but things were missing: the little artifacts that decorated her lamp tables, the books, her collection of porcelain animals. They were all gone.

He crossed quickly to her bedroom door and opened it. The closet doors were standing ajar. Her clothes were gone. He looked in the bathroom. Empty. He returned to the living room, desperate now and helpless. For an instant, he considered the possibly that he was in the wrong apartment. Maybe she'd moved to another floor while he was in France. Maybe into his apartment! He ran up the stairs and opened the door. Quickly he looked around for some sign that she had moved in with him. Nothing. Nothing but an envelope on the kitchen table with his name on it and the ring he had given her.

My dearest Jay,

I wish that time could have stopped for us in Paris or even here in Sheridan Square. These have been the most wonderful months I have ever known. In their whole lives, most people never experience the love and joy that you have given me in these few short months. For that, I will love you forever. I pray that God will always take care of you.

Yours, for life,
Joanna

P.S. I have taken the Montmartre painting. Something to remember you and these past few months by.

Like night fog rising, he was instantly enveloped in grief-stricken panic. "Oh, God, Joanna, don't do this! Why?" Jay ran from the room and then raced down the four flights of stairs to the street, almost as if he expected to find her at the curb waiting for a taxi. He ran around the corner, his rational mind knowing that she wouldn't be there. But he had to be sure.

He hurried back to the brownstone and rang the bell for the building super. After nearly five minutes, the man emerged from the basement, angry at having his dinner interrupted. No, he had not seen Joanna Olenska. When Jay told him that he thought she'd moved out of her apartment, the super got angry. "She has a lease, goddamn it. She's responsible for the lease."

Jay restrained the strong impulse to punch the man and ran back up to the fourth floor. In a near frenzy, he searched her entire apartment, hoping to find some clue as to where she might be. Where would she have gone?

Back in his garret, he forced himself to sit down and try to think logically and clearly. He took out a paper and pencil and made a list of all the people she knew from Ad-Film and in the neighborhood. He tracked down George Kukoris and discovered that Joanna had never shown up for the audition.

He visited Ad-Film and talked to Vivian. Then he went to see John Baskham. That next day, he stopped in every shop in the Village that he knew her to frequent. They all remembered her, but none had seen her.

A week later, desperate, he hired a private detective, but the effort eventually proved futile. For days, he checked the bank of mailboxes in the vestibule of the brownstone, in the hopes that she might write or that her mail might give him a clue as to where to look. As he walked the streets in the Village, he thought he saw her in dozens of different places. He would run to her each time, only to find that it was not Joanna at all.

She was everywhere, but she was nowhere.

34
Death of a Gran Prix Racer

John Baskham sat at the corner table in P.J. Clark's, waiting for Jay to join him.

"The Renault people love the Dauphine film," John said as Jay sat down. "We'll do more work for them, assuming the car doesn't fall apart first."

"You eating or just drinking?" Jay asked as he looked at John's martini.

"Just drinking."

"You sound like Elliott. 'I think I'll just drink my lunch today,' he'd say and then put away five Martinis. I'll never understand how he did it."

"No word, I guess, huh?" John asked after an awkward gap in the conversation.

"Nothing," Jay answered simply. "She's just disappeared. I don't know where to look anymore. I've called everyone she ever knew. I've even put personal ads in the paper. Nothing." Jay's drink arrived and he stared at it as if somehow it might provide answers. "I just don't understand why she left. It doesn't make sense that she'd just leave without explanation."

"Her note gave no indication of why she was leaving?"

"Not really," Jay said, making no effort to shake off the dark mantle of anguish that had draped over him

For a few moments, neither man spoke. Then John broke the silence. "I heard from Sherry Pierce, the other day."

"How's she doing?" It was an automatic response and he expected to hear little more than that she was doing OK.

"She sold her house and will be moving up to Boston to be with her parents. She asked me to ask if you'd give her a call."

That surprised him. "Me? I wonder why."

"No idea."

Jay called Sherry the next day. She told him there was something she wanted to show him. He agreed to drive up to Mamaroneck. At first, he got lost. Only when he recognized the hill that had all but killed him on the morning Elliott had taken him jogging did he get his bearings. He passed the house with the two large rocks, where he'd watched the woman put on her morning show. "Who's servicing your account these days?" he said aloud to the vacant window.

Elliott's house awaited the moving van. Inside, he let Sherry lead the way through the passages left between the stacks of cardboard moving boxes.

"I'm glad you came," Sherry said. "Elliott liked you."

Jay was not about to set the record straight.

"How are the kids?" Jay asked in an attempt to hold up his end of the conversation.

"Doing as well as can be expected. They're with my parents in Boston. As I told you on the phone, I have something to show you. Let me get it," she said, leaving the room. When she returned, she handed Jay an envelope. "I guess this is what they call irony."

Jay opened the letter. It was from Paul Newman's agent.

*Paul has read both the treatment and the book. While this
letter should imply no commitment from him, he would like
to discuss who you have in mind to write the screenplay.
Assuming the screenplay reflects the quality of the book,
he would appreciate the opportunity to discuss the project
further.*

"Well," Jay said, handing it back to Sherry, "I guess this confirms that Elliott was right about the book."

Sherry looked around the room and tossed up her hands in mild frustration. "Sorry, there's no place to sit down."

"That's OK, I can't stay long. I just wanted to stop in and pay my respects. I was out of the country when it happened."

"I heard."

Jay began to suspect that the Newman letter was not the reason she'd asked to see him. She seemed to be struggling to find a place to begin.

"Jay, I'd like to ask you a question and I want you to answer me honestly."

Whatever she was about to ask, Jay sensed, represented a personal risk to her.

"There were so many nights that Elliott stayed in the city, so many times he ended up spending an extra day on location. Was there another woman, Jay? I need to know."

Another woman? he said to himself. *How about dozens of other women?* Jay found it tempting to expose Elliott to his wife. Fitting and final retribution, he thought. But to what end? What would he really accomplish and whom would he hurt? Not Elliott. No, the sad little cheerleader standing in front of him would be the only one to suffer. So what did Sherry really want him to say? Her expectant expression was filled with latent dread.

She pressed him for an answer. "Was there, Jay? If there was, please tell me."

There was only one answer she could live with. "No. There wasn't another woman. I am quite certain of that. His only mistress was the company and, as you know, she was very, very demanding."

Sherry Pierce was visibly relieved. "Thanks, I appreciate your being honest." She gave Jay a kiss on the cheek. "I was just about to go to the cemetery. It will probably be my last time for who knows how long. Would you like to join me?"

Jay knew he could not refuse. "I'll follow you in my car," he said, wanting to avoid having to return with her to the house.

***

After Sherry left the cemetery, Jay stood a ways off from the gravesite, as if the distance would help speed separation from the few months he worked for Elliott. The section of the cemetery Sherry had chosen—or maybe it was all that was available to her—marked the graves with flat, ground level markers. Visitors would have to nearly step on a marker stone before they could read the name of the person who was buried there. From where Jay stood, the grave markers, including Elliott's, seemed to have disappeared beneath the grass. Who he was and what he had done mattered not one whit to the man on the lawn tractor who, Jay assumed, must have appreciated how much easier the flat headstones made his job.

It was if Elliott had been relegated to obscurity. As Jay thought about what he had done to Joanna, he wanted to shout

"Good riddance!" Joanna had been right about Elliott. He was a user. He hurt people and never felt any remorse for that damage he inflicted. While Jay was not one to mock the dead, he felt only contempt for the man in the grave.

It occurred to Jay that had he been more experienced and less impressionable he would have recognized that Elliott had been bent on his own destruction. His dream of making the feature was, in reality, a desperate fabrication designed to give his reckless meanderings the illusion of purpose.

Elliott, he realized, must have wrestled constantly with the fear that he might not have the ability to translate *Death of a Gran Prix Racer* into a truly great film. Maybe a John Frankenheimer or one of the French or Italian directors could have done it. But Elliott Pierce? His talent lay in making one-minute features showing people in a mindless America worried about what car they would buy. His gift was that he knew how to take ordinary automobiles and recast them into visual images that transcended what they would never—could never—be in steel. That was what he did in life. Maybe he knew that was all he could ever do. He must have harbored that secret deep down, where it counts, below the conscious reality, where those fears lurk that ultimately drive people to hide from the truth. Maybe that's what ultimately drove him to turn his car into the wall. No one would ever know for sure.

As Jay turned his back on the graves and walked toward his car, he recalled something Elliott had said once, which now seemed like a fitting epitaph. "Jay, you've got to understand that making commercials is not brain surgery. We work, we play, we get paid and we get laid. That's all there is to it."

Maybe he was right. At least about himself. In any case, Jay was glad that he'd had the satisfaction of walking out on Elliott. But even that bit of satisfaction was diminished by knowing that he had not escaped Elliott without injury. No, Elliott had managed to deliver his unkindest and most painful cut as he gloated while revealing that they were *cousins*. The scar would stay with him forever.

"Fuck you, Elliott Pierce!" he shouted to the distant grave. "I'm glad you're dead."

***

Three months passed and there was still no word from or about Joanna. Slowly, Jay began to resign himself to the fact that she would be found only when and if she chose to be found. One morning, on his way out of the brownstone, he met a young couple carrying cardboard packing boxes up the stairs.

"Do you live here?" the young man asked.

"Top floor," Jay answered curtly.

"My name is Charlie Betts and this is my wife, Jan. We've just rented 4B."

Joanna's apartment. The news fell on him like a shower turned suddenly cold. While her apartment had remained vacant, he had clung to the vague hope that one morning he'd pass by her door and discover she'd returned. Now that it was rented, he knew that what he feared was fact: she was not coming back.

It was time, he decided, for him to leave Sheridan Square. If, in that moment, someone could have shown him his future, he would probably have laughed in disbelief that he would end up doing exactly what he had promised himself he would never do. And he would have wept in despair at learning all the years that would pass before he would find her again.

35
Absolution

He sat in the library of the Greenwich house that once was his father's favorite retreat and realized it was in this room that many of the most important events in his life had taken place. It was here he had come to inform his father that he was ready to join the family business. That he had done so surprised even him. For two years after Joanna disappeared, he had drifted. He had worked for Baskham for a short time and then found he had lost whatever it was that had initially driven him to think he might one day become a filmmaker. The prodigal son had come home.

It was a little over a year later that, in this room, he announced his engagement to Brooke Whitney. And it was in this room, the day before they were married, that Brooke had come to him and said, "I know I can never be Joanna to you, but I promise that I will be a very good wife and I will love you as much as she might have."

He had assured her, "Joanna is past tense. Only you, Brooke, matter to me now." From the look on her face, he knew he had been convincing. But the words sounded hollow and he wondered if Joanna would ever really be just *past tense*. In the years that followed if Brooke had ever wondered whether he thought of Joanna, or suspected that he had attempted to find her—and she must have—she never asked.

Their two boys where seven and five and their daughter three, when his father handed him the deed to Deerfield Park and told him his mother and he were moving. They'd spend the winters in Palm Beach and live in their Newport *cottage* in the summer.

Two years later, after Wilfred Carraway's funeral, his mother announced she would stay in the Palm Beach house year-round—except, of course, during the summer months when she booked herself on extended cruises.

Finally, what he considered the last and most tragic event of his life had taken place in this library. For it was in this room that Brooke told him the doctors had concluded her cancer was inoperable and ultimately fatal. When Brooke died, he sat here and wept. He had learned to truly love her as he'd never thought he would.

At his wife's funeral, Jay's mother paid him what he would remember as her one and only compliment. It was a summation of his role as husband, father and overseer of the family fortune: "You have acted responsibly." In retrospect, he wondered if that was all that he could say about his life.

In February of 1989, he got a call from Ceci in Palm Beach saying the doctor gave their ailing mother little time and that he should probably come down right away. Jay caught the early morning fight to West Palm and was at his mother's home on South Ocean Boulevard in Palm Beach by noon.

Her bedroom was on the second floor of the seaside mansion. The large, ornate room had the look of an antique shop in which the owner had been unable to find enough space to properly display the abundance of period French pieces. The works of countless masters crowded the walls, seeming to jockey for position. On the far side of the room, floor-to-ceiling French doors, which could have been opened to let in the freshened sea air, were closed and locked. As a result, a pungent medicinal odor rising from the virtual pharmacy sitting on the nightstand hung stagnant in the room.

His mother was lying on a large, canopy covered bed. Her head and shoulders were propped up on a bank of silk-covered pillows. She smiled thinly and held out her hand as a sign of welcome as he approached. Jay noticed that she was wearing a very formal-looking, gold brocade bed jacket over a power-blue, laced-trimmed nightgown. Her hair was perfect as if the hairdresser had just left. Clearly someone, possibly a maid, had made sure that her makeup was carefully applied. Around her neck she wore a string of large south sea pearls. On her ears clumps of cut jade with diamond edging dangled on her neck. He found himself wondering if the attention she had given to her appearance was intended to impress her maker, much as she had worked to impress the guests she had greeted at her parties.

After several minutes of banal inquires about how she was feeling and who had been to see her, she announced to Ceci and the nurse that she would like to be alone with her son.

Once the door was closed, she said, "There's something I need to tell you. Even if you consider what I am about to tell you a confession, I think you will have to agree that it has a happy ending. If I were a Catholic, I suppose you might assume that I was seeking absolution. I don't subscribe to that kind of thing."

Jay picked up a chair from in front of an antique bureau, placed it beside her bed and sat down. "Mother, where are you going with this?"

"It's about that ..." her hand paddled at the air as though expecting it somehow to aid in the restoration of her memory. "That girl. Oh, what was her name?"

Jay immediately knew. "Joanna?"

"Joanna, yes. Joanna Olenska, wasn't it?

"What about her?" There was impatience in his voice.

"Please, do not force me to rush this," she said. "Now, as I recall, you'd had lunch with your father not long after Scott's passing. He was very concerned—as was I, of course—that you had no intention of assuming Scott's position with the company."

"Mother, what's this got to do with Joanna?" The sharpness in his voice demanded she get to the point.

"I will get to that," she said. "It was quite apparent that one of the reasons for your reluctance had to do with that girl. We felt she was, at least in part, the reason you did not want to come back to Greenwich. Your father suggested that we just let matters take their course and hope for the best. I found that unacceptable. I suggested—no, to be truthful, I strongly demanded—that he go to New York, talk to the two of you and do whatever needed to be done to bring you home so you could assume your responsibilities."

"Dad never talked to the two of us about my coming home."

"That's true. Because as it turned out, you were still in France, doing whatever you were doing with that film company." She coughed several times and then paused, appearing to gather what strength was left to her. "So, when your father arrived in New York, he went to your building and found the girl had returned by herself. He asked if they could talk."

"About what?"

"About you. Apparently, it was a totally unproductive conversation in so far as coming to any resolution. In fact, he told me he actually liked the girl and felt strongly it would be best if we just stepped aside and let nature take its course."

"What did you do, Mother?" He could feel his pulse quicken as he realized he might be on the verge of learning the answers to questions that had haunted him for years.

"Fortunately, I had listened to my own advice." His mother looked at him with an expression that said she intended to maintain a superior level of calm and refused to be hurried. "After I met the girl at my lawn party and you told me of your intentions, I enlisted the services of a very accomplished private detective. I felt for the good of the family—and particularly you—that it was incumbent upon me to look into her background. What the detective found absolutely shocked me beyond words."

"What did he find?" Jay was losing any residual patience.

"It seems that sometime in either the late forties or early fifties, Miss Olenska had an abortion. It was one of those disgusting, back-alley operations. Apparently, it went badly and she ended up in the Murray Hill hospital. All the sordid details were in the hospital records."

"Elliott!" The name leaped into his throat. "That bastard!"

"What? Who's Elliott?"

"Nobody. Go on!" Jay said.

"Well, I decided that I needed to confront Joanna with what I knew. So I met her in that terribly depressing apartment building you lived in. I presumed—and, as it turned out, I was correct—she had *not* told you about the abortion."

"She would have. I'm sure she would have."

"Well, I'm not so sure. In fact, I was under the distinct impression that she thought if she just ignored her past it would somehow just go away. Of course, things like that never do go away and the damage to one's reputation—in this case yours—can be irreparable."

"How could that have damaged my reputation?"

"What would your sister have thought? Our friends? People like the Whitneys and Brooke?"

"How would they know?" he asked.

"As I told Joanna, things like that always get out. People always seem to know."

"Only if someone tells them! Who was going to tell them?"

She appeared oblivious to the implied accusation. "I made it clear to her that, as a God-fearing family, we could not accept her—let me be kind—her *sullied* past."

"It was not for you to decide whether or not to accept her," Jay said, his jaw tightening. "You had no right! It would have made no difference to me." Then, more to himself than his mother, he said, "I don't know why she didn't wait until I got back from Paris to talk with me?"

"That was exactly what she told me she planned to do.'"

"But she didn't wait!"

"Only because I had the presence of mind to demand that your father, who had just been sitting there like some mute, to ..."

"Dad was there?" Jay did not attempt to hide his surprise.

"Of course. You don't think I would have gone to that place of yours alone?" She appeared shocked that Jay would have assumed otherwise. "I must confess that he was totally against my confronting Joanna about her past. But then your father was always, shall we say, *reluctant* to deal with anything potentially unpleasant. Not surprisingly, he left it to me to make sure that Joanna understood that he and I were in *complete* agreement..."

Jay stopped her, "'Complete agreement on what?"

"That the only way to protect you from having to suffer socially because of her … of her *unfortunate* past, was to end your relationship."

"I don't believe Dad agreed with you."

"Well, apparently, Joanna didn't either. She had the temerity to ask him exactly that."

"What did he say?"

"He didn't say a thing. He just stared at me for a moment knowing full well that contradiction was out of the question. Then, without so much as looking at Joanna, he nodded." Mrs. Carraway shook her head slightly as though recalling what she had regarded as her husband's less than adequate supporting performance. "At best his nod was little more than a feeble acknowledgement of what I'd been telling her. But apparently it was enough to confirm that we were in agreement."

Jay found that the matter of fact, emotionally detached, tone of her voice only added to his building resentment. It was as though she was recounting, with little or no feeling, a bit of inconsequential gossip overheard at one of her parties.

Mrs. Carraway paused and fumbled briefly on the bed table for a pill, found it and placed it in her mouth. She continued, "After what had been a very difficult and exceedingly uncomfortable conversation, I fully expected a flood of tears. But, I must say, to her credit there were no tears and not even a single angry word. She just stood up, went into her bedroom, closed the door and left us just sitting there. Just *sitting there*," she echoed as if still amazed at Joanna's socially abrupt departure. "When, after several minutes, she didn't return, I felt sure that we had been successful in saving you from ..."

"From what? Saving me from what?" he shot back, his anger now released and unbridled. "A life without the woman I loved?" His rage began to slide into depression as he thought about what the scene with his parents must have been like for Joanna. No shell to protect her. No armor to strap on to do battle. And then, in desperation, how she must have felt when she looked to his father, who she liked and respected, in the hope that he might say something...that he might come to her defense. Jay was sure that when she saw him nod, indicating his agreement with his mother, it was over. His father had delivered the coup de grâce.

His mother coughed again, her voice growing weaker. "After we got home, your father must have had some sort of ...what do they call it... 'guilt trip.' Two days later, without consulting me, he went back to New York to see her. He fully intended to apologize and say that we would not interfere in your lives. That whatever the two of you decided, we would accept." She rolled her eyes as though after all these years she was still stunned by her husband's audacity.

"Did he talk to her?"

"No, fortunately, she was gone. 'Moved out,' the landlord told him. And he had no idea where she was going. Several years later, after you'd finally given up looking for her, I was happy to point out to your father that I believed fate would show it's hand. I told him I was sure it would all work out for the best. And, as you know," she said with a sunny confidence, "it did. Brooke was the best thing that ever happened to you. What more could you have asked for in a wife?"

"Don't bring Brooke into this. This is not about Brooke."

"But in a way, it is. Brooke was a truly wonderful mother, raising three splendid children who have, in every conceivable way, been a credit to you both. Can you image your life without those children if Brooke had never brought them into this world?" She did not wait for an answer. "Of course you can't. So you see, in the end it really has worked out very well. Don't you agree, dear?" She was smiling serenely as she laid her head back on the pillow, her burden lifted.

Jay said nothing. What could he say? His mother had long ago perfected the ability to frame an argument in such manner as to leave no reasonable or even logical opportunity for rebuttal. To argue that it had not worked out for the best—that he would rather have married Joanna—would make him appear to be suggesting that he'd have been happier if his children had never been born, if they had never given him the pleasure and joy he had known watching them grow up and become successful adults. That would be unthinkable.

To argue with his mother would also be a dismissal of the devotion and love he had received from Brooke. That would not only be shameful, but a cruel and unfair homage to her memory. No, there was nothing he could say. No adequate response. His mother had cleared her conscience. Jay thought she actually looked at peace with herself as she called for Ceci and the nurse to return. She had left him feeling like a man set adrift at sea with no rescue in sight.

When three days later his mother died, he saw to the burial arrangements. He refused to offer a eulogy at the funeral service and left it to his sister to see that she was properly interred next to their father. As his plane left the runway and the long barrier island that is Palm Beach appeared in his window, he found himself with but one thought: There would be no absolution.

36
September Song

In July of 1994, his daughter Alesandra—everyone but her fiancé and he called her Sandy—came to him, as she often did, asking if she might offer the house for a cocktail reception in early September. She told him it was for one of the many charities she supported. Jay was, of course, delighted to accommodate her.

"Just don't leave me having to do all the dishes," he joked.

"I think the caterer will handle that," she said playfully.

On the night of the party, he took quiet pleasure in seeing the house alive with young people. It brought back memories of the parties Brooke and he had thrown. Most of the faces were young and he recognized only a few of those who had been friends of his children.

Jay was contemplating a retreat to his bedroom when a tall, seasoned woman who showed evidence of one too many surgical attempts to restore the old alignment of her face approached him tentatively. "Mr. Carraway, may I ask you a question?"

"If it's about this fundraiser, my daughter, Alesandra, might be better able to answer."

"Alesandra's not your wife?"

"No, no, that's my daughter. My wife passed away a number of years ago."

"I'm sorry to hear that. And I'm also sorry for assuming that your daughter was your wife, but with so many May-December marriages these days, you never know."

"Lots of men my age seem to think that a Ferrari and trophy wife can do wonders for the old libido."

"No fools like old fools," she said. Then, tilting her head toward him as if sharing a secret, she added, "That's personal experience talking, you understand. But, let me get to the reason I came to look for you. I have a question."

"Well ask away."

"Did you by chance, a long time ago, work for a film company in New York by the name of Ad-Film?"

Jay broke into a broad smile. "I certainly did. How did you know?"

"I'm Vivian Marsh," she said holding out her hand. "I was Vivian Abato then."

"Of course! Vivian," he took her hand. "How are you? It's been a while." Then he added, in jest, "I take it you've long since left Mr. Marty Oppenheimer's employ?"

"Years and years ago. Actually, three husbands ago." Her sweeping gesture indicated the entirety of the house. "I see you've done very well for yourself since your days at Ad-film."

"Yes, but I have to admit that I had a bit of a head start."

"Those were crazy days, weren't they? I'll never forget that party on the roof when you decked Mr. Cat Food, or whatever his name was. You became an instant hero to every woman in the company"

"I also became instantly fired."

Vivian prattled on about the Ad-Film party as he waited for the right opportunity to ask the question that had haunted him for so long. Did she know what had happened to Joanna? The words lay heavy on his tongue. It was as if he had shackled the question he yearned to ask, refusing, for the moment, to let it inject itself in their conversation. He feared that in the asking he might reveal the depth of his desperation to know where she was, how she was and to learn the answers to questions he'd asked himself a thousand times.

"Of course, Marty blamed Joanna for letting that slime ball come on to her. Marty was really an ass."

"Whatever happened to him?"

"Oh, he went to Hollywood and tried to produce TV shows. I think the sharks out there had him for lunch, if you know what I mean."

He could wait no longer. "Do you have any idea whatever happened to Joanna?"

"Well, as you know, she left New York without a word to anybody. Remember, you called me two or three times looking for her?"

"I remember."

"Then, it must have been five years later. I was, God help me, still working at Ad-Film. Anyway, I got a letter from her. She was living in California and had married a man who worked as a computer developer or something in Silicon Valley. They had two children. Unfortunately ... must be ten, fifteen years ago, I think ... they got a divorce. I guess the guy was a workaholic. When he wasn't working, he was drinking. So they split up. I called her when I found out about the split. Poor girl was very stoic about it. From what she said, I got the impression that their relationship was never all that great. She still sends me a note now and then, Christmas cards and things like that. We talked about someday getting together, but she never came east again and I never had any reason to go to California."

"Is she still there?"

"I think so. The last time I heard from her was about three years ago. As I recall, her two children lived nearby and she had no plans to leave." She thought for a moment and then blurted, "Saratoga! Like Saratoga water. That's where she lives. It's near San Jose, as I recall."

Jay did his best to appear that his interest was merely causal, like someone inquiring about an old college friend. "You know, I'd love to drop her a line. You don't happen to have her address, do you?"

"I'm sure I do. But, it's at home in my address book. I'll call you tomorrow with it."

***

"Scott," Jay said when his oldest son answered the phone, "I'm going to fly out to San Francisco tomorrow."

"Business or pleasure?"

"Business. Remember we talked about the possibly of buying a vineyard to keep me out of the office so that you and your brother wouldn't have to put up with my cockamamie ideas?" His proposed visit to a vineyard was a ruse, of course. He felt a white lie was better than admitting—and then having to explain—why he was chasing what had become almost an apparition from his past.

"Dad, you know that's not the reason we discussed it."

He laughed. "I know, but maybe getting me out of the office is a good idea. Anyway, I'm going out to look at one that I've heard may be up for sale."

"Want me to go with you?"

"No. I promise not to get lost."

***

As Jay sat on the bed in the Hyatt Hotel next to the San Francisco airport, he rehearsed what he had decided to say when he saw Joanna. Then it occurred to him that he had flown across the country without having checked to see if Vivian had given him the right address and, equally as important, whether Joanna was at home. There was only one way to find out. He called information, gave the operator Joanna's married name and address. The phone rang only twice before she picked it up.

"Hello?"

He said nothing. Nothing? He had to say something—anything. "I'm calling to see if you might be interested in a subscription to ahh … to *Women's Wear Daily.*" *Where did that come from*, he wondered?

"*Women's Wear Daily?* No, I'm afraid I'm not interested."

He was desperate to keep her on the line a little longer. "How about one of our other magazines?"

"No, thank you. I think I've got all the subscriptions that I need for the present."

The voice was definitely Joanna's. The tinge of her Brooklyn roots still faintly colored her voice.

"Good-bye," she said and hung up.

My God, he thought, I'm shaking. *Do I want to do this? Maybe coming out here was not a good idea. Maybe there's nothing to be gained —nothing but painful memories to be had from digging up the past. No*, he thought, *whatever the pain, whatever the result, I have to see her again.*

Whether it was his sub-conscious procrastination, the problem with the rental car company or his indecision as to what to wear, he did not leave the hotel until after two. The map showed that he only needed to drive a short way down Highway 101 and turn off on Route 85 to reach Saratoga. In all, it was a drive of about thirty miles. A half hour, maybe forty-five minutes with traffic, he calculated.

As he drove south, he found himself thinking about the first few years after that last afternoon in Paris—well before time had begun to fill the hollowness of separation. He had looked for her in crowds, searched among faces on the subway platforms and once or twice he thought he saw her among the ranks of actors answering a casting call for some vacuous, inane soap commercial. Once, he thought he might have seen her boarding an airplane; another time, entering a restaurant on the arm of some faceless escort. She was everywhere and she was nowhere. Illusory and real.

In the early years of his marriage, Joanna continued to be the phantom *other* woman—always in his thoughts, but never in his life. In time, as children arrived and the responsibility of being a good husband, a good father and a good businessman took charge of his life, he thought of her less. The years clouded his memory. Only now and again, when something reminded him of her, did he retreat to the place where he had hidden the picture that he had taken of her in Ceci's dress. At those times, as he held it in his hands, he let his mind rerun random takes from scenes that time and chance had long since relegated to the cutting room floor. Afterwards, he would wonder if his memory had become selective, choosing to save only that which he wanted to remember and filling the voids with a young man's fantasies.

The highway sign indicated that Saratoga was but seven miles ahead. It also pointed left to Cupertino. He recalled that Cupertino was the home of the Ridge Vineyards. If asked by his sons which vineyard he had visited, at least he would have an image to describe. It took him more than twenty minutes to find it. He drove in, parked in the visitors' lot and stared at the rows and rows of vines, heavy with grapes awaiting the vintner's decision to begin the harvest. *What am I doing here in a parking lot, for God's sakes? Why am I finding every possible excuse to delay what I've come to do?*

He wondered if possibly, deep down, he was afraid of seeing Joanna after all these years, a Joanna he might not even recognize. His memories were of a woman just turned thirty and, though he knew better, it was the image of that face he was bringing with him. There was an emotional risk in pursuing apparitions his rational self had warned. But he chose not to listen. The lost years demanded closure whatever the eventual price.

At just before four o'clock, he turned back onto Route 85 and within ten minutes, he was in Saratoga. He found the address easily. Her house sat on a tree-lined street directly across from a small park. He drove by the house several times. He saw that a car was parked in the driveway in front of the garage. He was relieved; she must be home. He drove to the end of the street, turned around and passed by the house again in the improbable expectation that she might have found some reason to step outside. She had not. He turned right at the next street and circled the park, not once, but twice. The second time he pulled his car over to the curb. He got out and walked slowly across the park. Wooden benches lined the sidewalk across the street from her house. He found one directly opposite her front door and sat down.

As he studied the house, he was aware of children playing on jungle gyms and swings behind him. Their voices squealing in delight were peppered now and then with crying, followed by soothing words from a mother. Joanna's front door beckoned, but he made no effort to move. Would she even remember him? Yes, of course she would. Would she have kept the painting they bought in Montmartre? Maybe she had tucked it away in her attic, maybe not.

Jay tried to picture Joanna's life. The house fit the image of the one she described that afternoon in Central Park. But, given what Vivian had told him about her husband, he guessed her life had not been a version of Ozzie and Harriet. How different it must have been from the one they had imagined for themselves and from the one they shared for those few months in New York.

It was after five o'clock when an SUV pulled into her driveway. The rear doors opened and he heard high-pitched shouts of, "Grandma, Grandma, look what we brought you!" A man and a woman emerged from the driver and passenger sides and followed the children into her house. A son? A daughter? One or the other, certainly.

Occasionally he could detect movement through the front windows and once or twice he heard the happy voice of a grandchild. He felt as though he had become a spectator at a play, permitted to watch but not expected to join the players on stage. What right did he have to go knocking on her door and invite himself back into her life? He would be a stranger to her after all these years. He was someone she had known, but probably had all but forgotten.

It was after seven when the front door opened and the children tumbled out. "Bye, Grandma, I love you," said one.

"Me too," echoed the other.

"Bye, bye, see you on Saturday." It was Joanna's voice. She was in the doorway now, a shadow silhouetted against the lights coming from inside the house. Her hair, he could tell, was definitely shorter, but from what he could see of her figure it appeared that the years had barely compromised it. Her face—if only he could but glimpse her face! But it was obscured by the diaphanous curtain of darkness that separated them.

The car doors closed and the car backed out. Joanna retreated into her house and shut the front door. She was alone now. The dusty light of the evening had long since faded and the sounds from the park had given way to the night songs of insects. He wanted to get up, to walk across the street and knock on her door, but he found he could not. The tacit fear that the memory of what had been would suddenly transform itself into an unpleasant reality kept him rooted to the bench as the minutes passed, one after another.

Just days ago he had thought that somehow, by traveling 3000 miles, he could beat his way back against the tide to the past, recreate what was no more and reclaim that which he had lost. He wondered now if it was too late for that. Life had moved on like a receding flood, leaving at best only a residue of faded memories. Joanna and he had been like two wandering stars, finding each other in the vast cosmos for a bright, incredible moment and then sent by forces they could not control into different orbits and different worlds.

He looked at his watch; it was nearly eight. He imagined her seated in her living room, her face staring out the window, thinking of ... thinking of he knew not what. For half a lifetime that face in the house across the street had belonged to other people. The image in his mind was that of her face the night after they had come home from La Bohème and she had come to his room asking to share his bed. That was his face. It belonged to him alone. Then, now and forever. Yes, it was his face and he would see it one more time.

As he stood up from the bench and started to cross the street, his heart began to race. *My God*, he thought, *I'm actually scared. No, petrified is a better word.* The evening had turned cool with a bit of bite in the air and he pulled his coat up around his neck.

As he approached her house, he saw her standing in the living room looking as if she were trying to remember where she had left something. Glasses maybe? A magazine? A book? She was wearing a dress that cut her at the knees revealing legs that conjured up memories of the first time he saw her.

He rang the doorbell and waited. The outside door lights came on. The door opened and she stared into his face. Those eyes that had mesmerized him from the very beginning were at it again. Jay felt slightly weak, like some pubescent schoolboy having come to call on the object of his affection.

Time had been very kind to her, he thought. Age had given a classic depth to her appearance. He who, even as he had grown old, had maintained his way with words could find none. He prayed that an inspiration would arrive to guide him through these first moments so as not to leave him blithering and appearing hopelessly incoherent.

Inspiration was not necessary.

"Hello, Jay," she said. Her tone was warm and yet there was a distinct melancholy in her voice. "I've been hoping you'd come."

The surprised look on his face asked the question for him.

"Vivian called. She said she'd met you and told me about your conversation. She knew so much about you. She also said that you'd asked for my address. I felt sure you'd come, one day soon."

Her greeting had caught him completely off-guard. He fumbled like an actor trying to remember his lines. "Joanna … .I … what I want to say is … I've been looking for you for a long time, Joanna. Most of my life, I think."

Her eyes searched his face like someone reacquainting themselves with old familiar surroundings after a long time away. "I'm glad you found me."

In that brief instant, standing where he was, looking into the eyes of the woman that he had promised himself he would love forever, it was as if the intervening years had suddenly disappeared. He was once again in the garret at Sheridan Square. She came toward him, he took her in his arms and for what seemed a very long time they held each other. Words became unnecessary, superfluous.

All these years he had imagined a moment like this. But, mixed with the elation he felt a tinge of guilt—as if his being here, holding Joanna, was somehow a betrayal of the love that Brooke had given him. No, he thought, I was a good husband to Brooke. I loved her and had she lived, I would not be here now. Then again, if I had stopped Joanna from getting on the plane at Orly, my life would have been very different. She would have been with me all these years.

She turned her head up toward his. "Are you still my same Jay?"

He pulled back slightly, looking directly into her face. "I think so. At least, I hope so." He grinned. "There's just more of me now."

"Not that much more," she said.

She pulled herself into his chest again and he could feel her grip tighten on him. Once again he pulled back so that he could look at her face. "You are still the most beautiful woman I have ever known."

Showing a flash of embarrassment, she deflected the compliment. "Oh, I do think you need glasses. Or did you just forget to wear them today?"

Jay decided it was time to say some of the things he had rehearsed during his plane ride. "Joanna," he said, taking her hands in his and looking down into her eyes, "I've missed you more than I can find words to express. I want you to know that it's not my intention to intrude on your life. You've probably got more important things than dealing with a refugee from a fifth floor walk-up on Sheridan Square."

"You under estimate your importance," she said. "I think maybe you had better come in before the neighbors begin to wonder if I've taken to entertaining strangers on my doorstep."

Jay followed her into the living room and immediately saw the Montmartre picture over the fireplace. As he walked over for a closer look, she said, "After Vivian called, I retrieved it from the box I'd stored it in, up in the attic. It's been there an awfully long time. I was afraid it might have faded, but as you can see it's the same as they day we bought it. My daughter—she was here earlier—wondered where it had come from. I told her I found it in an art store a couple of days ago. She loved it." Joanna stared at the painting and without turning back to him asked, "Have you ever been back?"

"Once, but it hurt a lot. Have you?"

"No, I've never even been back to Paris. After I married my husband, I decided certain memories were better left alone."

Jay did his best to compose his thoughts. For a brief instant he wondered if he should begin by apologizing for what his mother had done. No, he decided, an apology would only lead them to bitter memories and open the old wounds they both had suffered. In the scheme of things, that September was a thousand years ago.

What had happened then did not matter now—certainly not at this moment. *Only being here, with her—only that matters*, he thought. *We don't have time to regret the past, only to take what we can from today.* "Joanna, in coming out here I had no plan, no idea of what I would do or ask you to do after I saw you again. For all I knew, you might have told me to get lost and shut the door in my face."

"But I didn't, did I?"

"No, you didn't," he said, taking her in his arms again. "I may be a little less patient and more impetuous than I was back in 1957. I know we can't turn back the clock. We only have the time that's left for us now. How does the lyric in that song go? 'When you reach September one hasn't got time for the waiting game.'"

"That's September Song. It ends with, "And these few precious days, I'll spend with you."

"I know that after all these years asking you to pick up where we left off won't be easy. I mean, I'm not sure I'm that much fun to live with. I've got all kinds of bad habits that need fixing. I've gained a few pounds and lost some of my hair and, basically, I don't look much like that twenty-six-year-old that made love to you in Paris."

"But then, I don't look like the thirty-year-old woman you used to wake up with in the morning."

"You still look very good to me. And I would happily wake up next to you for the rest of my life."

"Even if you don't mean it, thank you."

"I do mean it. Hopefully, I haven't changed all that much— inside. I'm a little wiser, maybe. A lot less volatile. I haven't felt like punching an agency creative director in years. And, maybe most important, I still know how to row a boat,"

"Will you take me to Innisfree again and carry me off to Elysian Fields?"

"Just say when."

She reached up and took his face in her hands. "You are my same Jay. It's still you in there, isn't it?" she asked, touching his heart. The tears began to well in her eyes and she laid her head on his shoulder.

Finally, he thought, *she's come home. We are back in Sheridan Square.*

"Will you spend these few precious days with me, Joanna? However many we may have, will you spend them with me?"

Her cheeks were wet now with rivulets of tears. She looked up at him, her face aglow, her eyes searched his with a look that said she was ready to peel back the years.

"Yes," she said. "I'd like that very much."

END

16726912R00182

Made in the USA
Charleston, SC
07 January 2013